Danceland Diary

Editor: Susan Musgrave
Cover art: David Thauberger
Book and cover design: Tania Wolk, Third Wolf Studio
Printed and bound in Canada at Friesens, Altona, MB

The publisher gratefully acknowledges the support of Creative Saskatchewan, the Canada Council for the Arts and SK Arts.

Library and Archives Canada Cataloguing in Publication

Title: Danceland diary : a novel / by Dee Hobsbawn-Smith.
Names: Hobsbawn-Smith, Dee, author.
Identifiers: Canadiana (print) 20220397554 | Canadiana (ebook) 20220397783
ISBN 9781989274828 (softcover) | ISBN 9781989274842 (HTML)
Classification: LCC PS8615.O23 D36 2022 | DDC C813/.6—dc23

radiant press
Box 33128 Cathedral PO
Regina, SK S4T 7X2
info@radiantpress.ca
www.radiantpress.ca

FSC
www.fsc.org
MIX
Paper from
responsible sources
FSC® C016245

Danceland Diary

DEE HOBSBAWN-SMITH

Luka's Family Tree

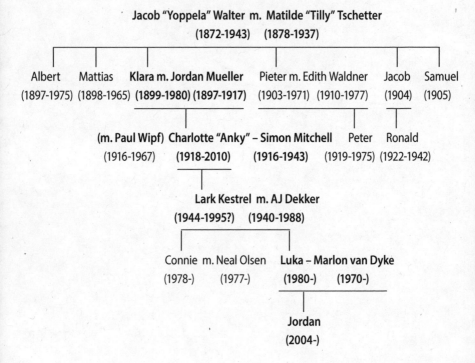

Jacob "Yoppela" Walter m. Matilde "Tilly" Tschetter
(1872-1943)   (1878-1937)

Albert   Mattias   Klara m. Jordan Mueller   Pieter m. Edith Waldner   Jacob   Samuel
(1897-1975) (1898-1965) (1899-1980) (1897-1917)   (1903-1971) (1910-1977)   (1904)   (1905)

(m. Paul Wipf) Charlotte "Anky" – Simon Mitchell   Peter   Ronald
(1916-1967)   (1918-2010)   (1916-1943)   (1919-1975) (1922-1942)

Lark Kestrel m. AJ Dekker
(1944-1995?)   (1940-1988)

Connie m. Neal Olsen   Luka – Marlon van Dyke
(1978-)   (1977-)   (1980-)   (1970-)

Jordan
(2004-)

"Without the past I can't learn to live in the unfolding present.
This bit of history called the new millennium wants to forget,
but forgetting means having to repeat everything that came before.
While the past can be a burden, it is also a gift out of time.
The clear moments of memory must be understood.
It is only then they can be let go."

Patrick Lane, *There is a Season* (McClelland & Stewart, 2004, p. 117)

For Floreen and Lila.

One

ANKY'S FARMYARD IS SOMNOLENT, the trees and buildings drows-
ing in the wavering late-August evening heat. No birdsong. No one about.
My son, Jordan, is as cautious as my Siamese cat Ming as we climb out of
the Beetle and enter the house. My grandmother, Anky meets us in the
kitchen. She's limping and carries a cane – that's new, but not surprising. But her greeting is warm as she waves us into the parlour without
ceremony or hug. Jordan hides behind me on the worn grey plaid couch,
clutching a cushion decorated with lions and giraffes. Ming is on my lap,
hiding behind my elbow.

Jordan is first to emerge. "Mama told me about you," he says as he stares
at Anky. When Ming hears his voice, she leaps free and prowls the room,
paying close attention to the riverstone fireplace dominating the north
wall. From there, she saunters past two spindle-back chairs and peers out
the shuttered French doors and windows, southward onto the deck and
patio. Then she leaps onto a delicate roll-top desk with its top down and
eyes the top tier of the book-lined built-in shelves along the other walls.
It's my favourite room of the whole house, cozy and welcoming, and still
familiar, although an old Hutterite schlofbonk has migrated from Anky's
bedroom and now occupies the northeast corner, its hinged wooden seat
stacked high with papers and books.

Anky pops a wide smile and says to Jordan, in her gruff mix of English
and Hutterisch, "Ich bin Ankela, your Great-Grandmother. You will call
me Anky."

Hutterisch is the dialect of our tribe, the gypsy Hutterites. It's an oral
language, nothing written, and I'm told it's similar in sound and colour to
Yiddish and Plautdietsch, or Low German, the languages of the Jews and

Mennonites, wanderers like our ancestors. I know maybe a dozen words of Hutterisch, some endearments and others curses, all learned from Anky. Something is redeemed each time I say them, just as something profound happens to my heart when my kid and my grandmother gaze into each other's face. "Us" suddenly feels real, the two of us transformed into three. It isn't the first time they've met – I brought Jordan with me when my sister Con married Neal – but he'd been a babe then, unaware, so this is their first real encounter.

Anky – Charlotte – has been my guardian since Mother rolled out of my life twenty-two years ago. Anky filed a missing persons report at the time, and she's spent much of the past two decades analyzing police records from across the country, setting aside her natural reserve to talk with cops from Sault St. Marie to Saint John's to Victoria.

We drink lemonade. When we finish, Anky says abruptly, "Do you need supper? No? Go take a look around, Luka. I need to sleep. We will talk tomorrow." Jordan sticks close to my side as I leave the house, ignoring our luggage for now.

Mother's spirit precedes me, gardening trowel in hand, her footing solid despite crazy-high stiletto heels, tight short skirt, ruffled blouse. She wore the damnedest things to work in the garden, what Anky calls city clothes. Anky, now, she lives in loose floral cotton dresses, most times with an old-style button-up bib apron. But Mother – crazy for clothes, she was. She ran up Dad's credit cards on dresses and shoes that she swore she needed, then she and Dad fought every month when the bills arrived.

Mother ditched us on a mid-April afternoon, 1988, not long after Dad died; I was eight, Connie ten, the air raw with stubborn winter despite crocuses peeping through the yellowed grasses in the fields and roadside verges. She collected Con and me as usual from the school bus at the corner of the grid road without saying a word, her face, usually so animated, as still as a snowed-in field. Down the long driveway, Anky's small house invisible behind the caraganas, past the just-waking strawberry fields and raspberry canes, around the corner and into the yard where Dad's truck and horse trailer still sat near the main house. Then she slammed the car to a halt.

"You girls climb on out." Her voice was flat, the tone we'd learned not to contradict. We got out, obedient daughters. She leaned from the car window. "Tell your Anky I'm going to the west coast. Be good." We started screaming as she wheeled the bashed-up Civic in a tight circle, gunned the engine and drove away.

Anky turned seventy that year, still straight-limbed, still whip-strong enough to keep her market garden – and her granddaughters – in tidy order. How have I spent my time since then? Looking for Mother. I followed her to Vancouver. It's true that while there I earned my hort and botany degrees, but initially, I went looking for her. I gave up searching just after I learned I was pregnant, when I decided I couldn't bear to think of her any more. Then I had Jordan. He's a nervy boy, and needs me. Jordan is as vital a presence as Mother ever was, and curious, like her.

THE MAIN HOUSE where Anky raised Connie and me hasn't changed. I remember Anky replacing all the windows and the French doors not long after she and Oltvetter Paul moved in with Con and me after Mother left. The exterior's been painted recently, a deep blue-grey, a welcoming shade, the perfect offset for those clematis and hollyhocks that still backdrop my roses and delphiniums beside the doorway.

Around the corner to the south of the main house stands a tiny wooden A-frame tucked into a meadow and surrounded by caragana shrubs, wild and jungle-deep, backed by elms and blue spruces, their tips brushing the sky. The glass in both windows has miraculously remained intact, but it's gone that wavery, milky shade, like eyes going blind; the house reveals nothing when the rusty hasp on the door refuses to yield.

Anky lived in this doll's house as a young widow during the Second World War, then she married Oltvetter Paul, and they inhabited it again, later, during the decade when Mother and Dad and Con and I occupied the main house. It's stood empty since Mother left. I loved visiting Anky there for tea and kuchen. A memory percolates up, of Mother sitting on the porch, rocking furiously, both hands clenched around an empty garden basket, her face a blank field. When was that? I can't recall, and the image fades, a disturbing sepia ghost.

Close by is an aging greenhouse, its glass walls still intact, interior tables empty except for Anky's gardening. Next to the greenhouse raised beds cluster, all at Anky's hip level, each bed lush with Swiss chard, carrot fronds, beans climbing past their poles, the leathery leaves of beets, tomatoes restrained by cages.

Tour concluded, Jordan and I return to the main house and unpack. I settle him in, then turn into my own room. As a teen, I plastered its walls with full-colour magazine photos of Freddie Mercury, tropical plants, and Olympic volleyball players, but now all the walls are bare. The familiar bed is freshly made. I crawl under the sheet. My body recalls the reverberations of the Beetle's engine during our long drive east, through the Fraser valley, climbing into the mountains east of Hope, through the closing teeth of Three Valley Gap, the climb to Roger's Pass, over the Golden Gorge. Skirting Calgary's expansive suburbs, sliding in and out of the great coulee of Drumheller. Then cruising the long stretch past Delia and Youngstown on the windward side of the Hand Hills, across the provincial border at Alsask, angling north through the flatland surrounding Kindersley and Rosetown. I fall asleep eventually.

WHEN I WAKE, I lie motionless for a few moments, listening to the chickadees' perennially cheery morning song. Tiptoe down the hall with my yoga mat under one arm. Jordan is still asleep, one arm dangling off his bed, the other snug around Ming. He looks so like Mother. My heart breaks and mends again, as it does every time I stop and really look at him. Anky isn't up yet. The deck's wooden floor is cool under my feet as I unroll my mat and lie down. Yoga outdoors has its own pleasure – horizon, mat, a limitless sky, the singing of birds. The deck's double-wide steps face south. As a kid they made me think of a dock at the edge of a lake, but instead of a lake they overlook the hay field, and a closer field where Anky's market garden used to soak up the sun. The hay field is clean-cut, its crop harvested. I complete my final asana and the call of caffeine kicks in just as I hear Anky moving about in the kitchen.

ANKY WAVES YESTERDAY'S *Star-Phoenix* at me after breakfast. I tell her I've already read Connie's column, a mostly well-mannered – for Con – rant about the irrelevance of the newly announced Governor-General, Michaëlle Jean, and the Crown in general. Anky directs me past Con's headshot to an ad for an old-style threshing bee she wants to attend. It's harvest time. On that long drive back across the prairie, just Jordan and me and Ming, I pointed out the big Martian monsters that modern tractors and combines have become, preying on quarter section after quarter section.

"Soon there will be no heavy horses, no threshing machines even in museums. The boy should see one in action. You, too. These are horses like my mother bred," Anky says, sticking to her guns, just like always, that jutting jaw and tight lips almost quivering with indignation.

So we go. Anky says jump, we hop to it.

After lunch, I pry open the passenger door of her rusty Oldsmobile. She shakes off my hand when I try to help her in, but she doesn't complain when I toss her cane into the back seat beside Jordan. Anky doesn't drive anymore. She's – what age now? Ninety-one? Ninety-two? Con and Neal – when their marriage is on-track – live in town. Anky has lived alone since I left. She has the help of a neighbour, Con said when she called to ask me to come stay awhile, maybe a few months, to keep Anky company and help her before she dies. It sounds morbid when you put it that way, but Con's blunt. And she's been pushed to the limit, driving out to the farm to see Anky every few days. So I sublet my apartment.

Anky and Jordan and I head north, up the gravel road towards the small town of Goodfare, then west along the Yellowhead Highway. It follows the North Saskatchewan, the river set in a deep, wide scrape made by the glaciers, water far below the lip of the escarpment. Goodfare, twenty-five miles west of the city of Saskatoon along the riverbank, is a straight-line prairie town: Main Street meets the railroad tracks where the Co-op elevator towers over a hotel with a bar and pool tables on the main floor. Anky has told me that back in the day, the town had a store that was stocked with what the area's Mennonite and Hutterite women didn't make themselves or grow in their gigantic gardens – rolls of yard goods, stout thread, bone buttons, needles and pins for making their families' clothing, glass quart jars for canning.

"Look, Jordan, see those buildings? By the grain elevator?" I say, waving my arm towards the town perched on the riverbank. "That's Goodfare. You'll go to school there, kiddo. Like I did. Just for a while." I don't tell him I hated it. Busted west as soon as I graduated. But I didn't have my mother. Con had left for university in Saskatoon by then, so it was just Anky and me, and she was a sharp-tongued woman back then.

Jordan doesn't answer. On our drive to Saskatchewan, he talked my ear off, asking questions, a shrill stream that betrayed his nerves about this monumental change, but this afternoon that familiar shy dragonfly lands on his head. He'll talk when he's ready. Just like Anky. In the silence, I recall his unexpected arrival in my life.

THE DAY I LEARNED I was pregnant, I slumped on the couch in my Vancouver apartment, listening to the summer rain pound the window. Earlier in the day, a blood test confirmed what my body had already told me in unmistakable signs, then I'd lain on my doctor's examining table, ankles and knees scooched up, trying to relax despite the speculum. My doctor had pursed her lips when she lifted her head from between my knees. "Need a referral to the clinic?" she'd asked quietly.

My heart fell. "I don't know." Every element of my body turned inward. I sat silently in the examining room, aware that my situation made me look gauche and woefully careless. A baby? How could I fit a baby into this life? Just the week before, I'd decided to stop seeing Marlon, but he didn't know it yet. Now what?

All afternoon at work, the yeses and no's of motherhood pursued me. I discussed my dilemma with my friend Cherie while we tidied orchids and hand-pollinated heirloom tomatoes. I'd met her when I found a part-time job as a labourer at the UBC greenhouse. She had this wild orange-and-red-striped silk scarf holding her hair off her face when I walked into that greenhouse, and she was gorgeous, skin the colour of a café latté, eyes like a jungle cat's. A tiger's muscles too, along her bare arms: when we met, she dropped her wheelbarrow and stripped off her gloves before holding out her hand. The girl had a grip worthy of a Klingon battle-queen. Within a week, we were sharing coffee and class notes and picking up each other's plant clippings at work. Cherie and her daughter, Keisha, lived in an apartment on Kits Point, a stone's throw from English Bay. It's tiny and bright, a hole-in-the wall bachelor with scant room for a couple of herb pots – one always brimming with arugula – on her balcony. I had a main-floor suite in an Edwardian house just off Main Street that I'd sub-let to a pair of hort grad students while I was away. Cherie grew crazy varieties of salad greens and heirloom tomatoes in an unused greenhouse on the university's back lot. Had her name on a waiting list for a community garden plot, wanted a house with a yard so she and Keesie could keep chickens.

Keesie was almost two; Cherie was noncommittal: "What do *you* want?"

I couldn't face an abortion. Such an act of finality felt like one regret too many, a regret with too many unanswerable questions radiating out, an irreversible decision I feared would balloon over time. What did seem clear was that I'd face parenthood alone. The rain pounded harder, the window black with water.

Just like that, my mind was made up. Now, how to tell Marlon? He and his wife had several kids – what would he say if I told him he'd fathered another? Maybe he'd call me careless. Fretting turned into guilt. Maybe I should just end the affair – what a terrible word! – without telling him?

Then there was Anky. Surely she'd scour the Bible for appropriate passages to quote if she knew I'd been seeing a married man – the Commandment forbidding the coveting of wives undeniably extended to husbands as well. Anky was old-fashioned. For sure she'd disapprove of having a baby out of wedlock. In the end, I didn't tell Marlon. I ended our relationship by phone, a terse conversation, without revealing my pregnancy. After I hung up, even Ming's muffled purr as I carried her from room to room didn't ease the pangs. Now what?

TEN KILOMETRES WEST, we turn north at a hand-lettered plywood sign: "Old-time threshing this weekend." Above the river, a small farm cuts into the hills. We round the corner, and enter the landscape of a painting – Millet's gleaners. Out in the stubble, farmers cluster by the threshing machine, their wives relegated to the edge of the field like poppies along the highway's verge. The women's cotton dresses are faded, the men's overalls straining across their bellies, and even at this distance I know that every face is sanded by hard living.

The coolness of the morning has given way to heat that hangs heavy against my skin. Anything could happen on a day like this, in this kind of heat. It's an incubator. Women finally say what's been brewing for years, men break free from patterns that have held them in thrall, in the field or on the road. Out there in the field, still and golden amid barley stooks and dust, ripeness waits. The wind-rows of barley create amber spirals, a labyrinth leading to the past.

Two

I SPOT MOTHER a couple of minutes after we drive onto the farm where the threshing bee is underway. The yard is crowded, dusty, an impromptu parking lot. My grandmother's rackety battle cruiser edges forward slowly, hemmed in by dirt-caked grain trucks and dusty SUVs jammed up as densely as any urban parkade. I ease the Olds parallel to a barbed wire fence, aiming for a break in the caragana hedge. One spot left. We nose in, and as I slip the gearshift into Park, my amber bracelet rattling on my wrist, Mother emerges from between a pair of lanky poplars.

No. It can't be. Mother left years ago. A drumbeat of adrenalin abruptly kick-starts against my ribcage.

Jordan's Spidey-senses kick in, too. "What is it, Mama?"

"Nothing, sprout."

The woman pauses between the trees at the fenceline, her back turned. I lower my voice, addressing my grandmother in the passenger's seat beside me. "Over there, Anky. See her? Is it Mother?"

"Can't be now, can it, Luka?" Anky's calloused hand on my arm is heavy and reassuring, but I pull away and heave the car-door open, squirm through the narrow clearance, shy away from the barbs waiting to snag me.

The woman doesn't budge or bat an eye as I march up to her. She resembles Mother, but only as a spaniel shares general canine attributes with a collie. My heart still kicks at my ribcage. A fair, fine-boned face. A tall, lean physique. Same tight jeans and high-heeled boots. Same flyaway hair exactly the same shade as Jordan's, coiled in an out-of-date honeycomb chignon, a style Mother loved. She's definitely not Mother. What a fool

I am. All these years gone by without her, how can I still feel hopeful? I retreat, muttering an apology to the stranger with the timeworn look and the brown eyes that should have been hazel.

Mother always claimed that the past was dead. That drums through my head as I make my way back to the car. Well, bullshit to that. Calling the past dead is a lame hobbyhorse, in my opinion, a poor excuse for burying bad behaviour and bad times. Mother wanted to cut free from the past, sure, I get that. I've done my share of ditching. Like coming home to Saskatchewan with Jordan, even though I'm just staying until Anky kicks her clogs. Leaving Vancouver was first-class ditching. I was afraid to live there any longer, and I'm relieved to be gone – Cherie's still there and she's frightened, living in a city where a human predator roamed without detection for years. The thing is that Anky needs me here. She needs Jordan, too, and to have a youngster on the place again after decades without.

My kid has helped Anky out of the Olds and is handing her the cane when I get back to them. I scrabble Anky's chair from the trunk and shove it and a blanket under one arm. Jordan grabs my free hand.

"Is that the thresher? Is it like eating a cookie and having all the crumbs collect in your pyjama bottoms?" he asks, pointing downwind, scrambling the description I gave him on our trip across the flatland to Anky's farm, of grain being shaken free from the stalks.

"No." I keep my laugh private, glad to have something in the moment to concentrate on. "It's like shaking all the crumbs onto the ground."

"I don't think I'll like this," Jordan says. "Anky, did you see that machine work when you were six? Was it scary?"

"Nothing to be afraid of, liebling," Anky says as she halts in the shade beneath a trio of mature elm trees. The chair unfolds like an octopus. I steady the metal arms while Anky settles herself on the blanket-covered canvas seat. A couple of minutes pass while Jordan and I debate whether we need another blanket. He finally concedes that no, he can't see any ants. We've just sat down cross-legged on the grass beside Anky when another ghost makes an entrance.

"Hey, Luka!"

The voice is unmistakable. Earl Hamilton. My oldest friend and former would-be flame. This day is like a flipping *Star Trek* time-travel episode.

"Who's he, Mama?" I have to bend close to hear Jordan's reedy voice.

"A friend," I say in a whisper, and immediately know why I whispered:

how to explain old flames and the past to a child barely turned six?

Jordan tightens his hold on my hand as I turn to face Earl. He was always as tall as me, but his body, once as gangly as a fly rod, has filled out, his legs still as long like a sand hill crane's. Most of his face is concealed – by sunglasses, the visor of a baseball cap, a close-clipped black beard singed with red – but it's the same aquiline nose and elevated cheekbones.

Jordan's next whispered question shocks me into stillness. "Is he my daddy?"

"No!" Why would he ask now, and about Earl of all people? My voice has sputtered up the scale, and I have to concentrate on dropping the volume and pitch. "He's not."

Earl takes off his shades, and those storm-grey eyes welcome me before the hug engulfs me. He smells of sweet alfalfa hay. It's a shock to realize that my body so clearly remembers the last time he hugged me, a dozen years ago, dancing at my high school graduation, the voltage of his fingers on my back the same now as when we were both still green. For a moment, I relax. My breathing eases. My hands spread tentatively across the muscles in his shoulders. A second heartbeat, and then a third, drags by before I pull free.

"I'd have known you anywhere," he says and reaches across the years, gently ruffling the wispy hairs on my forearm. "When did you get back?"

"Yesterday"

Earl looks past me to Anky. "Mrs. Wipf, how are you, ma'am?"

"Don't call me ma'am, young man. I might be old but I am certainly not used up." She peers up at him, then her face clicks into recognition. "Earl Hamilton. I don't suppose you've met my grandson Jordan?"

Earl drops to one knee to Jordan's eye level. "No, ma'am. Oops." A grin, then he sticks out a hand toward my kid. Jordan ducks behind me, but Earl doesn't give up. "Hey buddy. I've known your mom since she was about your age."

Jordan eases from behind my hip, clutching my leg as Earl straightens. Even for Jordan, this seems exceptionally clingy. Then Earl waves his arm like a magician, and a girl steps forward, long-limbed and lithe. Glacial blue eyes study me from beneath all-but-invisible eyebrows, sun-bleached hair waterfalling past her jawline. She looks about thirteen or fourteen, as handsome as Earl, with a Nordic coolness that could never be his. She clutches a kite.

"Is she yours?" I can't help myself. Then could kick myself for being so blunt, for being so rude, talking as if this beautiful child were a cyborg, or not even present.

"I wish. My step-kid, Claudine."

So he's married. He introduces us. It takes me a minute, awkward silence as I study the girl's face and then it comes to me: her mother is Suzanne Hébert. Head cheerleader back in the day. Blonde, a face of distinctive angles and planes, and a supple body, impossibly sleek, carving effortless backflips and cartwheels down the hall in school. No one could have been further from the gawky, awkward Amazon I'd already begun to grow into. Somehow I'd never thought of Earl as married to anyone. Never really thought he'd marry.

We shake hands, then Claudine half-steps away from me, her impatience politely contained still palpable, her kite whispering in the breeze.

"Where's Suzanne?" I ask Earl.

"At home with a nanny about to kid."

"Excuse me?"

"Go ahead, Claude. I don't think there's enough wind to get that thing aloft today, but go ahead and try. Don't get close to the horses! As if she needs telling," he says sideways as Claudine lopes away, heading toward the distant riverbank. "Sorry. I meant that a female goat is about to give birth. We farm Sue's folks' place about five kilometers west of your granny's farm. I care for the sheep and goats, and she's a cheese maker, and helps with the hard deliveries – the animals need a smaller hand than mine. Claude takes after her mom – she's good with animals too." His boots scuff a trough in the loam. "You're as pretty as ever, taller 'n I remember, maybe."

"Yoga."

Amusement creases the skin beside his eyes. "Is this a move or a visit?" He takes my elbow, my skin prickles under his hand as if his touch is a jumper cable, and my shrug frees my arm from his grip. "Well, about time either way," he says equably. "C'mon, let's go watch the horses."

I hang back, making a pretence of fussing with Anky's chair.

"Go," she says. "I'm not moving from this shade. Hannah is just over there – you don't know her yet, but you will. She has been my Kronka Kechin. You ask her." Her brisk wave indicates a pair of women talking a few meters away. "Go say hello."

Earl laughs. "Come on, Luka. What have you been up to, other than making a kid with hair the colour of a strawberry roan? He look like his dad?"

"No. Like my mother." I scramble for a safer topic than Jordan's origins. "Do you remember her?"

"Who, your mom? I hardly knew her. She dressed pretty sharp, I do remember that," he says.

We stroll to where the threshing machine growls, Jordan wordlessly hanging onto my hand as if he expects me to leave him behind in the stubble. Earl's sunglasses now perch on his ball cap like a frog's eyes.

As Earl stoops toward Jordan, in my son's tight shoulders I see my dad, the muscles bunching in his back as he strode around the house after Mother, trying to calm her. Jordan's hazel eyes squint up at me, concern swelling behind the irises. I crinkle my nose at him. His exhale is a palpable release as he asks, "Why are those horses so big?"

"They're draft horses, Jordan. They're bred to grow that big," Earl says, squatting beside my boy.

This day suddenly feels too big to contain or hang onto.

Three

TO GAIN A LITTLE breathing room, I take up the opportunity Anky cre-
ated. "Stay here and watch the horses with Earl for a few minutes, sprout,"
I tell Jordan. "I'll be right over there talking to those women." He looks
worried, Earl says something – some joke – in his ear, and Jordan's features
unwind a half-notch.

The women are heading toward Anky. When I cut off their approach, the
face of the farther woman constricts and she half-turns away.

"I'm Luka Dekker," I say as I get closer, holding out my hand. "Charlotte
Wipf's grand-daughter?"

The woman nearest me beams and takes my outstretched hand in hard
fingers. She's almost eye-to-eye with me, as sturdy and straight as a cedar
tree. She's channelling some crazy '60s flower power: strands of fair hair,
loose and long, peek out in tendrils around her round face, her purple and
pink headscarf the only flash of colour amid the grey bobs and braids; hers
the only shorts and tank top, a garish splash of primary-colour geometry
among the garden of old-lady floral dresses blooming around the edges of
this field.

"I'd have known you anywhere," the cedar tree says, smiling. "You look
like your grandmother. I'm Hannah Wurtz. Me and Mick and our boys
live across the road from Charlotte. She's been telling me about you for
years. Great to finally meet you." She shifts slightly, a tree uprooting itself,
to include me as she indicates the woman next to her, still half-turned
away. "Luka, meet Pauline Waldner." Pauline straightens, and her stony
face eases a degree. "Pauline went to school with your mom and farmed a
stone's throw from Charlotte's place until she and Andy sold and moved
to town."

Pauline makes no comment, so I jump in. "I just drove back from Vancouver with my son," I say, pointing at Jordan. He's standing quietly, sheltered within the curve of Earl's arm, safely anchored by Earl's grip on his forearm.

"Charlotte said you were coming," Hannah says. "Cute old Beetle you have, eh? I saw you drive in We see everyone up and down that road, kind of like a rural telegram service." At Hannah's laugh, I feel my tight-pulled wires begin to loosen. She's still holding my hand. "Anyhow, we hay the quarter south of Charlotte's yard in exchange for Mick plowing out the driveway and yard when it snows." So she's Anky's unnamed help. A sigh escapes me without my really noticing as she asks, "Staying long?"

Pauline leans in a little to hear my answer.

"A little while," I say, thinking of the long drive from Vancouver. Nothing about this day – not the familiar landscape, not the soil blowing into dust, not the horses, not Earl's unexpected appearance or even Mother's looka-like, or this surprising, likeable woman holding my hand – has altered my original idea of a brief stay. How brief I hate to consider.

When I finally ease my hand free, Hannah grins. "A while, eh? Your little guy going to ride the school bus with our boys come fall?" My nod doesn't slow her down. "Charlotte's been hoping you'd come home. She's getting on, and Connie doesn't get out as often as she might. I've been doing Charlotte's grocery shopping and running her to her appointments for a few years now."

"She said you've been her Kronka Kechin? What is that?"

Hannah laughs, a big roll that shakes her body. Then she dries her eyes, where tears of mirth had started to flow. "Only Anky would equate my kitchen skills with a Hutterite cook for the elderly. I've brought over noo-dles and soups and the occasional kuchen and dumpling. Nothing special. You don't speak Hutterisch, I guess."

I shake my head, wondering. More karmic debt to work off. Hannah holds up her hand to halt my thanks. "She'd do the same. I'm glad to help out. Charlotte's been good to me."

I abruptly stop trying to analyze the day and look directly into Hannah's face. Love and affection, bright as her clothing, shine through the wrinkles. A bit of the guilt I've hauled through every day of the last six years chips off and melts. "Con's been after me for ages to come back," I admit.

Hannah's laugh ripples like whitecaps. "Connie's a crackerjack."

"Anky used to call her Nuckela. A dumpling, because she's sweet on the inside," I interject.

"Exactly. And helping out's just good manners. Right, my girl?" she says to Pauline with a nudge. Pauline nods in silence.

I decide to take a chance. "Can you tell me anything about my mom?" I ask both of them. "As a kid? As a young woman?"

Pauline's cotton dress suddenly flaps in a brief gust of wind. Behind her, outlined against the sky, I spot Claudine's kite climbing.

Hannah fills the silence. "Paulie, you're the same age as Lark – what, sixty-five now? Weren't you school pals?" Pauline, stone-faced, doesn't respond. "Well, she always was an odd duck, your mom. At least that's what I've heard. Maybe she rubbed a few folks the wrong way. You must miss her."

"You can't imagine," I reply, struggling to speak as a wave of loss washes over me, my breath caught somewhere beneath my sternum. I've always known Mother was off-kilter, so Hannah's words come as no surprise. Do I miss her? Her absence is a constant ache that flares from time to time into full-blown misery blanket-stitched with hot threads of anger. We've only been back a day, and already Mother haunts everything I do. I've seen her ghost drinking vodka at the breakfast table. Wandering in the yard. Crouching in her fancy clothes in the strawberry patch. Patrolling the upper hallway past Jordan's bedroom. Over the years in Vancouver, her absence subsided to a dull ache. Now, back on the prairie where her presence is so vivid, the loss of her feels like a tidal wave. My renewed hope she's still alive, that she might yet be found, makes it worse. I miss Dad too, but he's dead, and there's no coming back from that.

"Later, my girl." Hannah pats Pauline's shoulder, then takes my hand again and leads me a few paces away. "Don't fret about her, she just doesn't know what to say, what with Lark always being so strange and then leaving so sudden and all. You know what your Mom was like. No one wants to throw a stone. At least, not in front of you." She appraises me, top to toes, and briskly rubs my hand. "Here, you look a bit peaky all of a sudden. Don't worry. You and me, we'll sit down over coffee and some of your Anky's kuchen if you like and yak about your mom and you and your little guy. Next week, maybe. All right?"

Some unseen rope has constricted my chest and all I can do is nod like a fool. Then the wind picks up, and I imagine Claudine's kite cutting capers high above us. My chest and ribs spring free and suddenly I can breathe again. Sweat collects on my throat and forehead, under my breasts, as tangible as this woman's generosity. Across the field, the threshing machine groans and clatters, all belts and pistons, dust and chaff rolling in cloudbursts. Stalks of barley disappear into its maw. Kernels cascade in bursts from the chute. The horses pulling the barley-heaped wagons trundle without stopping, their eyes rolling at the racket.

I surreptitiously wipe away the sweat beneath my top and release Hannah's hand – I didn't realize I was still holding it – but the comfort lingers.

"Now it's high time I go say hi to your gran. We'll be in touch, my girl," Hannah says, and turns away.

Pauline is still standing a few feet away. Waiting, it seems. She catches my eye and nods. Her face is as spare and deeply carved as a totem pole, grey braids swinging alongside her cheekbones. Her voice rasps like barley in the threshing machine. "Your mom was my best friend back when we were kids," she says. "We lost touch."

"Did something happen between you?"

"No. Well, yes. She was a hothead, I'm guessing you know that already. In grade nine we stopped being friends. Then your grandmother sent her to Saskatoon."

"What happened in grade nine?"

"She got into trouble for – oh, something or other, it's slipped my mind now. Long time." She frowns again, her face creasing as if in pain, and I realize that she remembers well enough but doesn't care to say.

"What was she like?"

"A firecracker, fearless, funny, took all the risks. She badgered me into walking across the train bridge in Saskatoon with her one winter after we skipped school and thumbed into town to see a matinee at the Roxy, then we ate fries at some joint on Twentieth Street. We couldn't have been a day over twelve. My mom gave me a royal walloping after I called her to come get us." She cocks her head to look up at me, a sparrow assessing a possible threat from a hawk. "I heard she finished high school in Saskatoon."

"She did."

"Then I heard she took off for Vancouver. I stayed here, settled down, raised three kids." Her hands flap helplessly in circles, then fold across her chest.

"Why didn't you –"

"What? Stay in touch?" Pauline's laugh is a raven's croak. "No Facebook or cellphones back then, Luka. I did call the farm after I heard she'd come back with a cowboy in tow, but she didn't return my calls." The indentation between her eyebrows deepens as her voice turns wistful. "We were just fool kids. I always wondered what happened to her." She looks up at me again. "You don't look like her."

"No. I always wanted to."

"Your little guy over there is the spit of her. Well, I've always regretted how things turned out." She turns away abruptly.

Pauline has obviously skirted what really happened, something more serious than a spat. Was Mother already sick in grade nine? I return to Anky and squat beside her, letting my questions join Claudine's kite, still climbing above us. Earl sends me the high sign, then turns back to Jordan, gesturing at the horses still circling the field, men behind them shouting as they fork bundles of barley onto the wagons. A coyote slips past the aspens, brazen explorer from the river valley. By the threshing machine, frenzied howls and yelps break out as the neighbours' dogs catch the coyote's scent. Jordan's head goes up, looking for me, apprehensive until Earl lays a hand on his shoulder in reassurance. I wave, and my kid grins and turns to Earl, saying something I can't hear.

"You met Hannah then," Anky says.

"She's cool. I like her."

"Thought you would. Saw you talking to Pauline too."

"She said Mother was a firecracker. And she said something happened, Anky."

Anky sighs. "Let it be, liebling."

Fifteen minutes ease by, the heat building around us, before she turns to me. I read her face, and help her stand. Too hot, time to go. On the river's high bank, Earl's step-daughter has reined in her kite. Anky leans heavily on my arm and her walking stick. No sign of the tall mystery woman in the parking lot.

When we reach Earl and Jordan, my son is talking to Claudine, waving his arms, his face a bright candle. The girl's smile looks genuine as the two of them bend over the kite in his hands, an elaborate Chinese dragon with a long tail of orange and yellow satin ribbons.

"Amazing kite," I say. "Where did you get it?"

"Dad made it," Claudine says, her pride evident. "He's made dozens. This one's mostly silk." I belatedly realize she means Earl. Claudine holds out her hands to repossess her kite, and Jordan's face dims a little as he releases it.

Earl swings Jordan into Anky's car. He catches my eye and smiles. When he steps into his truck, I have to restrain myself from tugging at his sleeve, sixteen again.

He leans out of the open window. "Drop by sometime. We can have coffee, and Claude can show Jordan the goats and sheep, maybe kick around a ball, put up a kite if the wind's right."

I don't have a chance to ask about his kite-making expertise. As he drives away, the truck's taillights catch the sun, winking out a code of regret.

As we roll east on the highway, Anky raises her eyebrows and purses her lips. "Mind your manners, Luka. You had your chance with him."

Her bluntness grounds me. We've known each other too long to take offense. "Not the kind of thing a woman necessarily discusses in a car," I say. It's a phrase Anky is fond of, and then I ruin the effect by giggling.

Anky just grunts, her dark eyes half-closed but her wit still sharp. "Lesson learned?"

"Lesson learned." I catch my breath, then add over my shoulder, "What about that incredible kite, Jordan?" No response. He's nodding in his seat.

Anky and my son both sleep on the drive back to her farm. Me, I'm bedazzled by the day and its mysteries. I've got one arm out the window, the dry hot prairie air on my skin entirely different from the damp, cool air of Vancouver. So odd to be back, as if time has somehow looped into a knot that leads to the past. The inevitable, unavoidable past.

Four

IN GRADE TWELVE, back in 1998, on the rare days Earl didn't have university classes, I cut my own classes to walk the four blocks to Bill's Downtown Grill in Goodfare for coffee with him. We'd meet at the corner in front of the community centre where Earl parked his truck, then walk to the café side by side, in perfect cadence as we talked. Earl dreamed of studying history and literature; I wanted to tend flowers, gaudy things that thrived in hothouses. The intimacy between us, not sexual, but a friendship of over a decade, felt like a flower I had no name for, a tender tropical, foreign and unusual, fragile when I compared it to my classmates, boys and girls with no thought for anything beyond getting loaded and laid on a Saturday night.

That spring, one day while we were driving to the university, I spotted a yellow lady's slipper in a ditch just northwest of Saskatoon. It was minutes from death by backhoes digging out a new subdivision from what was previously farmland. Earl did the hard part, hauling a shovel from his pickup and digging deep into the ditch to get as much of the flower's taproot as possible while the dump truck drivers cursed. After he'd uprooted it, he replanted it for me in the meadow on Anky's farm. Its hooded bonnet bobbed like a beacon, content in its transplanted home.

A month or so later, ten days before graduation, I perched on a stool at the café's counter, idly spinning in slow circles, the tail end of a DuMaurier between my lips, debating where to plant rosebushes and delphiniums on the farmyard. The bell on the screen door chimed. Earl walked in, taking up a stance close behind me, both his hands on my shoulders as he spun me to face him.

"Lovely Luka," he said, and although he usually teased me, this felt different, his voice tight, pitched lower than usual, and a new current surged, something unsaid that hovered between us.

"Earl, what are you doing?" I shied away and stubbed out my smoke.

"Luka? I want –"

"Earl, don't. I'm leaving in a few weeks, remember?"

Everything mixed into a jumble, thoughts of my dead dad merging with the look Earl gave me, and a recollection of my classmates' voices, telling a recent arrival about me: "Call her Luke. She was supposed to be a boy. Or a plow horse." The comment had stung; I had strong legs Anky had always called sturdy, legs so long I towered over almost everyone I met, and worker's hands with garden soil permanently embedded under my fingernails. Who'd want a sturdy dirt-grubbing plow horse? Earl couldn't possibly want me. Everyone left, as Mother had, as Dad had by dying. The best strategy was to forestall the pain of eventual loss. After Earl walked out of the café that day, I made my way back to school. I kept my head down, looking at the sidewalk, shuffling my feet to discharge the electricity that had coursed through me in the café.

Earl called repeatedly in the days leading to the end of high school, but each time, I refused to take the phone from Anky's hands, retreating to the outdoors, where I busied myself by planting shrubs, burying any thought of Earl with their tender roots. I attended my graduation ceremony with Anky and Con. After the speeches concluded, the DJ set aside the country tunes and defiantly put Queen on the CD player. "Crazy Little Thing Called Love" flooded the auditorium and dancers surged to their feet as Earl strode through the door, past the tables filled with twittering students and their parents, and pulled me onto the dance floor. I closed my eyes and let the magic flicker up my arms, along my torso, through my midriff where Earl's hands lay quietly. He kissed my neck when the song ended. At the end of the evening, I couldn't bring myself to say goodbye, and two weeks later, I boarded a westbound Greyhound without a word to him. I was eighteen, on a mission to find Mother. I didn't have time for men, not even good guys like Earl. I didn't realize just how scarce the good ones were.

Five

ANKY AND JORDAN ARE STILL sleeping when we arrive home, Jordan's fingers twitching as if they clutch a kite-string, so I park, then ease the car doors open for better airflow while they nap. I tell myself again that Mother was wrong about the past being dead, and here's proof – I planted those delphiniums and climbing roses a dozen years ago, and now they could use a good pruning to keep from overrunning the front stairs. Ming lolls in their shade, looking relaxed, her eyes are wide open as she studies a quartet of barn kittens tumbling across the yard.

Within a few moments Jordan and Anky emerge from sleep. I help Anky up the steps, and Jordan jiggles from one foot to another as he holds open the front door. It's like training a pup, having a kid. Same thing over and over until it's habit and they don't question it. Good manners. Polite unasked-for help offered to folks who need a hand. Hold the door and wait your turn, listen and don't interrupt, say please and thank you. Anky would have my guts for garters if my Jordan had arrived on her doorstep a rough hooligan.

Anky leads the way indoors, through the mudroom into the long, sparely furnished kitchen. One end of the planked harvest table where she taught me to roll out cookies is set with an unfinished jigsaw puzzle and a vase brimming with sunflowers I cut this morning. Anky takes a chair at the table as Jordan skids past in pursuit of Ming.

"Jordan! Feed her instead of chasing, please," Anky says as she turns to the puzzle. No raised voice, no movement. Same general's iron fist in the velvet glove she adopted when she took charge of Con and me. Jordan slides to a halt, looks sideways at me, and then rummages for cat food in the lower cupboard while Ming carves slaloms around his shins. Once Ming is fed, Jordan perches on a nearby stool and silently watches Anky.

"I'd forgotten how beautiful this house is," I tell her. "Who built it?"

"About a hundred years ago the house and the barn were both built by my grandfather, Jacob Walter. That makes him your great-great-grandfather, Luka. Everyone called him 'Yoppela.' In Hutterisch that means 'Long Jake.'" She raises an eyebrow at Jordan. "He was a short man, barely taller than me. Lots of folks had nicknames back then – so many had the same given names. There must've been a half-dozen Jacobs in the district."

"Looks like you've sold off some land – I saw a few new homes out past the south field when we drove in," I say.

"I sold a few quarters over the years, yes, subdivided for city folks who don't farm. What do commuters need with eighty acres? Waste of good farmland, but I needed the money."

"The place is still as tidy as an army barracks. Why isn't everything coated in dust? You can't do housework anymore."

"Mick and Hannah help out. She gets those boys of hers over here to dust and work in the yard every week. I plan to have them carry on. You've got your hands full already. What say we have salad and grilled sausages later? Jordan, go help your Mama pick salad."

"In a minute," I say. "Hannah said you were good to her."

"It was nothing much. I took those boys of hers off her hands a few afternoons a week all spring. Painting the house. When they finished that, I found other chores."

"I bet you did!" Easy to imagine a crew of tall boys, Hannah's cedar saplings, shovelling compost and digging weeds while Anky sat impassively on the deck, a miniature taskmistress with an implacable eye.

Jordan sidles over to me as we head out to the raised beds. "When will we see Keesie and Cherie, Mama?"

"We just got here, sprout."

"I miss Keesie."

"I know. You'll make new friends."

"I don't want new friends. I want Keesie. I want to go for a bike ride."

"We didn't bring our bikes, remember? It's impossible to bike on these sand and gravel roads." A tactical error. As his face clouds, I hand him a few small black-skinned tomatoes and direct him to pick some carrots. Moments later, he surfaces from the jungle of carrot tops, clutching a fistful of orange, mouth full, his jangles soothed for the moment. The spicy aroma of arugula fills my nostrils as I clip leaves for salad. Cherie's fave. THE SUN IS STILL HIGH in the evening sky and the chickadees scratch and chirp at the feeder near the deck's wooden table as we fill our plates.

"It's good we came back, Anky," I say.

"Of course," she says. "This is your home." She reaches out and flicks a piece of amber on the double-strand bracelet adorning my left wrist. "You still wear this old thing? I'm glad."

"I miss her."

Anky cuts up her sausage, then Jordan's. When she raises her head, her smile is gone. She flicks a glance at Jordan, then back at me, and lowers her voice. "Your mother is most likely dead. All these years."

"I know that. But that woman we saw." Letting go of Mother means abandoning the image of I how I imagine her to be – safe, gorgeous, loving. Everything I doubt about myself.

"Your mother's gone." Anky's serene face tightens. A core of sadness lies within my grandmother, something familiar that I only partly understand, but the mask of pain that shadows her face is new. She has aged from a steely guardian into frailness with a limp; she barely comes to my shoulder, her face and arms that I recall as strong as iron finally corroded by time, sun, and wind. Her long grey hair is still a thick and unruly mane. Like mine used to be. When I turned twelve, I cut off my braids with the garden secateurs. I've kept it short and curly ever since. Convenient, and maybe it softens the width of my forehead. All through my teen years, wild black hair notwithstanding, my mirror whispered, "Plain" in a reversal of *Sleeping Beauty*. If I were ever to audition for a Trekkie TV series or movie, I'd want a Klingon role on a Bird of Prey warship – warriors don't need to be beautiful.

When we finish eating supper, Anky gestures to Jordan. "Let me show you something, mein katzle." She limps into the house, Jordan at her heels like a faithful pup. When they return, Jordan carefully carries an unframed black and white photograph, one I've never seen: my parents, dressed to kill in a three-piece suit and a wide-skirted flowing dress, caught mid-stride in a waltz, long legs perfectly matched, her face turned to his. Both smiling, handsome, aware only of each other.

Jordan hands me the picture. My fingers trace the faces of the parents I barely know, regret and longing bittersweet, as tangible as Anky's lemon tarts.

"Who are they, Anky?" Jordan asks.

"They're your Ankela and Oltvetter."

"But you're my Ankela."

"They're your Mama's mother and father," Anky clarifies. "I'm actually your Mama's Ankela. Your Great-Ankela. Luka, have you not shown the boy any photographs of his people?"

"I just had the one of Mother, in my wallet." I know I sound defensive.

"All those years away and you had no pictures? How did I not send you pictures? Well, that will change. That one was taken at a wedding in Goodfare." She waves a vague hand at the house. "More pictures are put away somewhere. You keep that one. For the schatzie."

Jordan pipes up again. "Who am I?"

Anky cocks an eyebrow at him. For a moment, her face lightens. She has only smiled a few times since we arrived, and the deep lines around her mouth seem permanently sculpted downward. For one heartbeat, I can imagine what she is thinking – how her great-grandson looks so much like the daughter she lost. As she eases him onto her lap, her face slips further downward, as if pulled by unbearable sadness.

"Hasn't your Mama told you? My schatzie is who. A Hutterite boy. You would wear a Katus – a cap – if we lived on a Colony, and your Mama would wear a Tiechel, a polka dot head scarf." Jordan starts to giggle, and Anky gently tickles him before carrying on. "But we are Prairieleit. The Prairie Folk. No colonies for us!"

"What's a colony?"

She gives him a nudge, so he climbs off her lap and onto the couch, leaning against me. "You do not know about the Hutterites, Jordan?" she asks. When he shakes his head, Anky frowns and begins in the unmistakable storyteller's singsong voice. "Yoppela was a toddler when his parents took a long ship's journey from Hamburg. That's in Germany, far away. They took a train before that, from south Russia, even farther away, and before that from Austria," she says.

Anky goes on to tell him that in 1874, the *S.S. Hammonia 3* was one of eight ships carrying over a thousand Hutterites who were persecuted for their pacifism and religious beliefs. Poor people like our family travelled in steerage, below the main deck. Yoppela's parents died on the crossing, so his uncles and aunts took care of him until the ship arrived at Ellis Island in New York City. They joined a wagon trek of Hutterite families moving west to buy farmland. Along the way Yoppela survived an outbreak of dysentery that killed many other Hutterite children. In South Dakota, the families decided against joining the Colony there, and headed north across the border, to Canada. They became the first wave of Prairieleit, the Hutterite Prairie Folk, who still live off-Colony in Canada and own land independently. Yoppela's aunts and uncles settled south of Goodfare, and he apprenticed as a carpenter. When he met my great-great-grandmother Tilly at church, he bought land and spent two years building this house before they married.

"I never knew all that!" I say.

"You never asked, Luka. You should know that Hannah across the road is Prairieleit, too. She was Colony-raised, but her family left when she was a child. Mick is Métis."

I nod, then rise. "Stay with Anky, sprout. I'm just going to do a little chore before it gets dark. I'll be a bit."

Anky doesn't look up, just gathers my kid close, next to her lap. "Now, young Jordan, tell me what you like to do more than anything in the world."

KNEELING AT THE westernmost point of the meadow behind the wee house with the blind windows, I ruffle my hands over aromatic leaves and stalks. Fescue, chickweed, lamb's quarters, wild sage, wild mint, Queen Anne's lace, yarrow. A few minutes of careful hunting pass before I find the yellow lady's slipper that Earl and I rescued a million years ago. I head to the greenhouse for a spade, then back to the house. In the parlour, I examine the orchids that rode east from Vancouver with us, among them another lady's slipper, a long-ago gift from Marlon. Out in the meadow, I dig a deep hole close to its wild cousin and tip the potted plant from its container. Peace. New life. Settlement. The soil packs like a mantra round the roots.

Blue-black magpies argue like bar brawlers in the spruce trees surrounding the deck when I return to my son and grandmother a few minutes later. Jordan is telling her about Claudine's kite. When he finishes, Anky looks up at the sky, gestures at me to come closer, kisses me, then Jordan, gets heavily to her feet and limps through the French doors into the house without a word.

Jordan sits quietly on the deck chair, stroking Ming. Then he twists around to study my face, his eyes round. "Mama, what did she mean?"

"By what, sprout?"

"The cap. And colonies."

"Ah. Hutterites are our ancestors. Our long-ago family, like Anky said. The little boys all wear homemade black cloth caps. Many Hutterites live in big groups called colonies, aunts and uncles and cousins and grannies and parents and kids all together. But not every Hutterite. Not us."

"Why not?"

"I'm not sure. Because my great-great-grandparents didn't start a colony when they moved here, I guess."

"Is this our home now?"

"For a little while." He puckers his lips. I can't tell what he's thinking. He doesn't say anything else about missing Keesie.

Later, as we climb the stairs to our bedrooms, a beam of light catches the stylized initials – M.S. – carved in slashing curves into the newel post on the landing. The slightest suggestion of a heart indents around them. I've wondered all my life – Whose initials? Whose longing?

After Jordan is asleep with Ming snuggled under one arm, I survey my own bedroom. I've mounted a large cork bulletin board on the long west wall. It contains one photo of my boy, taken by Cherie on Kitsilano Beach. I pull Anky's snapshot of Mother and Dad out of my pocket and pin it up beside Jordan's smiling face. The wall still seems unbearably empty. Rummaging through the shelves and cupboards in the other bedrooms reveals nothing except a solitary box of Mother's old things, the rest all bare. Not even dust. The rooms echo. What will I do with all this space? How can I rock my kid's world so he doesn't feel lonely in this rattling big house? Just how large a family originally lived here after Yoppela built it? Maybe Anky has a family tree tucked away with her photos. How is it that I don't know our history?

Earl knows his family tree. Back in the day over coffee, he described his ancestors' arrival in Nova Scotia from Scotland's beleaguered Highlands in 1778 on a "coffin ship" named the *Hector*. From there, Hamiltons moved west, helped build the fur trade, served as *coureurs du bois*, lumbermen, navvies building the railroads. It's such a typical white Anglo-Saxon Canadian settler story; the details have never left me. Earl thinks he might have Métis shirttail cousins somewhere, he hasn't had any luck finding them. He has a family tartan, too, and likes to indulge his Scots background. Even as a university student, he was a curler, and drank

Speyside single malt when he had the scratch to buy a bottle. All talismans of his family's origins. He can't speak Gaelic, but he knows who he is and where he came from. I turn on my laptop and poke from site to site, reading about Hutterites – us, the wanderers of central Europe – looking for simple ways to explain our ancestors to Jordan. I've never cared about my history before, never thought of myself as a Hutterite, never listened to Anky's stories. Seeing her and my kid together has changed something. I, too, want to know who I am.

Six

I'M ON THE DECK absorbing the morning light when Jordan wakes. After breakfast he is keen to dispense fresh coffee.

"Can I take a cup to Anky?" He returns a few minutes later, still carefully carrying a cup, now half-empty. "She's not awake."

"Set that cup in the sink while I mop up. No, don't drink it, you monkey! We're going on a road trip. To Goodfare. Remember the town I showed you yesterday? It's market day." I scribble a brief note, thinking as I do. Maybe that odd woman I met at the threshing, Pauline, will be at the market. Maybe she'll get past her bullshit memory lapse if I have my shy smiling boy along to spark some maternal goodwill. A longshot, yes, but worth the gas. Plus Anky needs a chance to sleep in.

Our short drive is made briefer by Jordan telling me his thoughts about the draft horses at yesterday's threshing. "We should stay for winter, Mama. We could get some big horses, and a sleigh. Or maybe a wagon! We could drive all the kids to school! You always say we have to be greener. But someone would have to clean up behind us. Those horses make a lot of poop." He subsides. A minute later, he pops back up. "You said you want a garden, right? The horses could eat the weeds. Or is there something the horses can pull to dig the holes so we can plant the seeds?" The entire ride to Goodfare, he obsesses about how to make heavy horses a reality in our lives, and he doesn't run out of equine ecology until we roll down the town's dusty main street.

These days, Main Street is much as I remember: the café is still there, along with a convenience store, the post office, a hair salon, the hotel's pub and pool hall, and three churches – a plain white Mennonite rectangle, a steepled Presbyterian church fronted with smooth river rock, and a Catholic chapel with a bell tower and a statue of Mary. I spot a new gym and a daycare at the corner, geared to the occupants of new houses in a small subdivision on the east side of town.

I go straight to the curling rink at the west edge of town. The rink's double doors stand open and half a dozen pickup trucks are parked outside. Inside the rink, a dozen battered folding tables arc around the inner wall past the empty concession stand. A handful of shoppers stand before the tables. Jordan tugs at my hand and I wonder if he will gallop ahead, reconnoitring, but no, he puts me between the tables and himself. "Look, bread, and big cookies, Mama, can we get some? You haven't made cookies in ages and ages. And that lady has jam, and that one has honey. And carrots."

"Anky has carrots in her garden, remember? We want to buy things we don't grow or make ourselves. Here's ten bucks, go choose some jam. No cookies!"

I have a jar of clover honey in one hand when I recognize Pauline, paying for berries at the adjacent table. She nods warily. Within moments Jordan slips back to my side and shoves a jar into my other hand, then fidgets with the change, counting it over and over under his breath. I grab the coins before he drops them.

Pauline pinches my arm. Such strong fingers, I bet she leaves bruises.

"So here's your little boy. He really does look just like Lark." She turns me loose and extends a basket of raspberries toward Jordan. "Here, help yourself."

Jordan snags a handful of berries, then, with a scrunched-up look of dubious approval directed at Pauline, hunkers down a few steps away on a bench to eat them one at a time.

"She was so beautiful, Luka, even as a girl," Pauline says in a low voice. "We all thought she should have been a model. What became of her after your dad died and she left town?"

"I don't know. We lost contact. I was hoping that someone here might have stayed in touch."

"Not me. Before that, during school, Charlotte – your granny – sent her into town to live for awhile, with that woman, what was her name?"

"Anky's god-mother, you mean? Marina. Anky's never told me the details."

"Yes, her. Charlotte packed Lark off to the city during the winter of grade nine. She was suspended for something she done on the school bus. But even before that she got it into her head that I stole what she thought was hers, a guy she fancied. I didn't even like the guy, but she was flat-out mad about him, and she wrote my name and all kinds of nasty words on the school wall one day in red paint. It took the janitor weeks to clean them off."

"What happened on the bus?"

"It wasn't pretty. But I don't want to tell tales to her kid."

"But she claimed you stole her boyfriend?" It's an effort not to laugh.

"Sounds petty now, don't it? You should've seen her – she couldn't stop talking, all sorts of crazy nonstop nonsense, and always rhyming. And those words! Leaves a bad taste in your mouth, that kinda language. Sweet one day, sour the next. Your mother got so weird no one wanted anything to do with her even though she was the prettiest girl in school. You wait and see, your young lad here might not be so sweet as a teenager. We heard rumours about her as an adult, sure enough."

"What kind of rumours?"

"Nothing that amounted to nothing. She moved to Montreal. She got a job as a model in New York. She dated Robert de Niro and Billy Joel. Stuff like that. Just gossip." Pauline appraises Jordan. "Poor wee lad, lost his granny, hasn't he? But he'll have his other grandmother, surely, your husband's people? No?" She purses her lips. "A single mom, then? Our kids are pretty much all grown and gone, to Calgary or Fort Mac or Toronto or Winnipeg. None of our lot has grandkids nearby. The trouble with small towns, isn't it?" Her tight grimace that is not a smile, freighted with disappointments. "Here, dearie," she says to Jordan, holding out a carrot from her bag.

He considers the carrots and selects one. "My Anky's are better," he mumbles through a mouthful of orange pulp.

"Course they are, take some extra for when your Anky's are all gone, dearie. Nothing lasts forever – just take a look at me. Old before my time. That's farming."

Pauline pushes her grey hair from her forehead and scratches her nose. "Luka, you tell Charlotte to take it easy now she has you home. You'll be glad to be back from the coast. Nothing good about that place on the radio, all those missing and murdered women. I hear on the CBC that they've rejected that terrible man's appeal for a new trial."

A shudder tightens my skin. I suddenly want to be far away from Pauline and her news. While we lived on the coast, the pig farm trial was all over TV and radio. She follows us outside. "Some things are best left in the past, Luka. Worry about your little one here." She swings Jordan's door closed with a decisive click.

At the empty schoolyard a minute later, I sit on the swing while Jordan scuttles across the monkey bars, up the ladders, down the slide. *Best left in the past.* Being here has made it clear that I don't want to leave Mother in the past any longer.

AT THE FARM, we find Anky awake and sitting in the shade on the deck, an open book and Ming on her lap. Jordan scrambles over, legs thrashing, and ends up in a sprawl at Anky's feet. At her flinch, Ming bolts, followed by Jordan.

"Can we talk, Anky? Pauline told me that Mother lived in Saskatoon for most of high school. That was with your god-mother, Marina, right? You've mentioned her before. What happened?"

Anky goes white. "I couldn't manage her." She's suddenly near tears.

"I didn't mean to upset you." It's only a few steps into the kitchen and I return with a glass of lemonade. "Drink this."

What a fool I am! I shouldn't have mentioned Pauline. Just how much can I ask Anky? Close behind the worries crowd my everyday fears about her aging, her inevitable death, my finding work, the challenges of raising a child. Surely such fears are old hat to a woman who brought up her grandchildren after she'd passed her seventieth birthday. How much of a burden do I want to be? Abruptly, I decide that my problems are mine, not Anky's.

"Um. I was just wondering about finding a short-term job. But it'll keep. What about those old photos?"

"You want to look at them now?"

I shake my head.

She smiles, as sweet as Jordan's impish grin, but that reservoir of sorrow hasn't receded. "Good. You're learning."

ANKY AND I SIT ON the deck again that evening, stars above us in that brilliant canopy I'd forgotten exists.

"My mother didn't have time for me," Anky says suddenly after I return from checking on Jordan, asleep in his bed.

"What do you mean?"

"Just that. She spent her time and energy on her horses. Whenever she tended to me, I felt like one of her foals – worthy of attention as a small and defenceless creature, nothing more. I never did think she loved me." She pauses. "She named me after my father."

"Charlotte?"

"Not that name. Jordan. My middle name."

"I didn't know that! Tell me about him."

Her face clouds over. "Not much to tell. I never knew him, Luka. He disappeared before I was born. He was an American, came up from a Dakota Hutterite Colony during the First World War. Maybe he was a draft dodger, I don't know. The story is that he showed up with a string of horses that might not have been his to sell. All that really matters anymore was that my Ma – Klara, you know her name – became a studhorse woman after he disappeared. Women didn't do such things back then, and my mother went against her father to live her own life. She lived in men's clothing – pretty remarkable in that time. I've told you about Yoppela. He had a terrible temper, was said to throw his hammer at his apprentices. Yoppela hated Jordan, my ma told me. She said they were both violent men."

"So this Jordan, your father, he just disappeared? How's that possible?"

"A permeable border," she says drily. "Or a dry well. Take your pick. The stories were pretty wild. Men didn't just disappear. But Jordan did. I remember Ma telling me that she had a theory involving murder. The details escape me, such a long time ago, not sure it matters anymore. After Jordan vanished, Ma's family wanted her to work as their maid and cook. But she refused. Her best friend Marina Shevchenko was Ukrainian, and when her brothers and father were sent into detention in the mountains during the war, Marina had no choice but to go to work as a maid in Saskatoon. Ma got regular letters from her, and there was no way *she* wanted to be a maid. So she became a studhorse woman."

"But how, Anky? What horses? Did Yoppela give Klara a horse?"

"Marina did. Her father's Percheron stallion and mares. All the property on their farm was confiscated, but Marina hid the horses and sold them to my mother. For a dime. Ma didn't love anyone or anything except that stallion."

My mouth frames the words, "*We* love you, Anky," but my tongue locks and refuses to hand over the key. So I turn my face away. The stars. Look at the stars.

"I hated those horses. Especially that stallion. Marko, his name was. Ma loved him. She said he was her freedom. She rode that infernal livestock breeding train with him all over the province. Took Marko to the CNE in Toronto, to Chicago, even hauled me along on the train to Boston to see about selling some of her young stock to a circus. Then Marina took me in so I could go to high school in town. That was during the Depression, and I'd have been stuck on the farm for good if Marina hadn't offered. After I left I don't think Ma even missed me. She as good as gave me away. I never forgot." Anky fidgets with her teacup, then sets it down with a clatter. "It nearly broke my heart when your mother left you and Connie. Marina, now, she knew how to be a mother, even though she didn't have any kids of her own. She was more a mother to me than my own. And she was a good mother to Lark, too."

She doesn't want a reply. I nod, one hand clutching my amber bracelet. The bracelet reminds me of a time when Anky intervened between Mother and me.

IT STARTED WITH SEEDS. Mother sat at the kitchen table in a ruffled voile blouse and leopard-print capri pants, a muddle of seeds before her, three teacups aligned to one side. Her hands flashed, and she dropped flat squash seeds into one cup, oval bean seeds into another, tiny brown radish seeds into the third. Each time I tried to help, seeds would skitter between my fingers to the floor. Mother's face tensed. When I knocked over a teacup with a crash, seeds and porcelain shards scattering across the floor, Mother jumped up and grabbed the broom.

"Luka! Leave well enough alone. Go watch TV. Don't wake your father."

Dad was snoring in the parlour, Connie in an armchair beside him, reading. He'd arrived home the night before. His horse trailer was parked in the yard and his horses had snorted through the paddock's rails when I'd gone outside for a romp with Anky's dog, Max. Whenever Dad was awake, he and Mother would kiss. Then they would argue. I would scuttle outside in tears or go find Connie, terrified of what might happen next. "Next" was always another kiss, then another rodeo, and Mother, left alone, would fall into her darkness.

My stomach churned with anxiety as I hovered in the doorway. What should I do? To my relief, the front door opened and Anky walked in, her rubber boots caked in clay, mud-footed Max at her heels. Anky looked at Mother's tight face, the broom she clenched in one hand. Then she met my eyes. Off came her gloves and boots. "Love" was not a word that my family used – I can't remember ever being told I was loved – but the expression on Anky's face was a watermark, incandescent with love and forgiveness, for me and for Mother.

Anky pulled off the necklaces she always wore. One was a treasured wedding gift from Marina – a gold chain with an old coral cameo carving of a woman's head and shoulders, lilies in her arms. The second, a double strand of Baltic amber, my favourite, had originated with Tilly, my great-great-grandmother. She wore it and a matching bracelet as she journeyed across the ocean, from Tyrol in the old country, and gave the set to her daughter – Klara the studhorse woman– when she married. The amber pieces were of graduating sizes, smooth knobs in uneven polished shapes, each glowing like a harvest moonrise, a tiny helix of seashell floating in the necklace's largest chunk. Whenever Anky held me on her lap, I loved to gently touch each necklace, my fingers moving from the slickness of the amber to the bevelled edges of the coral cameo.

"Here, Luka." Anky held out the necklaces. "My jewellery got vershimmeled in the garden. It would be a big help if you'd untangle them."

I crouched at the table, ignoring the low-pitched argument behind me. When I had the necklaces separated, I carefully carried them to Anky. "Give them to your mother," she said. "She likes such things. When you are older, I will give you my amber bracelet."

Standing between Mother's bare feet, I stretched up and draped the jewellery around her neck. She pecked my cheeks with her dry lips, left and right, once for each necklace. Mother was long gone when Anky gave me the amber bracelet for my sixteenth birthday.

Seven

"I'M GOING TO TOWN, to the market, Anky. Should I take Jordan or leave him here with you?" A drive might shake off the haunted sense I've had all morning – Mother following me as I move through my yoga practice, water the garden and feed the barn cats and wash the dishes.

"Leave him. I will tell him stories about Yoppela and the first Jordan. While you're in Saskatoon, visit your sister. She'll want to see you."

Anky can't see the face I pull. It's invariably stressful, talking to Connie. She's always got her knickers in a twist about something, and she always interrogates me like I'm the subject of her latest political potboiler. Maybe she won't want to see me. Maybe we'll do nothing but argue. Maybe –

"Maybe I should take Jordan along?"

"Call Connie."

I call, but her message cuts in as usual, so I record a brief admission of our arrival, that I am coming to town. That I'll stop in.

I try to avoid comparing Saskatoon's farmer's market with my former market of choice, Vancouver's Granville Island public market. They're different worlds. Business at this market is brisk, a far cry from the quiet country market we visited yesterday. It's easy to see why: the Saskatoon market is vibrant, perched by the river and its popular walking path, and a long row of locked bikes attests to summer transportation preferences in a city famous for relentless winter. The lot beside the building is filled with marquee tents and vendors selling soaps and sugar bowls, freshly roasted coffee beans and hand-curated spices, samosas and sausages. I buy a coffee, all of the tables in the market's café section are occupied, so I lean against a pillar, close to a busker who picks out a good rendition of an old bluegrass banjo classic as I send a quick email to Cherie, telling her about meeting Earl after so many years. Cherie knows all my secrets. When I told her I was going back to my grandmother's farm for a while, she nearly fell over with laughter. "Saskatchewan? Too cold for this girl, Luka. Although I'm sure there's plenty of space. The final frontier." A true Trekkie.

When I finish my coffee I head to the big reefer truck from the Okanagan that's parked at one end of the market's parking lot, with clusters of people buying cherries, peaches, and apricots. As I pick through the Red Havens, I recall that Earl's wife makes cheese. This is where she'll have a booth. But there's no sign of a cheese stall.

Maybe one of the market's oldtimers knew Mother? As I make my rounds no elderly vendor interrupts me, exclaiming how remarkably similar to the young Charlotte I am. Never mind. Maybe I can get short-term contract work at the new greenhouse at the university's experimental farm – breeding hardy plants for the prairie climate could be a dream job, similar to what I did at UBC. Cherie and I discussed the possibility before I left, this whole Saskatchewan project suddenly seems daunting. Poorly thought out. How will I raise a child, care for Anky, drive to and from a city job?

I pay for the peaches and make the turn indoors through the door, then spot the cheese stall, its counter stacked with wheels and wedges. The woman behind the counter taking money and offering samples is not Suzanne. I've tasted half the samples when the clerk suddenly chirps, "Here's Suzanne now! She can tell you all about all the cheeses!"

I'd have known her anywhere. Same cartwheel-worthy limbs and lean body, same sharp-angled face and gleaming hair, same pianist's fingers. I don't know how to respond when Suzanne wraps me in an unexpected hug.

"Luka! Earl said you were back. He said you have a little boy?"

"Jordan's at home with my grandmother. You haven't aged a bit, Suzanne. " My words sound limp after Suzanne's exuberant greeting.

"Ha. Thanks," Suzanne says. "I'm definitely aging inside. You obviously haven't gotten to the teenaged parenting stage." Her laugh is contagious as she hands me a fat wedge of cheese wrapped in parchment. "Here, put this in your bag. It's aged gouda, really the best thing I make. Does your little boy like cheese? Maybe the chèvre for him, it's not so sharp. And I know your grandmother likes my smoked cheddar. But those are all goat – here, you have to try my Manchego. It's sheep's milk."

36

"I met your daughter. She's cool."

"Too cool, maybe. She doesn't like coming to the market anymore. Teenagers. She used to love it. Earl's the shepherd – well, him and the dogs. We had a couple of late lambs and kids dropped this week, and one needs bottle-feeding. So Claude's playing nursemaid, and today it's just me and Carly." She indicates the clerk, busy serving a trio intent on buying some of everything.

As Suzanne wraps the cheese, I hide my face as I dig through my purse for my wallet. That spark. It threatens to ignite each time I even think of Earl. Surely my face is an easy read. But her gaze as she puts several packets in my hand is even and straight, without the guile I associated with her as a teenager.

"No, it's a welcome-home present." She waves off my cash. "You can be a paying customer next time. Make sure you come back and tell me which you like."

The man waiting beside me nudges my arm. "Don't argue. Suzanne makes the best cheese this side of Calgary."

"There you go, unsolicited praise," Suzanne says, laughing again. "Welcome back."

Such uncomplicated kindness. I don't know it yet, but visiting her stall becomes a weekly occurrence, as much for the pleasure of getting to know Suzanne as for her cheeses. Her high-wattage grin brings to mind the long line of hopeful boys she held in thrall as a cheerleader – and Earl. I have to stop thinking about him.

Suzanne's warmth stays with me as I tour the remaining stalls. Doubling back to the fruit truck, I sort through new-crop Macs and Galas, swivel to reach the perfect Gala just out of reach – and collide with a tall denim-clad man. A black beard shot through with streaks of red. Storm-grey eyes under a faded ball cap.

"Luka," Earl says, his voice climbing the second syllable of my name. "Your granny said I'd find you here. Got time for a coffee?"

Finding the right tone takes me a moment. "How's the lamb?"

"A kid, actually. Fine. The nanny figured things out. Coffee?"

"A quick one, maybe. I just saw Suzanne. Needed apples to go with her cheese."

I wave my bag of cheesy comestibles. A half-beat pause hangs long enough for me to wonder what unspoken words wait to fill the silence.

"Honey and cream?" Earl asks, a coffee mug in each hand, his expressive face impassive for once.

A few minutes later, our coffees cool on a tiny tabletop. My heart under my shirt is a hummingbird trapped beneath a fabric net. Hush. His wife has long fingers, gentle as she tends her goats. Pooling milk, racks of creamy cheese rounds, breezes and butterflies. Hush. My body has proved to be such a disloyal creature. Untrustworthy. There's no denying the man is hot. But off-limits.

He rests his hands on the table. Stillness emanates from him in a way it hadn't as a younger man. What hard lessons has he learned to generate such calm? He tells me he earned his history and literature degrees as he'd hoped, but – "Who needs a historian specializing in sixteenth-century Scottish literature? All I could do was teach or write, and campus politicking turned my guts to water, so... I started writing a book." That half-body-shrug gives me goose bumps. "I haven't finished it. Yet. It's about a Scottish poet named William Dunbar. Life kinda highjacked me, I pick away at it when I have a few minutes to myself."

"A writer! Earl, that's great news. Surprising, but great. Can I read it?"

He looks sheepish. "Yeah. Surprised me too. I'll let you read the final draft before I send it out. If I ever finish. You've got a kid, you know what I mean. Lifetime projects. Sue and I got married a while after Gerrit died. It was unexpected – a heart attack. Claude was pretty little yet. The farm came from her folks, a little organic mixed farm. Then there's the sheep and goats and Sue's cheese-making gig. It's a lot, tending animals and making cheese, way too much work for one person. It turns out I like being a shepherd as much as I like growing things. I figured out, maybe, what's always attracted folks to farming – growing green plants makes me feel hopeful in a hopeless world." He takes off his cap and fiddles with it, head down. When he meets my eyes, his face has the brooding look I remember. "I didn't forget you. And you left. No note. Never wrote. Didn't call."

"I was a kid." Listening to myself, I hear a half-assed belated apology.

"We both were."

"Do you remember the lady's slipper?"

His laugh rings like an orchestra cymbal. "The flower you spotted in the ditch north of the city? What were we doing out there anyhow?"

"You wanted to find a shortcut to campus."

He shakes his head in disbelief. "You made me dig up that poor flower with backhoe operators fifty feet away, just dying to plow me under."

"I found it out in the meadow where we planted it. Blooming."

"That's good." When Earl raises his eyebrows again in silent question, that same quirky tilt, my words find their way out. My life in Vancouver. My searches for Mother.

SOON AFTER MY ARRIVAL in Vancouver in 1998, I visited the downtown police station. The desk sergeant leaned on the counter, twirling an unsmoked cigarette. When I told him I was looking for Mother, he didn't quite laugh. "Last known address?"

"Our farm. Near Saskatoon."

He stuck the smoke behind his ear and scowled. "Then how do we know she's in Vancouver?"

"She said she was going to the coast. She'd lived here earlier, before she married Dad."

"Big city. Any friends?"

"None that I know."

He didn't bother to respond, just pointed to the wall where dozens of photos were aligned in tidy rows, "MISSING" inscribed above each. Most of the faces were Indigenous women, but none looked familiar. I pulled out the only photograph I had, of her as a young mom, tall, with high cheekbones and long reddish hair, her amber necklace at her throat, her daughters at her knees. Even in jeans, she looked like a model.

After a cursory glance, the sergeant asked, "Got anything more recent?" When I said no, he told me that dozens of women disappeared into the Downtown Eastside, Vancouver's underbelly. "Low Track, we call that patch. Lots of women go missing down there."

"What do you mean, women go missing?"

"Read the news. She a junkie?"

The thought hadn't occurred to me. I tried to sound casual as I reviewed the photos on the wall. "I don't know." I concentrated on keeping my voice steady.

"A hooker?" I must have gone pale. "Sorry," he said, not sounding sorry at all. "I gotta say it. You look on the stroll at Pain and Wastings?" I could only glare at him, too green to call him out. Then, as another cop in uniform walked past, he relented. "Look in Chinatown? Gastown?"

"I never thought –"

"No one ever does. Look there. And keep an eye for sharps."

"What?"

"Used needles. All over the place." As I turned away, he added, "Take a friend with you."

I ignored his advice. Something shameful, an uneasy frankness and brutality, clung to that first search. It took me to the city's guts and grease pits, a side of life I didn't want to even admit to knowing existed. The bus trundled north up Main, rainwater splashing onto the windows, and I pulled the cord before Hastings. Past Oppenheimer Park. Past the Marr Hotel, where a dozen motorcycles lined up like renegade soldiers. Garbage tumbled from bins. Seagulls and crows pecked and picked. I saw Mother in the slumped shoulders, needle-tracked arms, and scoured face of every woman hanging out in front of the Asian apothecaries and near the greengrocers, their cut flowers sitting outside in water buckets. Beside the restaurants that smelled of garlic and something sweet and delicious.

My hands still shook when I halted several blocks west on Hastings. My eye caught an orange gleam against a bed of ice in a window. The sign, a blue neon seahorse, read "The Only Sea Foods." It had been hours since breakfast. I stepped inside, admitting in a small corner of my mind that I wanted to fill myself with something to dull the pain of what I'd just witnessed. Salmon seemed a better bet than dope.

Even I could tell the place was a joint. A counter curved in a double loop, a few booths, a stool at the counter the only empty seat despite the place's grime, a half-swabbed floor. As I sat down, on either side dockworkers and lumberjacks in worn jeans and steel-toed boots glanced briefly at me, then back at their heaping plates.

The chipped nametag pinned to the cook's stained apron read Dick. He slapped a saucer heaped with bread and butter onto the counter.

"So?" Dick said. "You want the chowder?"

"What's chowder?" Anky's cooking – borscht, cabbage rolls, pot roast, apple kuchen, strudel, pork chops with onions – had never ventured into seafood.

"Soup. Onions and bacon, potatoes, celery, clams, cream. You know clams? Here." He sloshed some thick white soup into a mug. "Try it."

The chowder was sweet and briny, unlike anything Anky had ever made. I slurped the cup empty and held it out with a nod.

"Atta girl." He set down a brimming bowl and heaped more bread in front of me. As I ate, he shuffled from stove to deep fryer without wasting a step, piling enough fish and chips for a stevedore onto every plate.

My nerve finally returned. I hauled out the snap of Mother. Held it out. My hands were shaking. "Ever see her? She's missing."

Dick set down his spatula and squinted at the picture. "Your ma? A looker, hmm? She's a bit like a high-class girl comes in sometimes, 'cept her eyes are different. And her mouth. Maybe I seen her. Wait a sec, gimme that snap. Sal might know. She's been here longer'n any of 'em."

He plucked the picture from my hand, shook it between two fingers before a blonde Vietnamese woman who hunched on the farthest stool. "Hey, Sal, know this girl? Daughter here looking for her ma."

She flicked the picture's edge with chipped nails. Then she shook her head. Her hoarse whisper: "I have seen her some times."

My first positive clue propelled me off the stool toward her. The unshaven man beside Sal's stool sloped away at my approach, his breath reeking of tobacco, his body of stale sweat. I edged closer to Sal, clumsy as I leaned in and reclaimed the picture. Face to face, my fears swelled into ferocious, terrifying bloom: when I looked past the long jagged scars on Sal's face, I could see the beautiful woman she had been.

"That's my mom. You knew her?"

"She do not look like you."

"No. Her name's Lark."

"Fancy name. Girl calls herself something else. Laura, maybe?"

"Where did you see her?"

"Out. Around. I have not saw her for long while." Sal spun around so all I could see were her thin shoulders and back, an impervious wall of denim.

Dick jerked his head toward my stool. "Have some coffee," he said, slopping a full mug on the counter. His rough concern reminded me of Anky. The tears hung, waiting for a chance.

Dick's counter at The Only became a regular hangout. I stopped in for Dick's awkward moral support as much as for food, textbook open on my lap, notebook jammed against my plate. The women and men at the tables and curved counter constantly changed, and after a couple of months, I asked Dick about Sal.

He stopped, ladle suspended over his chowder pot, and looked at me as if I'd asked about a Klingon traitor. "Ain't seen her lately."

I kept going back. It wasn't just the food; maybe I'd finally catch a glimpse of Mother's face in the windows, the puddles, the raindrops. But I always returned to campus with my belly full, heart empty and aching, mind wandering. Over coffee, I'd tell Cherie what I'd seen, and ask questions she could never answer: Where had Mother slept? Had she eaten at The Only? Had Dick been kind to her? Was she all those things the cop had suggested? I could never ask if she was still alive.

I CAN'T GO ANY FARTHER. My coffee is gone. My back is drenched in sweat. Earl sits beside me, his head tilted down, face nearly invisible beneath the brim of the ball cap. "So I can guess that you didn't find her," he says quietly.

"No."

The silence hangs. "So," he says at last, his tone considered, careful, like a man feeling his way forward. "You're back. Living with your granny and your kid and your cat. If I can help – just let me know."

I nod. I've told him all I can. Can't imagine asking for help. "Your folks?"

"Both passed. Cancer. Dad's chewing tobacco, Mom's uterus. It's been years now."

"I'm so sorry." I have to restrain myself from blurting out anything that might hint at attraction. Our old bond still calls me, and I want him to know something that only Cherie knows. "I haven't told Jordan who his father is," I say in a low voice, leaning forward over the table so his face is close. "His father's married."

"Your business. I won't say anything if you're intent on keeping it private. You'll have to tell him sooner or later. He has a right to know. So does his dad, whoever he is." He pulls away, his hands stilled on his lap. "Luka, there's something I want to tell you."

"Sorry." I am, but I mean to keep him at arm's length. "It's great to see you, Earl. I need – I need a little time to get settled in and all. You understand?"

"You haven't changed, Luka. You still don't want to hear what someone else has to say. What is it you're so afraid of? And are we ever going to talk about why you left?"

The heat rushes across my face. I stand up and shake my head ever so slightly. My shopping bag falls free and thuds to the cement floor. I kneel, concentrate on the bruised skin and damaged flesh of the fruit. No words come when he kneels beside me and helps retrieve them. Then he nods, raises one eyebrow and smiles, a cotton candy half-grin with sadness at its core that reminds me of Anky.

"I know," he says as he puts a peach in my hand. "More bad timing, eh?"

Just like that. I keep my head down until the clomping of his cowboy boots across the market's cement floor fades.

Eight

CONNIE'S HOUSE IN SASKATOON is a snap to find, a traditional dark green two-storey on Colony Street with a glassed-in front porch and a red picket fence festooned with sweet pea blossoms. I park a few houses away and sit in my Beetle before I go down the sidewalk to Con's gate, remembering the time that followed Jordan's birth as I discovered a new way of living life in Vancouver. I bought a trailer for my daily bike rides on the seawall, and after Jordan was born, he went everywhere with me. He was two when he tossed his first Frisbee on Kits Beach, and even younger when he first visited Granville Island market for cheese and olives and everything in between. Some weekends, Cherie and I loaded the kids and our tired asses onto the ferry to Victoria, restoring our senses by telling each other stories on the old quarry's hillside at Butchart Gardens while Keesie ran circles around us and Jordan slept in his stroller. Sometimes we drove up the Squamish highway to Whistler, or retreated to Harrison Hot Springs without the kids for evenings of sushi and sake. Hanging over it all was the pall of the pig farm horrors, women missing and murdered, and the trial and sentencing that followed. Every woman in the Vancouver area must still feel its effect. Cherie and I tried to keep current, but the details were grim, and I had to turn off the television. I couldn't duck my own worries – where was Mother? She'd fallen through the cracks and disappeared. Every time I heard a news story about another woman gone missing or another body found, I prayed.

Then Con called me back home when Anky started to fail. I had to do one last hunt before I drove to the prairies. "My last search, I promise," I told her. She surprised me with her response.

"Yes, of course you have to. We've just avoided talking about it. The Downtown Eastside is a tough neighbourhood. Women have vanished there. Maybe Mother was one of them. She may have been one of that maniac's victims. I think both of us have suspected that's a possibility for some time. I know I haven't had the heart to admit it. Whatever you turn up won't be pretty. Are you sure you want to know?"

"Which is worse, knowing or not knowing?"

"Knowing," Connie said promptly, surprising me again.

"But I need to know."

"I understand that," Connie said. "Now listen. I'm going to tell you a few things about being a good investigative reporter. There's no trick to it. All reporters are what Anky called Neisheerich, you know, nosy. Like me." She half-paused. "It's okay, Luka, I know what I'm like. It's about asking questions, and not being afraid to ask. Asking the right people. Start with the databases where newspaper articles are archived. I'll text you a couple of good sites to save you some time. You'll find tons of stuff about the inquiry. Look for articles that identify the cops involved in the cases, then locate the cops through the police station. Are you sure you want to?"

"I don't know. I've got this stomach ache."

We'd had this conversation before, but it was different this time, with more at stake, more than one life. I chided myself at the same time Connie did. "When you get stuck, get some air," she said curtly. "Go for a walk. Or call me."

FOLLOWING CON'S hard-headed coaching session, my online research turned up an appallingly long list of names catalogued by the Missing Women's Inquiry, along with relatives' names – sisters, sons, mothers, cousins of the vanished. More digging revealed a few contact numbers. One morning I dressed Jordan quickly and headed out with a glance down the slope toward Kits Beach, then made a quick stop around the corner to drop him at daycare. Rain turned the sky into melted pewter, fine drops that settled into mist and masked any sight of the ocean. The sea, that smell, still foreign after over a decade of living on the coast, deeply saline, bracing iodine. I filled my lungs as I hopped a bus across the Burrard Bridge, through the streets between downtown skyscrapers, past the SeaBus terminal. Anxiety settled in as the bus cruised east along Hastings, the rain so heavy that I couldn't see more than a few feet through the foggy window. I looked hard, squinting for sight of the big neon sign, the seahorse. I hadn't been to The Only in years.

The bell rang and I jumped out of the bus's rear door at Main and Hastings. My path took me past the old Carnegie Centre, where kids half my age hung out, the sweet, pungent reek of pot hanging in the air. I skirted the steps, hurrying. Mother's high-planed features floated into my memory. She'd gone to The Only, I was sure of it. A tenuous link, yes, but a link I needed to follow. All I had was memory.

There was no neon seahorse sign, no window full of fish, no Only. What had happened? I had the address right, I'd been there dozens of times. It had to be there. I leaned against the damp window and studied the building, the Loggers Social Club. Old brick, high windows, and definitely no neon seahorse. I'd thought The Only would always be there. Why would I bother to check online? The sinking feeling in my chest felt like a personal betrayal. I remembered how my searches for Mother had radiated out, fuelled by my meals at The Only – chowder, salmon, pan-fried halibut, my first oysters. When I peered through the filthy window, stained and torn paper hanging inside on the glass obscured the interior. I couldn't see the counter, the stove, the stools. Now what?

But it was gone. When my stomach rumbled I headed around the corner to a Cantonese place on East Cordova. Half an hour later, belly full, empty rice bowl and clamshells stacked on the table in my booth, I pulled out my cell phone and Googled The Only. Sure enough, it had been closed by the city for selling undersized crab and fish it couldn't produce invoices for, the fabulous neon seahorse sign hauled off to a museum. The sky darkened, grey clouds turning black, closing off the horizon. It was time to dial one of the numbers that I'd found during my hunt for the families of that murdering madman's victims.

"Shannon Petrie." At the sound of that clipped no-nonsense voice, I wondered how to introduce myself. Excuse me, I want to pry into your family's past. Pardon me, I need to know about your missing mother or aunt or sister. Mea culpa, I need to cause you some pain. There was no way except straight off the high board. "You don't know me. My name is Luka Dekker. I found your name on the Missing Women's Inquiry website. My mother is missing."

Silence on the other end. I counted to almost ten before I resigned myself to the abrupt click and dial tone.

Three more attempts failed. On the fourth, my fingers stumbled across the digits. The voice that responded was a man's soft tenor. "Roger speaking."

"Roger Arnett? Mister Arnett, I am so sorry to trouble you. I found your name on the list of relatives of missing women on the Inquiry website."

A definite silence. "Are you media?"

"My mother is missing. Since – oh, I don't even know how long now. Since I was eight. My name's Luka Dekker. Do you have a minute to speak with me?"

I could make out a voice in the background, husky, male, interrogative. "No, it's fine, Mason. Ms. Dekker, I've spoken with too many reporters in the past five years. How can I help?"

"I'm not a reporter. I'm looking for my mother. And call me Luka."

"Well, you have my sympathies, Luka." A whispered debate interrupted him. Then his voice returned. "I'll help if I can. What do you want to know?"

"That's the thing. I don't know. Can you maybe just tell me –" Reluctance slowed my words. How to ask him to replay his own pain? "I'm sorry. This was a bad idea."

"No, not necessarily." He paused and took a breath. "My sister's name was Amanda. She was seventeen when she vanished ten years ago. Five years ago, DNA identified her as one of the women attacked and murdered by that pig farm monster. I won't use his name. He doesn't deserve to be named."

"I am so sorry."

"It didn't go to trial. I'm not sure what good another trial would have done anyhow." My question finally framed itself in the pause, but he resumed speaking, answering my unasked question. "Missing Amanda doesn't stop. What *does* help is knowing. Maybe that's what you need. Call the cops, the lead detective. I don't remember his name, Porto, Park, something like that, a guy with a PhD, but his bosses didn't have much time for him; they said that hunches were better than deduction. It sounded like something out of early Sherlock Holmes. Anyhow, he figured out the serial killer thing. Talk to him."

"How do I say thank you?"

"Here's how: make a memorial for your mother. Something to remember her as she was, and as the woman she might have become. Don't let her get frozen as a victim in your head. You've got to melt the ice, then bury her, and establish a memorial that isn't *her*. My thoughts, for what it's worth. My partner and I host a soup kitchen in Amanda's name every few months at the women's centre."

Just before I hung up, he added, "Have you gone to the Inland Hotel on East Hastings? It's in the same building as Insite – you know, the safe injection site. It provides housing for people who can't find any other housing. They have a doctor on staff who's written books about mental illness and addiction. Maybe he met your mom."

When I called the Inland Hotel's clinic, I waited on hold for almost ten minutes. Finally a voice with an East Coast cadence came on the line. "Inland. Can we help?"

"I'd like to make an appointment with your doctor, please."

"Your lucky day, dear. I just had a patient cancel with Doctor Matthew for tomorrow, nine A.M. What's this regarding?"

"Doctor Matthew may have treated my mother."

There was a moment's silence. "Bring government ID."

My hands shook I disconnected. It took a few minutes to calm myself enough to resume my online search. A site slid past, and I rolled back to it: "The Blue Blog: A Walk on the Wild Side," a Downtown Eastside blog by a working Vancouver cop, a beat cop who walked the streets and likely knew the street kids and predators that preyed on them. Excerpts that I browsed showed that the guy had seen some stuff. I closed the entry, appalled. This could be about Mother. How could voyeurism into such private pain help? I returned to the blog's home page. Overwhelmed by the despair the blog couldn't disguise, I noted the cell phone number of the cop behind it, then stared at my keypad. Finally I tapped out a brief text message, outlining Mother's disappearance, asking to meet.

I was about to step out the door when my phone chirped. The text read: "Got yr message. Noon @ Waves, Main & Pender. Look for badge. Constable Blair Smith, VPD. Blogger cop."

For the first time since I'd risen, I saw blue sky.

The rain slowed just before noon. As I approached Waves, I spotted a muscular cop in a blue uniform beside the circular window by the door. He sat alone, openly studying each person who walked in, just watching, pale sharp eyes, and a hedgehog's eyebrows and moustache beneath the taper fade haircut. "Luka?" he asked as I stepped inside. His mouth seemed stapled shut, his teeth barely parting as he spoke.

"How'd you guess?"

"That look. Going to meet a cop you don't know gives a person a particular look. I've seen it dozens of times." He stood six inches shorter than me when he got to his feet and held out his hand. "I'm Blair Smith. Constable. Call me Blair."

By the time I seated myself at his table with an espresso, Smith had pulled a tablet from his backpack and tapped away at it, two-fingered. "You said you're looking for your mother? What's her name? Maybe we've had her in the system."

"Lark Dekker. But..."

He interrupted brusquely. "Don't start second-guessing. How long has she been missing?"

"Hang on a sec, Constable. I'm curious about this blog of yours. How is it that a policeman has a blog? Is it official? I mean, are you sanctioned by the police department? Or are you some kind of rogue?"

"I don't have anyone vetting what I write, if that's what you're wondering." His tone didn't lighten and his eyes were chips of grey ice. "You had a look at my posts. I present the neighbourhood, show folks what really happens here from the perspective of someone who walks the streets every day. It isn't pretty. Now can we get to it?"

As I told him the story of Mother's disappearance, Smith's eyes narrowed. "So you were, what, five?"

"Eight."

"You remember her?" I nodded. "What you have to remember is that her disappearance fits the timeline of when that maniac started killing women down here."

Hearing Mother so casually classified as a possible multiple murder victim shocked me into silence. Smith didn't seem to notice. "We've found forensic evidence and DNA of dozens of women on his farm," he continued. "The sick fuck brags he killed forty-nine. There've been no names attached as yet to all those victims, but you'd know that too, eh?" He eyed me from beneath his bristling brows. The look verged on hostility. "You and your family didn't begin to wonder when the news about the pig farm started to come out?"

I squirmed on the tiny chair, feeling like a chastised child, and made an effort to keep my tone neutral. "Yes. No. We filed a missing persons report ages ago, and I looked high and low when I moved here. But my grandmother's getting old, and I'm a single mom."

Smith leaned back and crossed his arms. "No one's pointing any fingers. It's tougher after this much time, though. Chances of finding her are long at best. Hundreds of women disappear. Most never surface."

"So I'm just supposed to give up and go home?" My voice rose. Several people glanced at us, then averted their eyes as Smith scowled.

"You're too late. I've been a beat cop in the Downtown Eastside for seven years." He snorted again. "I've got a good idea of how things play out. The place is an open-air drug market."

"I know that." I bit down the frustration rising like bitter medicine. "It is my mother we're talking about."

"You don't have a monopoly on mothers. Every dickhead junkie out there has a mother. Some of them are just as messed up as their kids."

My temper sparked, but I spoke as evenly as when I addressed my son. "I know that too. Maybe there's someone else I can talk to. Another cop who knows the ground?"

Smith shrugged and tapped his pad. "The real work on this case was done by a hotshot detective, first one on the force to earn a Ph.D. Rockmore, his name is, a Geordie, from the north of England. He works in Homicide, did a stint in Missing Persons, knows the case cold. He's the man to talk to."

"You know him?"

"He's an okay dude. I'll ask if he's free. Hang on."

I swallowed the last coffee in my demitasse. This cop was helping, but his anger was contagious. Did all cops acquire that unsympathetic shell? Smith seemed to read my mind. He looked up and cocked his head at me like a bantam rooster. "He says to send your mom's details and he'll get back to you. I'll text you his email."

I nodded, relieved to have the whole thing deferred and at the same time horrified at how simply human lives were categorized and shelved. Smith tapped at his tablet again while I stared out the window, watching the parade of people going by, my brain sorting through all the possibilities I'd avoided considering, all the ways Mother could have come to grief.

"It's all happening so quickly," I said when Smith looked up from typing.

That snort again. "Welcome to the digital age. We've got old-timers on the force tell stories that curl my hair about how long it used to take to get information from one person to another." One more tap on his tablet. "The computer has revolutionized police work." The tablet beeped and Smith bent to read the screen, then bundled the tablet away into a messenger bag.

"Send a full description and photo of your mom to Rockmore. He'll get back to you. That's all he can do right now. I've sent you his contact info. Now excuse me. I'm on duty." He waved off my thanks. "Just doing my job."

Standing on the sidewalk's rutted pavement moments later, I gazed at the dome of the Carnegie Centre half a block away. An open-air drug market, Smith called the area. It was ironic that the district included The Only, where I'd fortified myself in my own way.

Nine

I'M HEAD DOWN, scuffing the grass like memories as I pass through Con's gate. How will Con greet me? Is Neal in residence? I don't even get a chance to ring the bell. Con flings open the door, leaps down the stairs, throws her arms around me, then tugs me into the house. "Oh, prodigal you, welcome home!"

Newspapers and magazines lie open across the kitchen counter and dining room table. Books are stacked on the floor and coffee table, and beside her laptop on the overstuffed armchair. Some are by Saskatchewan authors whose names I recognize: Martel, Birdsell, Campbell, Margoshes, Slade, Vanderhaeghe. Quilts hang from every wall, tidily folded over backs of chairs and couch. Connie follows my eyes. "Those quilts are all new. Making them helps me concentrate."

My sister looks more and more like Anky, her hair longer, her edges rounder and softer than when she was a teenager. She's no taller than my shoulder, but she still moves like lightning loosed across the sky. "How's that nephew of mine?"

"A little anxious. School starts soon."

"Why don't you send him to school in Saskatoon instead of in Goodfare?"

"Too much driving, Con. We're only staying a few months, remember?"

"I hadn't forgotten. I thought you might like him to get a better education."

"It's just a few months, Con. Just until..."

"You really think Anky's at death's door? Cynic. She's a tough old bird. Whatever, I'm glad you're back. I've got a job interview in Toronto coming up at *The Star* and Anky's going to need someone."

"Where's Neal?"

"How's Jordy taking to rural life?"

"He loves the farm. He loves Anky, too. What about Neal, Con?"

"He's away."

I can't crack this code. Away, at work? Away, in a different home? Away, permanently? I know that if I press her, Con will only duck and weave. So I let it slide. "Speaking of Anky, she showed us this old picture of Mother and Dad dancing. She says she has more pictures. She told me about her mother, Klara, and Yoppela, and the first Jordan. I want her to tell me something about Mother as an adult."

Silence. I just struck a nerve. And committed yet another tactical error: I forgot that Con can't keep track of more than one thread at a time; she gets flustered and talks in circles. How she manages at work baffles me.

"Luka," Connie's voice cracks with barely contained exasperation, "what came of your last hunt for her? We spoke a few months ago, and I haven't heard anything." She nudges me. "Sit down. Let's hear it."

The retelling takes longer than I'd expected. Emotion rises up in waves as I recount my trips through the Downtown Eastside.

THE DAY AFTER MEETING Blair, my third coffee of the day in hand, I stood in the shadow of an angular concrete and aluminum building on East Hastings. The sign read "Insite," with a diagram of a hypodermic needle, then "Inland Hotel Society." Beneath it, a smaller sign: "Gabriel Matthew, MD."

The clinic was already busy, every chair occupied. I checked in with the receptionist, and recognized her thick Newfoundland accent from my phone call. Then I waited. After an hour, I started looking for ways to bust through the paper queue that the receptionist had lined up on her desk. How would Connie manage such a situation?

A slightly built dark-haired man in a white lab coat with a stethoscope over his shoulder finally emerged from the hallway, his hand on the shoulder of a woman in a tank-top and short denim skirt, her heavily pregnant belly protruding.

"I'll see you next when you deliver that baby, Daphne," he said. "Won't be long."

The man sitting beside me burst into applause. "Doctor Matthew," he called, his voice a broken drainpipe, "you're the best." The rest of the people in the waiting room started clapping too.

"Thank you, Aloysius," Doctor Matthew said. "Just a few more minutes, and I'll be right with you."

"Sure doc, sure."

"Luka?" the receptionist called, and I followed Doctor Matthew into an examining room.

He didn't wait for me to sit. "How can I help?"

"I need to ask if you know my mom." I pulled the photo from my bag. "She's been missing since I was eight years old. Please, Doctor."

"What's her name? Missing since... when?"

"Lark Dekker. Since 1988, when she came to Vancouver."

"That's a long time. She's past middle age by now. In all likelihood, if she's been living rough and doing drugs, she's long dead. I'm sorry." His voice was accented, Central European, maybe. "I can check our records if you'd like to wait. Please spell her name?"

He left the room. I heard a loud chorus of jeers and catcalls when he reappeared a few minutes later. "They thought I was done with you," the doctor said, flipping through a file. "We only ever had one Lark. I remember – she was an explosive patient, tall, red hair, threw things, plants, plates, whatever came to hand. I caught her threatening to throw a cat at another patient once. I remember her telling me that she had two daughters she missed terribly, then she started crying. That sound like your mother?"

I nodded, reeling inwardly.

"She lived at the Inland, and I had her taking lithium and olanzapine, but whenever she started feeling better, she stopped taking her meds. She disappeared. That would have been back in 1995, not long after we opened. Now, if you'll excuse me..."

I walked out feeling lightheaded. 1995. That was before I even moved to Vancouver. The load of blame I carried shifted slightly. But why didn't I find this clinic when I first arrived in Vancouver in 1998?

"That'll be ten Hail Marys and five Acts of Contrition," the receptionist said as I emerged into the waiting area.

"What?"

"For taking so long." A grin briefly softened her face. "Just joking, dear. Pretend you're in St. John's. We all get down on our knees and repent regularly there. Have a lovely day."

At home that evening, I emailed Detective Rockmore a photo and a detailed description of Mother – her age, date of birth, date she disappeared, height, hair colour. Her jewellery – just the necklace. Her habits – mah jong, vodka, cigarettes, clothes. Her medical history. Her disappearance from the Inland. Everything I could think of. I hadn't heard back when I loaded the car and drove east with Jordan and Ming two months later.

"SO ARE YOU DONE with this obsession?" Con asks when I run out of words, her voice surprisingly soft. "Mother is gone. No news. Nothing."

"But Con, since I've come back it's like living with a ghost. She's everywhere."

"She's dead. And you've got your Jordy to think about."

"I know, but –"

"But nothing. You couldn't find Mother in Vancouver during twelve years of looking. Every time I called, you'd just come back from some hunt or other. You said that you'd just do that one last search. Give it up now. You're done."

"I don't expect to find her. Not her, just... some sign. Maybe she's left something. A clue."

"Anky spent hours combing through missing persons' reports from across the country, don't you remember? She talked to cops from Vancouver, Calgary, Victoria, Nanaimo, even Seattle, and back east too. What clues could you possibly turn up on the farm? Twenty-two years after she ditched us? Get real, Luka. This isn't some stupid fairy tale."

"Connie, you're not listening." I wonder again how Con has prospered for so long as a journalist. She's deaf to anything that doesn't suit her view of the world.

Ten

DURING MY DRIVE HOME, I use memories of our childhood to diffuse my anger with Connie. Dad spent his time on the rodeo circuit; Mother's moods coloured everything. Some mornings, she would laugh and tickle Con and me and run up and down the kitchen, shrieking. Other days, she wouldn't move from her bed. Those days, Connie called Anky out from her little house across the green. Anky was literally our anchor. She kept the market garden immaculate, weighed the fruit, made change, and said "Thank you" to the well-dressed city ladies who came to pick berries and salad greens. She eventually enlarged the shack, adding refrigerated drinks and ready-picked vegetables and berries, lemonade, and ice cream. "We need them," she said when Mother finally noticed. "There are other farms those ladies can visit." Mother just twirled the beads on her necklace, then tugged her lower lip.

When Mother left a few months later, Anky and Oltvetter Paul moved from the tiny two-room house to live in the big main house with Con and me. We helped haul clothes and books, trip after trip until we both collapsed on the porch in tears. I had no words to express how I felt. Late that night, the coyotes yipping from beyond the fields, I did my best. "Anky, did I do something bad?"

Anky shook her head, her answer oblique. "Your Mother's sick, liebling. She has been for a long, long time."

WHEN I REACH the farm, my body aches as if I spent the morning throwing rocks. I climb out of the car with the bag of peaches, apples, and cheese slung over one shoulder.

Jordan leaps at me. "Mama! Anky's been telling me stories!"

"What kind of stories?" He squirms onto my hip, and I bury my face briefly in the crook of his neck. Something about the sweet scent of child is grounding. His hair has gone spiky in the heat, and I smooth the ends into a semblance of tidy. I catch myself mid-motion, mirroring Anky. She always uses her hands to express her feelings. I often find myself smoothing Jordan's face or hair, straightening his shirt, snugging his scarf, without uttering a word. Despite all the love that wells up every time I look at him. Despite telling myself repeatedly to speak. Do I want Jordan to pick up the habit of not talking? Habits, good or bad, are hard to break. "Where's Anky?"

"Stories about when she was a girl. And about you! Mama, did you really drive a tractor when you were my age?"

"No, sprout, I didn't. Where's Anky?"

"Sleeping."

"Okay. Let's be quiet, then."

Anky's asleep in the parlour, her small frame a compact comma on the couch, her hair unbound and falling over the edge. Guilt pricks at my eyelids. I should never have asked her to mind Jordan. As Connie reminded me, she's old. Frail. She's already raised a daughter and two grand-daughters. The last thing she needs is responsibility for another youngster.

"ANKY, I'M CURIOUS," I say over tea in the kitchen after tucking Jordan into bed later that evening. "Why did you send Mother to live with Marina?"

Anky's broad face thins and tightens. "I've told you this before. I couldn't reach her. She was ill. You know that."

"How could you send away your own child? It must have –" It must have been painful, I was about to say, but the look on Anky's face tells me it was far worse.

"Marina offered to keep her. I trusted Marina more than my own mother, and it made sense at the time, but I've lived with the regret ever since. Now let's talk about something more pleasant. You said you wanted to see some pictures, yes? Bring me that album on the top shelf in the parlour."

Anky's hands shake when I hand her the album. She flips it open to the front page, pointing at an array of photos. "There's your mom, your dad, you, Connie." I know these images. I've seen them dozens of times, but not for a dozen years. Maybe I'll see them in a different light today. "Take them," she says, insisting. Several loosen easily.

"Anky, I want to know more. What was Mother like?"

"You lived with her, Luka. You know what she was like."

The moment passes. Anky seems to shrink, and announces herself worn out and ready for bed soon after. I return to the album and find an unfamiliar photo, a black and white image of a middle-aged fair-haired woman, round-bodied, with Slavic cheekbones and wide eyes beneath plucked eyebrows set in a broad forehead. "Marina, 1955" in Anky's familiar slanting script at the bottom of the page.

Upstairs, I pin the photos on the corkboard between the shots of Jordan and of Mother and Dad dancing. The gallery is growing. Anky said she trusted Marina more than her own mother. Anky has secrets, but her time to share them is slipping away.

OVER THE NEXT WEEK, Anky and I often discuss rural life. I want to know how she coped with raising two kids on a farm. She tells me that all the nearby families work off-farm so they can afford to live on the farm. It sounds crazy, and I begin to wonder if a revived market garden like Anky operated might have potential. And school – a bus will take Jordan to and from Goodfare each day.

On Sunday, when I return to the market, I stop at Suzanne's booth to rave about her Manchego. "That's one great cheese!"

She laughs, and we spend a few minutes trading notes on cheeses we love. When I leave, my bag contains more Manchego and a fat slice of a sheep's milk blue she's experimenting with.

All that week, we lay down the basis of new rhythms. We harvest carrots and the last pole beans, freeze rhubarb, make strawberry jam. When the breeze rises inexorably each day, I want to fly kites with Jordan, but I refuse to consider asking Earl about his kites or kite-making. Instead, I teach my kid how to choose ripe tomatoes for picking.

Hannah arrives alone on Monday afternoon as I embark on making my first-ever batch of dill pickles. "The boys are haying the south field," she says briskly. "I'll do the week's cleaning. Luka, don't even think about helping. It's obvious you're busy." She hands me a cake pan. It's warm. "Here, I made peach kuchen. Let's have it later, eh, my girl?" She peers into the parlour at Jordan and Anky, asleep on the couch, and disappears upstairs. I can't resist the caramel on the kuchen, and sneak a tiny taste. Later, when we congregate on the porch with kuchen and lemonade, Jordan tells Hannah stories about the barn kittens he chased, hoping to pat them.

"Come over when you can, Luka," Hannah says as she leaves. "No rush."

Jordan has relaxed since we arrived. He seems happier, calmer, runs all over the farm all day long. He hasn't cried for Keesie since that one time. He walks when he's around Anky, and is quick to bring her whatever she needs – sometimes before she asks. After supper the two of them settle on the couch in the parlour, and from the kitchen, clearing up pots and dishes, I hear her voice in that storyteller's cadence. I try to listen, but her voice is pitched too low to catch. Each evening after Jordan is in bed I walk the farm, looking. Just looking. The landscape is as familiar as my own hand.

I worry more at night. I tiptoe into Anky's room as well as Jordan's to check on safe breathing and sound sleep. Anky's spring has finally loosened. She sleeps later and later, and takes longer to wake. By mid-afternoon each day she and Jordan crash in the parlour, toe to toe on the couch with Ming slung across a hip or ankle or curled behind a bent knee. Did she wait for me to come home so she could let go? I can barely think about it. I take to brushing and braiding Anky's long hair at bedtime and before breakfast, as if for a child. One day she sits down to lunch still in her nightgown, and I nearly choke on my sandwich when I realize that she needs help dressing. For years, she's been the unstoppable wellspring of energy in my life. I'm not ready to think otherwise. Each morning, I pray I won't need to pick up the phone and share the inevitable with Con.

Anky isn't the only one on my mind. I dream of Earl, and often wake in a stir of sexual energy, imagining his hands on his keyboard. Holding a pen. Leafing through stacks of pages. And during the day, everywhere I look, I see Mother. The air smudges and blurs, and each morning, as I walk to the barn to feed the barn cats, time slips out of focus. I can't tell if it's 2010 or twenty years earlier, if I am an adult leading my son, or a child looking for Mother's shape ahead of me. This farm buildings and yard and fields feel haunted, by her absence, and her presence.

ONE SATURDAY AFTERNOON in late August, after we return from a visit with Suzanne at the market, Jordan and I walk over to Hannah and Mick's house while Anky naps. Jordan carefully carries a homemade peach pie, but halfway down the driveway, I take charge of it. Hannah meets us at the gate, three broad-shouldered boys of varying heights at her heels. They all have straight black hair and bangs. At a guess, their ages range from ten to sixteen.

"You Jordan?" the tallest asks. When Jordan nods, he sticks out his hand. "I'm Nash, this is my brother Stills, and my other brother Crosby." I start to laugh. Nash scowls, only half-heartedly. "Yes ma'am, my dad thought it was a pretty funny way to name us. Good thing there aren't four of us, or the youngest would be Young."

Hannah chases them all off to play soccer, then ushers me to a bench in the shade of an old elm. We sit facing the garden, a pair of black and white collies watchful on the grass at our feet. Small hills studded with aspens swell west of the garden and long-horned Highland cattle graze among the trees. A scarecrow wavers in the breeze, trapped in the tomato patch. Her garden spreads untidily but sensibly. Bulging squashes shelter beneath corn stalks where pole beans climb. Marigolds and calendula flutter yellow and orange flags among the beets and carrots.

"This is so lovely, it reminds me of Anky's market garden back in the day."

"Have you thought about reviving it?"

"Well, yes," I admit, "I'm not staying for more than a school term, two at most. But if I were to stay, I'd launch a CSA, maybe." I explain the term.

"Pre-sold crop shares? Smart! Every farmer needs that! If you were to take it on, you could rent a stall at the farmer's market to build up clientele. You should call and get on the vendors' waiting list right away. Just in case." Then she asks how I feel, nods when I don't immediately answer, her bright eyes scanning me unabashedly. "Rural life is a big change. You must be lonely, my girl. Anyone in your life? Will Jordan's dad swing by for a visit?"

I don't answer. Hannah launches into a long story about her first boyfriend. Then she casually drops in a short phrase: "I hear Earl bumped into you at the market." I must look shocked. "It's rural life, Luka. Word travels fast. Your grandmother has told me that you were sweet on him as a youngster. If you want to talk, I'm right here."

I feel the warmth in my face. "Nothing to discuss. So you thought you might have some school pictures of my mother?"

"I'll dig those photos out and bring them over sometime soon. Now should we try that pie?"

"You knew Mother?" I ask a few minutes later around mouthfuls of peaches and pastry.

"I never met her, but my mom – she died a few years back – rode the bus with her back in the day. She told me stories about how Lark flirted on the school bus, had all the boys eating out of her hand. One boy brought her records of Elvis and The Everly Brothers and Little Richard because she loved to dance. For months, Mom said, she had a crush on – now what was his name? – the principal's son, a cute Polish boy, a little wild himself." She pauses. "Something happened on the bus, Mom said. People talked."

"Pauline mentioned the bus too, and a boy. I asked Anky, but she almost cried."

"Not my place to say if Charlotte hasn't. She's had a load to bear, your grandmother. No, I don't mean you, sweetie! Now, will that sister of yours be visiting more? Now that you're back, I mean." Hannah raises her eyebrows and tips her head back, looking at me along her long nose when I don't respond. "Family can be tough."

"She blames me for not coming home sooner."

"Has she spent the past six years raising a little boy on her own? No? Then she's got nothing to do but lighten up. And you can tell her I said so."

As we walk home past a flash of volunteer calendula in bloom along the driveway, I think of the unexpected spark of yellow that Earl dug up for me the spring before I left for Vancouver. I've tried to simply avoid thinking of him. Now I bite my lip, remembering his face as we had coffee at the market. How he leaned toward me across the tiny table.

Eleven

THE DAY AFTER LABOUR DAY is another mild one, all the leaves still hanging, and green as summer.

"You are big now, Jordan," Anky says. "No more Klanaschuel – kindergarten," she explains when he looks puzzled. She hands him a small wooden box. "Pencils, all colours," she tells us. "Like I used to use. The box was made by my brother Albert." Jordan slides the lid in its grooves several times, peers inside, thanks her, tucks it carefully into his backpack. He seems calm as I drive him to school in Goodfare. At the classroom door, I smooth his hair, surprised at how choked-up I am. Before I retreat into the bustling hallway, I see that he's smiling as he advances toward the gaggle of children. He looks so small, so young. How can he already be starting school? His feistiness reminds me of Anky.

I spend the rest of the morning walking the farm from one end to the other. Mother's spirit, clad in her amber necklace and silk finery, follows. I pace the grounds, notebook in hand, assessing *terroir* and its inscrutable elements – soil, slope, sunlight, aspect, exposure – and measure potential spots for possible new beds and orchards, raised beds and greenhouses. Looking. Just looking. Good practice for when I actually do start my own garden back on the coast. As I walk I talk to Mother, about Jordan, mostly, and my worries for Anky. When I have lunch with Anky on the deck, I don't mention this.

"I found a lovely spot for an orchard, Anky," I say over our tomato and pickle sandwiches. She doesn't look up from her plate, and I wonder if she heard me.

"An orchard needs an orchardist. You could stay." Her tone is mild.

"Well, yes, just for a little while." Until she dies. The unspoken reason for my deadline hangs in the air.

"Your boy needs roots, Luka." Her voice has that level matter-of-factness that I've learned is unassailable.

Chastised child, me. I finish lunch without speaking.

NEXT MORNING, BEFORE Anky wakes, Jordan and I walk the length of the driveway to find the bus waiting. A half-breath later, the boys run up from the yard across the road. Nash escorts Jordan up the steps, then he hangs out the door, his grin a double for his mother's. "Mom says to stop in for coffee."

I am grateful.

"The boys will look out for him," Hannah says as I walk into her house. She looks more closely at me. "It's a hard truth for parents, to realize they need their children more than their children need them. It's our job to ready them, then let them go. Here, think about this instead. Mick's father was Goodfare school's unofficial photographer back in the day. Mick found a few of his pictures in the box of his dad's stuff. I recognized your mom right away – she looks so much like Jordan! Come look."

I don't have it in me to tell Hannah that the real cause of my grief is Anky, so I sit down and study the first picture. It was taken in the same era as the one I carried to Vancouver, and shows my young mother, seated, legs crossed, sleek in an elaborately embossed satin suit with matching pumps. Behind her, barely in focus, sits a coltish girl that I recognize as me.

"That's the grade three classroom," I say in surprise, "the last parent-teacher meeting she came to. I was so embarrassed that I slid my chair as far from hers as I could manage. Mother never cared what people thought."

I am grateful again for Hannah's restraint as she passes over another photo. Mother wears a sleeveless yellow linen dress, sandals laced to her knees, pearl drop earrings, and the double-strand amber necklace that matches my bracelet.

"Your mom really knew how to dress. What was the occasion?"

"I don't remember, yes, she had style. Once Dad came home from a rodeo and found her picking swiss chard in patent leather stilettos."

I purse my lips at Hannah's incredulous look. "Exactly. What do *you* wear in the garden? Not high heels. She went on big-money binges, shopping sprees that drove Dad and Anky to despair."

An hour later, the photos join the growing gallery on the bulletin board in my bedroom, and I go walkabout the farm in the vain hope that brisk movement will still the ghosts. Two hours later, exhausted, I join Anky while she watches the midday news. She's drawn all the blinds, and the poisonous blue glare of the television provides the only light. The feature report analyzes the recent announcement that B.C.'s Crown prosecutors have stayed all the outstanding murder charges against Vancouver's infamous serial killer. I can't stand to hear more about the pig farm. It's been months since I sent Detective Rockmore the information about Mother. No word. It feels like a lost cause. A few minutes later I find myself outside again, walking aimlessly across the farm. I end up at the meadow, staring blindly at the pair of lady's slippers.

NEXT DAY, AFTER seeing Jordan off, I finally call Connie, feeling completely alone.

"How's Anky? Her knee bothering her? She need anything?" Connie leaps into the conversation, her words in a rush as always, too much to say in not enough time, her staccato voice a creek in full spate, like Mother on her manic days. It's a workday, which means she's at the newspaper's office. I prefer imagining her in her sunny home office beside the dining room, imagine her pacing up and down, her boots clattering.

"I didn't get the job," Connie says. "So I'll just keep writing about politics from the prairies, I guess."

"So you'll be staying in Saskatoon, right? Good. Oh, sorry, Con, I mean –"

"Never mind." Her tone changes, and she says briskly, "Now then. I'm pleased. Want to know why? My editor just asked me to write about the missing Indigenous women in Vancouver's Downtown Eastside. The B.C. Attorney-General has announced a commission of inquiry. My last piece about Saskatoon police and their rotten record in dealing with First Nations women really got some traction, I think. You know, strip searches, harassment, but never the starlight tours they saved for the men – abandoning them barefoot at night in fields outside of town in thirty below zero. At least three men died."

"Why do you want to live in a city like that?"

"It's the same everywhere, Luka. It'll change. I have to believe that. You think Vancouver's any better, the way the city turned the Downtown Eastside into a ghetto? And what's worse in my opinion is that when housing prices go up in Vancouver like they always do, the yuppies will move in and gentrify it, and all those down-on-their-luck kids and low-income families will be forced out." Then, as abruptly as Mother ever did, Con changes channels. "Hey, why don't you bring Jordan and Anky into town for supper one of these days? No, maybe not, too much for her, right? I haven't come out yet so you could settle in without me breathing down your neck, it's high time I had some face time with my nephew, don't you think? Let's set a date. Soon. Deadlines are good. I've got a housewarming present all lined up."

"We aren't staying, Con. And no presents, please." Connie's last housewarming present was Ming, delivered to my Vancouver apartment by a Langley breeder as a fluffy spitball of three months.

Connie laughs. "Try not to worry. Anky's a tough old bird."

I hang up, feeling guilty and overwhelmed. My longing for Mother has upgraded from background breeze to tropical storm. And there seems little I can do about it. When I go to Anky's bedroom, there's no response to my knock, so I ease the door open and peer in. Anky is on the bed, facing the window, her torso rising and falling in the even rhythms of sleep. I retreat to the kitchen table, suddenly remembering her kindness the first time I went looking for Mother. When I first heard Marina's name.

MOTHER HAD BEEN gone a year. I tiptoed past Connie, busy doing geometry at the dining room table, Anky snoozing in her platform rocker beside the fireplace, and Oltvetter Paul on the couch, his book on his chest along with his glasses. I laced on my sneakers, put an apple and a chunk of cheese in my pocket, pulled on a jacket, and headed into the yard. It was early September. The elm trees curved above me, a high arch of trembling green leaves that softened the morning light as I passed under their arms to the driveway.

A few minutes later, I reached the gravel road. Mother had said she was going west. So I headed west on the grid road. As I walked, I called, "Mother!" So tiny I felt, under the vast blue awning of sky, my words vanishing, the horizon and the west so far away I simply couldn't imagine them.

A second intersection. Sweating in my jacket, the sun climbing overhead, I had just finished eating my snack when Anky found me. She rolled up in the pickup truck, Connie jiggling on the seat beside her, Joni Mitchell's voice fuzzy on the dashboard radio.

"I'm going to Vancouver," I told them, determined to ignore whatever arguments or reasons Anky gave, a little deflated when she acquiesced.

"Okay, liebling. We'll all go."

Con grabbed my hand and held it too tightly. The spot between her and Anky made a welcome nest, made safer by Joni's plaintive guitar.

Anky drove for a while before she pulled off the highway and parked. We were on an escarpment where the highway overlooked the North Saskatchewan River.

"Look," she said, and pointed. "That's west." The highway dropped into the valley to a bridge and rose again, disappearing in a haze of dust. I clambered over Connie's legs, banged open the passenger door, and ran, screaming and crying, to an old blue spruce on the hilltop. A few minutes later, Anky came up behind me and put her arms around me.

"I want Mother!"

"I know, liebling," Anky said as Connie dashed up and hugged us. Anky took our hands. "Vancouver is a long drive, two or three days away." I stared and stared into the disappearing blue until my eyes ached, then Anky led us back to the truck. "When you are bigger, you will go look," she said. "But for now I will show you something else."

She started the truck, turned around and returned the way we'd come, into the yard, where she motioned us to get out. She led us across the field, east, through more fields and past the slough, through an open gate and down a lane and onto a knoll with a tiny house. Its windows boarded up, a rusted hand pump standing sentinel duty over a worn wooden platform in the centre of the yard. Distracted, I looked around in curiosity. Con and I galloped all over the farm and its adjacent fields where gates stood open, and we had always obeyed Mother's and Anky's primary rule – never cross a barbed wire fence.

"This is where my friend Marina lived as a girl," Anky said. "She lost her family too. So she adopted ours."

I'M STILL SITTING at the kitchen table when I hear Anky limp down the hall. Slowly I follow her outside onto the deck. She takes a seat in the sun, leans back and closes her eyes, her face and frail cheekbones relaxed into the contours of peace. A rush of panic cascades through me. What will I do when Anky dies?

"Don't pray over me until I'm gone, child," she says in a hoarse voice that I barely recognize. "And stop beating yourself. Children grow up and leave, parents die. You'll see soon enough. I'm just glad you've come back. Now, how about some fresh coffee?" Nodding, voice caught in my throat, I don't move. Anky, eyes still closed, with the sensory awareness that I'd forgotten from my childhood, simply shakes her head.

"I've had a long life," she says. "I'm ready to let it go." She looks it, too, as if she has exhaled for close to the last time, her body contracting and her cells shrinking. "I want a nice funeral. A viewing. A lunch. Nothing fancy. And don't let the Prediger give a long sermon. No fuss."

"Anky, don't."

"Hush, Luka. You have your young Jordan. He'll carry you through. Put your faith in –" She opens her eyes and takes a hard look at me. "In your own wits. Trust yourself. Now, where's my coffee? What have you done today? How's your garden plan working out?"

I want to take her shaking hands, re-infuse her with hope for the future. But her wan face, lines carved deeply at eyes and nose, warns me otherwise.

"One more thing," she says. "I read somewhere that remembering is holy. It may be, but don't get bogged down in the past. Now help me into the shade."

Contrition and humility temper my touch as I lead Anky to her porch chair, bring her coffee, and brush out her hair. "Don't braid it today," she says when I start plaiting the long strands. "I think better with it loose."

All afternoon I watch her. Anky seems impervious to the scrutiny. She sits peacefully in her deck chair under the Amur maple, the tree's wine-coloured leaves falling free and floating to rest on her shoulders and long silver hair.

Twelve

WHEN I COLLECT JORDAN from the bus on Monday, Hannah's boys follow us home, cracking jokes among themselves. I notice Jordan listening attentively, and when they report directly to Anky for instructions, he joins them, his mouth still full of crackers and peanut butter. She sets them to weeding, and it's evident from their no-nonsense manner that they've been well-schooled on chickweed, quackgrass, and other pests versus edible plants, so I duck into the kitchen and make lemonade and slice watermelon for the crew. The boys work diligently for an hour, chow down, then wave goodbye, lugging home their weeds in several bags for Hannah's chickens. Jordan joins Anky on the couch for a nap, and I slip out to the deck for yoga, assisted only by Ming. True to Hannah's and Anky's comments, the three boys will show up once a week until the garden begins to wind down – when Anky will pay the visitors handsomely and send them home with instructions to "help your mother put her garden to bed." To Jordan, who will pitch in on each of their work sessions, Anky will hand a fat envelope, with instructions to "put it someplace safe for Schwisem Gelt." At his questioning look, she will add, "Back-pocket money, I mean. Spend it!"

"I TOLD YOU I had a housewarming gift all set up, remember?" Connie says on the phone a week later, almost shouting with excitement. "A pup. Anky always had dogs, remember? She'll love this dog. So will you and Jordy."

"What the hell, Connie! I don't want –"

"He's the royal dog of France, a Great Pyrenees. He'll be a guardian. You can't say no, I've already paid for his first series of obedience classes. I'm bringing him this afternoon."

WHEN I SEE CON'S car on the driveway, I take off at a mad gallop up and along stairs and hallways. I stuff Jordan's forgotten socks and t-shirts into his closet, and my sweaty yoga clothing under the covers of my bed. Knowing Connie, she'll want to inspect every room. She runs up the steps and into the house with a bottle of wine in one hand and a cake box in the other. A string bag crammed with balls of all sizes dangles from her wrist. She sets everything on the kitchen table, goes straight to Anky, and whispers something in her ear that starts Anky laughing. Con pulls a DVD from her jacket pocket and hands it over. Then she turns to me to explain. "One of my colleagues interviewed Anky about her life as a young working woman during the war for a documentary she filmed last year."

Jordan bounces into the kitchen and skids to a stop when he spies a stranger.

"Nephew!" Con points at the collection of balls on the table. "Here's something for you and your puppy." Jordan grins, but makes no move toward her. "Now come over here and let me hug you properly."

"It's your auntie Connie," I reassure him.

He looks dubious but briefly submits to her petting before addressing the real reason for her visit. "Where's our puppy?"

We troop back to Con's car and she coaxes a long-legged pup out to meet us. He is mostly white, a fuzzy bundle of bounce, the tan and black mask on his face divided by a white blaze, a grey and fawn brindle patch on his back like a saddle. Jordan names him Scout, and I can only shrug at my child-less, dog-less sister's naïveté and thoughtless enthusiasms. Do I have the time for a puppy? The energy? It's like having another baby. And my suite in Vancouver is definitely too small for a dog, and doesn't have a fenced yard. What will I do with him when we return to the coast? Plus the fact that I drive a Beetle. But the deed is done. Scout seems sweet-natured and, I soon learn, a quick study. He and Jordan immediately chase Jordan's soccer ball around the yard until both lollop indoors and collapse on the parlour floor. Ming hisses, spits, bats at the pup's nose, then later, after Con's departure, curls up between Scout's paws.

"You and Jordan will do well with a dog to love," Anky observes. "Did I ever tell you about the dog my uncle gave me when I moved back to the farm? He was a handsome brute, like this pup. Smart, too. Showed me where the birds nested. What was his name? He was a comfort to me."

Scout rouses and whimpers. I get him outside quickly. Puppy classes are an immediate necessity, so I call the school Con engaged. It has an open intake policy and space available starting next week. Sheer dumb luck. I confer with Hannah – Jordan can sleep over on Friday nights for the duration of puppy school.

A WEEK LATER, in Saskatoon, I spot two tall frames at the dog school – a girl with waterfalling hair and larkspur eyes, and a man in aviator's sunglasses and a black cowboy hat bringing up the rear, leash in hand, a gigantic raw-boned Newfoundland pup loitering at his heels. It's been a month since we met at the market, Earl looks thinner, hair clipped short, beard gone, the skin of his cheeks pale. He seems genuinely pleased to see me, draping a long arm around my shoulders. I try to keep calm as I gently pull free, conscious of Claudine's cool stare. He hands the black pup's leash to Claudine. Scout scrambles over my feet to sniff the other dog.

"His name's Scout," I tell Earl and Claudine. "He's a present from my sister Connie."

"He's gorgeous, isn't he?" Claudine says, crouching and rubbing Scout's ears. "Such soft fur, like a bunny's. He looks like one of the livestock guardian dogs we have. Is he a Maremma?"

"No, close. A Great Pyrenees."

"I want to be a dog breeder and trainer. Can I take him in?" At my nod, she takes Scout's leash, chirps to him, and leads both dogs down the hall. Dogs in kennels bark at our passing.

"That's Lennox." Earl points at the inky behemoth lumbering at Claudine's heels. "Sue says a dog's cheaper than another baby. That one's too big for a house pet, I told her, but no. What she wanted. Where's your kid?"

"At Hannah's. Having him here would be a disaster." I catch myself staring, envious. Dogs, kid, Earl. The whole enchilada. "He's soccer-mad," I say, and hurry into the arena, anxious to fill the air. "I've got to get him into a kids' league or something. He wants to learn how to do a bicycle kick."

"Claude can teach him. She's been playing for years. Ask her."

"Great! I bet you guys have lots of fun. And the kites – I've been meaning to ask you."

Earl takes off his shades, tips his cowboy hat back and looks at me. For once those eyes are grey lakes instead of rivers, focused and still. "How's your granny?"

"On the verge of slipping away. I'm feeling unanchored."

"I know what you mean. When my folks died, I felt like the earth had slid out from underfoot. You coping?"

"I'm anxious. I don't know how to plan for it. And I'm overwhelmed by the change. Farm life, you know." Stop babbling like a fool. Next I'll be telling him about imagining Mother everywhere. About the growing collection of photos on the bedroom wall. About wishing he and I –

Earl's smile makes me wonder if he read my mind. "The good part of it is that you're a farm girl at last."

"Only sort of. I'm not staying, Earl. But if I was going to be anything here, I'd be a market gardener."

"Owners! Leash your puppies!" shouts the trainer standing in the centre of the arena. The tangle of animal legs and noses resolves into identifiable pets.

We smile at each other. Then I catch my breath and turn away, abashed. Later, we sit on the floor in a circle. Scout ends up in a heap across Claudine next to me, and Lennox's long legs scramble for purchase as he tries to perch on my lap. Earl reaches over to stroke thick black fur and paws the size of saucers. When Scout is restored to me, Earl puts his hand on my forearm. I don't pull away. Claudine registers our contact.

"Let's have coffee. I could swing by." His hand moves up my arm, tentative as a new father. "Just coffee."

"Kites, Earl. I want to learn about those kites."

"Okay. I'll bring makings for kites."

I drive through the evening light in a daze.

At home, Anky rouses when I bend over her. "Bandit," she murmurs.

"What, Anky?"

"Bandit. The dog's name." She closes her eyes.

In the parlour with a glass of wine. On the couch in the dark, thinking about puppies and Earl. That gentleness with children and animals seems an innate part of him. Maybe Mother saw the same quality in Dad.

They met in Vancouver. AJ Dekker was an orphan, raised by an uncle on a ranch near Williams Lake, high plains country, and he came to the coast for the Cloverdale rodeo, the same rodeo where he would die years later. When he heard that Mother came from a Saskatchewan farm, and had a family there, well, nothing would do but to move back when they got hitched. Better than Vancouver, he said, a soft city. When I moved to Vancouver at age eighteen, I would learn that he was right and wrong. The softness of the coastal climate could not hide the harshness of life on the Downtown Eastside, where I hunted for Mother.

Dad's rodeo trophies cluttered the house. Mother hated those things. They must have reminded her of the risks, and all the time that Dad spent away from home. Whenever he travelled, she'd cover them with old table-cloths and sheets. Once I asked her how Dad had won the biggest trophy, a glittering golden bull with wide-flaring horns. She sipped her vodka and scowled. No answer. So one afternoon while Mother was out in the garden, I climbed up onto the back of the sofa and tugged at the sheet draped over the trophy where it sat on top of the bookshelf. The trophy crashed down on top of me. The horns broke off. Then I read the engraving: *El Paso Rodeo Championship Bull Rider.*

Mother laughed so hard when she came inside, then she hugged me and gave me a slice of chocolate pie with whipped cream. A fitting result, she called it. Dad laughed, too, on his next trip home.

"I got plenty more where that came from," he said as he gave the fragments back to me. "You make your own trophy outta these. That might be worth something."

When he came home between rodeos, he disappeared into the bedroom with Mother for the first couple of days, emerging for meals and a smoke on the steps. Evenings, I would tiptoe in and find space on the foot of the bed to watch old westerns with him, only to wake past midnight to hear him snoring, Mother cuddled and asleep under his arm.

"You still up?" he'd mutter when the creaking floorboards betrayed my passage on trips to or from the bathroom. "Get off to bed, you."

The last day, as he backed the horse trailer to the barn, Connie and I ran from the house, shrieking. "Wait, Daddy! Don't go!"

"Hey, you two, you'll spook the horses. Haven't I told you that before?"

We quietly stood by as he loaded both horses, then piled on as soon as he latched the trailer door.

"I'll be back in ten days. Take care of your mama. She needs your help, girls." He got in the truck and leaned out of the window. "Quick kiss." He smelled of alfalfa. "Bye!"

He waved as he slowly drove down the driveway. I could just see Mother, bent over the newly seeded carrots and radishes. She straightened slowly, adjusted her hat, brandished her trowel, walked to the edge of the drive. The truck stopped and Mother's arms went around Dad's neck, vanishing inside the cab. When she stepped back, Dad's truck and horse trailer resumed the long trek to the road. He stopped at the end, the outline of his arm visible outside the window as he took off his cowboy hat and waved it.

Mother returned to the garden and ferociously ripped up strawberry runners. That evening, she went to bed and didn't get up for a week. The second day, Con ran for Anky. She disappeared into Mother's bedroom, closing the door behind her.

I peeked through the crack at Anky sitting on the side of the bed, Mother's hand between hers. Anky's customary sharp tone flowed with honey. "They need you, Lark. Take your pills. Get up, liebling." But it did no good.

Anky stayed, filling the house with the scents of roasting chicken and cake. She sent me to the garden to pick strawberries and dig new potatoes. Mother remained in her bedroom when we ate supper.

"Luka, make a plate and take it to her," Anky said. "Connie, liebling, make up the spare bed for me, then run tell Oltvetter Paul that I will stay here tonight."

When the phone rang a week later, Mother knelt in the garden, weeding like a dervish, as if to exorcise the ghost that had swept her into the doldrums. I ran to her, unknowing message-bearer.

"Mother! Phone!" She set down her trowel, stood up, walked slowly toward the house. I couldn't see her face.

Dad's funeral was in the rain, at the small cemetery three kilometers away, where the rest of our family lay. Mother sold the horses and had Dad's spurs embedded in his gravestone.

SEVERAL TROPHIES STILL occupy the second shelf above my head. Maybe tomorrow I'll have a closer look at them. I am still on the couch, under a blanket with Scout at my feet, reading Anky's battered copy of Wendell Berry's agricultural essays when the phone rings, startling Scout awake.

"Hannah? Is he okay?"

"It's me." Earl's husky voice. "Still up?"

"Just settling down to read."

"Called to say glad you're in the neighbourhood. Makes me want to finish that book so I can start on a new one. I'm writing like crazy. This draft is close to done. Thanks for that, you're an inspiration! And I have an idea for a kite I think you'll like."_

"Cool. Good night." I choke on the words, guilt thick in my throat. My concentration is gone. It won't be thoughts of Mother that disturb my sleep.

SATURDAY AFTERNOON, Jordan slides down the banister and across the wooden floor like a flopsy bunny. Lying on his belly on the landing, he spots the initials carved into the newel post. His eyes get as big as Scout's paws. "Can I have a jack knife, Mama?"

From my seat at the kitchen counter, I offer a diversionary tactic. "How about we get a slide and a swing?"

"Can I have monkey bars too? A fort?"

Online, we examine photographs of possibilities. A farm can be dangerous for kids. No matter how long or short we'll be here, he needs his own place, a refuge and play space. For all our sakes.

"Thanks for the dog," I say to Con later on the phone, working hard to avoid sarcasm or irony, and surprise myself by inviting her to supper.

"How about tomorrow? I'll get a cake from the bakery. Anky loves chocolate."

CONNIE LIKES TO ARRIVE EARLY. I'm halfway through my yoga practice on the deck when I hear her car's tires grinding through the gravel along our long driveway. She sets a fat chocolate cake on the table and clatters over to Anky, gives her a quick squeeze, turns to face me.

"Neal didn't come?" I ask Con.

"He's gone." She pulls a face at me, ruffles Jordan's hair, bends to greet Scout. "I'll tell you later."

Gone? I ponder the mysteries of attraction. The people we love sometimes love people we simply don't twig to. An image of Earl starts to coalesce. I chase it off by leading Con upstairs and down, through the gardens, ending up on the deck just as Scout and Jordan manage to knock all the glasses and plates off the table.

Anky eats chocolate cake with gusto after only picking at her salad and grilled chicken.

"A perk of age," she says tranquilly when Jordan protests that he has to finish his chicken first. "When you are in your nineties, Jordan, you can do what you like, too."

On her way out the door, Con reaches up to pat my face, surprising me. "Let's see more of each other." She pulls me out onto the front steps. "I sent Neal packing. He's too fond of sleeping with other women. But he'll want to try again. He always does. This time I've started divorce proceedings." She brushes off my concern. "I'm better off without him. Don't fret."

I do, though, guilt coming home to roost. In the past I've been that "other woman." Never with Neal, but all the same. Con must be more devastated than she's willing to let on.

Later that evening, Scout doesn't return after I let him out into the dark. Cell phone in my pocket along with treats and a leash, I kick myself for not staying with him. Or putting up a fence. Pups need fences. It's a relief when Hannah calls a few minutes later.

"Scout's out in our back pasture, barking at the coyotes," she tells me.

I haven't met Mick before, but when he arrives, he doesn't say anything, just a sharp wave and a grin before he reaches across the bench to open the passenger door, and Scout tumbles out, home from his adventure.

Thirteen

ON THE SUNDAY MORNING before Thanksgiving, I have a coffee in hand when Jordan clambers to his feet on his chair and reaches across the table to click a piece of Anky's jigsaw puzzle in place – Monet's "Irises." Ming, perched on the table, pats at the loose pieces. Anky, who is still in bed, often claims that puzzles keep her eyesight sharp. So far, though, Jordan has constructed most of the entire outer edge, snapping each piece in place with the satisfied air of a master builder. The puzzle has become a bridge: Jordan's taken to chattering to Anky after their naps, telling her his theories on how to build moon-mobiles and space ships in the late afternoon of each day, what Anky calls "the witching hour" and worthy of a short pour of dry sherry as she sits in her rocker and points out likely puzzle pieces. On afternoons like those, the fading light turns the surfaces of her face into a study in shadows.

It's been a busy month, with cool mornings, mild days, and warm evenings, the best possible prairie weather. I've gone to town for groceries once a week and made a stop at the market each time. It seems – how unlikely is this! – that Suzanne and I are becoming friends. I never mention Earl's name as we gossip, and I've noticed that she doesn't either. I've canned and frozen the last produce from the garden. I look forward to my evening stroll around the farm. Jordan and Scout like school. Both are making progress. Jordan is learning how to read. He and I practice with *Jelly Belly*, chattering rhymes in between our work in the garden and kitchen. Scout can "Sit!" and "Stay!" for a minute before he wavers. But when I forget to put him on a leash and let him out alone at night just before bed, he runs off into the dark. I've taken to calling Hannah before I head out with his leash – turns out he likes to lie upslope in the field and oversee their Highland cattle. My online hunt for a slide and swing for Jordan is coming along, punctuated by promises I've made to myself: to not fret about Mother or Anky, and to sign off on Earl. He's emailed a few times, checking on our progress and volunteering to make me a kite, but I've forced myself to cool down, and I've put him off. When I see him at puppy class, we laugh and joke, but I keep an arm's length away from him, and avoid sitting beside him in the final circle when we pass puppies from lap to lap.

My coffee finished, I knock twice on Anky's door, then enter. "Morning, Anky, breakfast's ready. Would you like coffee in bed?" The drapes sound like marbles gone wild across an aluminum roof as I tug them open to let in the sun. "I'm taking Jordan to the market. Want anything?"

No response. Anky lies on her side, facing the east window, duvet up to her chin. A slight quickening, a tattoo of air on my ribcage, a tightening like a scarf, provides the only warning that life has woven a new pattern.

FIVE DAYS LATER, Con and I sit side by side on the front bench of the old Hutterite country church a few kilometres from the farm. Jordan sits at the end of the pew, playing with a string of tiny metal streetcars Con brought him from her recent job interview in Toronto.

"It wouldn't have helped to know when," Connie says under her breath. "You knew it was coming. Think of it this way, Luka: she got to know Jordan. Right?"

But not well enough. I should have brought Jordan home sooner.

The days since Charlotte's death have slid by in a haze. Connie, Mick, and Hannah showed up at the house soon after my phone calls, Con with an overnight bag in hand, Hannah gathering me into a monumental hug that unleashed tears, Mick bareheaded, an abrupt line of white on his forehead where his ball cap habitually sat. "Charlotte knew her way around a garden tractor," he said, nodding gravely. I suppressed a small giggle at the tribute. Con made a million calls and had an online obituary posted in the paper within hours. Hannah came back the next day, her hands full of turkey, vegetables, gravy, and pie, enough to feed dozens for days. Mick brought his fiddle and played softly on the porch while Hannah, Con, and I sat in the twilight.

Jordan has reverted to his early levels of anxiety. Anky wouldn't have wanted me to sugar-coat the news of her dying, so I didn't. "Anky has gone," I said to him that morning after finding her.

Jordan nodded, his face grave. "Is she coming back? Is it my fault she's gone?"

"No, sprout, she died of old age."

"Will you die soon?"

"I'm not old. So don't worry."

He nodded again and didn't ask any further. But each night since, he has tossed in bad dreams, muttering until I rise and soothe him, Scout at my knee licking his out-flung arm. During the daytime, Jordan sticks so close to me that I worry I'll step on him.

Pauline and several other elderly women from Goodfare arrived together at the visitation, held yesterday at the Goodfare funeral home. They all wore black pantsuits with big cheerful fake flowers pinned to their bosoms, like charms against dying.

While talking to Pauline, I spotted an old woman in a wheelchair, parked at the end of the front row of chairs in the visitation room, an attendant in the neutral garb of caregivers standing beside her. The woman was wrapped in an ankle-length black fur coat that she kept buttoned to her throat, with an incongruous fascinator of green feathers and maroon ribbons pinned to an implausibly red head of hair. She had dark violet eyes and a look that I couldn't decipher. She didn't stay long or speak to anyone, just rolled silently out of the room, her attendant pushing the chair. Who was she?

Half the county has come. Earl and his family have shown up, and I'm relieved at their silent support. Even the balcony is full, the congregation's hair lit by the light pouring through the church's windows. Those rectangles of stained glass emphasize the cracked drywall and rough floors. This church is old, used mostly for funerals, plus an annual harvest celebration and a Christmas service. Anky used to complain that she had to go all the way to Goodfare for church services instead of just up the road as she did as a kid, accompanied by her uncle Albert and the rest of her family.

The organ chokes into a wheezy rendition of "Wayfaring Stranger." We sit and stand and sit again, singing hymns I thought I'd forgotten, Anky's favourites, their words coming automatically into my mouth: Amazing Grace. Blessed Be. Lilies of the Field. Peace in the Valley. Beside me, Con's voice sounds subdued, slightly off-key. Mick, a Métis sash around his middle, plays his fiddle, no mournful dirges – a reel that Anky would've tapped her toes to. Reverend Waldman's sermon makes me cry, and afterward I can't recall a single word of it.

Connie gives the eulogy. We spent hours deciding what she'd say, what to acknowledge, what to keep private.

"Luka and I were raised by our grandparents, Anky and Oltvetter Paul," she says, on her tiptoes behind the pulpit. She scrunches her nose, sniffs, pauses briefly. "Our Anky wouldn't have wanted us to stand at her grave and weep. She'd have kicked us all back to the garden to finish harvesting the tomatoes, or into the kitchen to make a batch of bread." Laughter rolls through the church.

"Poems weren't her thing, either, so I didn't bother looking for one. Keeping this thing real, right?" More laughter. "She was a private woman, and I'm not sure she'd appreciate my standing up here telling you about her, but all Luka and I have left of her now are our memories. She always had a dog beside her until her last few years, a string that included Max, Angus, and Bandit, Junge Mandl, Captain, and Stella. She loved dark chocolate. Disliked fish, except for the trout that Oltvetter Paul would catch and they'd fry up right there on the riverbank. And there was nothing Anky couldn't grow.

"One of our favourite memories is the surprise Anky packed in Luka's suitcase when she moved to Vancouver to go to university. Luka, as you know, is tall, and she has a hard time finding clothes she likes that fit. She's also a horticulturalist, a gardener, and you can imagine what that means." More laughter swells. "So as a teenager, Luka mostly wore men's shirts that Anky bought at the thrift store. Anky knew the power of pennies, and she had a jar in the kitchen that we tossed all our coins into. The year before Luka went away, Anky and Oltvetter Paul filled that jar twice, and when Luka unpacked her suitcase at UBC, she found a brand new silk tunic folded on top."

Con looks down at her notes, then at me, her face slipping out of true. She hasn't quite finished, and I half-stand, afraid she might come unglued, but she finds her balance. "We'll miss her. Thank you for helping us remember her."

Reverend Waldman pronounces the benediction, and I lead the way out of the pews, Jordan's hand sweaty in mine. Regret prickles at me like a thistle – I *never* told Anky that I loved her. Damn this Hutterite breeding and its hidebound customs that choke out expression like a weed!

Reverend Waldman falls in step with us as we walk outside. Up close, I realize he's old enough to be my father, a faded, narrow-gauge man in a freight train of a tweed jacket two sizes too wide. His wispy voice barely gets clear of his throat before dissipating into the air like a spent train whistle.

"I'll miss her," he murmurs. "Charlotte was one of the stalwarts who came to Goodfare for bingo and fowl suppers even after she got on in years. Hannah drove Charlotte to church after she stopped driving, so it's because of Charlotte that Hannah joined our congregation. We've missed your grandmother this past while. I wonder, can we look for you and your little guy at church any time soon?"

When I ignore the question, he leads the way to a row of familiar headstones. "Luka, you might remember, here's your dad's grave." A rope of longing catches around my ribcage and jerks a tight half-hitch. "And here's Paul's, and here are the Walters – Yoppela and your great-great-grandmother, Tilly, and their three infants. And over there is your great-grandmother Klara and her brothers and their families."

I stop in front of Klara's and Albert's graves. "I wish I'd met them," I say to Connie. She just takes my arm and backtracks to Dad's headstone.

Jordan squats at our knees. He spins the set of spur rowels, buckle ends buried in the cement. "Mama, what are these?"

"Spurs, sprout. Your Grampa AJ was a cowboy."

On some of the headstones, all that remains is the anonymity of settled sand and accruing dust. Dates and names have vanished under the eternal prairie wind. Our family, our bloodlines. Before Jordan was born, I thought cremation the best end, and I still want to be cremated, but this little graveyard is filled with the dust and bones of my family. Perhaps my dust should end up here, with them.

None of the headstones bear the name of Klara's husband Jordan, my boy's namesake. And there's no one left to ask why not.

The interment service is mercifully brief. I worry at the end that Jordan, fidgeting in his new jacket and shoes, will forget himself and tell a joke or maybe leap forward and grab one of the spades the other mourners are passing from hand to hand ("Just a symbolic gesture, really," Reverend Waldman assured me, "a holdover from traditional Colony services.") and flail at the pile of dirt beside the grave. Jordan, distracted by hundreds of snow geese in a shifting skein of light above us, their voices carrying them south, stands quietly holding my hand and looking skyward.

Reverend Waldman turns to me, a half-smile on his face. "Any word of Lark? We were classmates, and I still wonder..."

I should have expected it. "Maybe we can talk about her another day, Reverend?"

"I'll call you. I'd be glad of the chat."

Jordan pulls free of my grip at that moment, waggling his feet, one at a time. The blessed child has a knack for timing. "Look at my new shoes!"

Con snags Jordan by his shoulder, and in seconds she has us turned around and crossing the yard toward the church. In the kitchen, she shepherds us to the buffet table, heaped with sliced ham and coleslaw and homemade buns and squares and colourful jellied salads. As I survey the table, Suzanne elbows through the crowd, holding an enormous platter of cheeses decorated with grapes and crackers, blowing me a kiss as she sets it next to the sweets. When she and Earl reach us in the receiving line, she puts a brown paper bag in my hand. "Cheese for later. And a nice bottle of wine," she whispers as she hugs me. Then Earl buries me in an embrace that I never want to end, and I force myself to pull free. From his post by the door, his eyes stay on me as the line moves inexorably past.

"Your grandmother was loved," Jeannie Waldner, the organist, says, clutching an overflowing plate. "We all cooked this lunch for her and everyone drove out from Goodfare to say goodbye." Jeannie eyeballs Jordan. "Is that your little boy? He looks just like – "

"Like Mother. Yes, he does, doesn't he?" Connie intervenes.

I see a few familiar faces. Others introduce themselves as cousins and shirttail relatives. No sign of the elderly woman in fur who attended the visitation, and I hear no more mention of Mother from the rest of the aging men and women who queue up to press my hands with their wrinkled palms. They all start with "I remember Charlotte..." and finish with nods. No tears. Questions will be asked behind our backs, later, in other homes: "Kind of Mutt and Jeff, aren't those girls? Why is the one so tall, where'd that come from? Can't think of any other women quite so tall in that family. They do both have the look of Charlotte. And the little guy, isn't he the spitting image of Lark?"

WHEN WE WALK BACK into the house, Anky's absence echoes.

"Okay, Luka," Con says. "Home free. You can cry now."

But no tears flow. It's sad, but not a tragedy. Anky had a full life.

Connie sets glasses and Suzanne's wine and cheese on the counter beside the jigsaw puzzle. We raise glasses in a toast, and Con and I tell Jordan stories about Anky.

"Remember the time she lined up all your clothes before you went to university, Con? She made you decide which ones to keep, and you said you needed them all? She said you were in danger of becoming a clothes horse like Mother."

"But then she said that my taste wasn't as good as Mother's, so that went nowhere. And when we went on that summer picnic to Batoche the year I turned fifteen, she decided we had to sing songs to the fallen Métis before we could eat. All I had in my head was 'God Save the Queen,' which hardly seemed right, given the circumstances. Now let's put on some tunes and finish Anky's jigsaw puzzle for her. Jordy? You're the puzzle king. Come on over here and let's do this thing."

Several hours later, the wine bottle empty, puzzle completed, pup and small boy tucked in, Connie drives away, leaving me alone on the couch, wrapped in a blanket. The chair opposite looms empty. Loneliness catches my hand. Then I remember Anky's comments about her distant relationship with her own mother. I couldn't reply at the time. I wish I'd spoken up, forced the words out despite my reticence. I whisper them now, facing the sky: "You were more than a mother to me, Anky, and I love you."

Hours pass. No sleep. I lie quietly in bed, listening to the small sounds from Jordan's room, remorse washing over me. Anky is gone. Not just the sad and iron-willed woman who cared for me all her life, and the fierce young mother she must have been, but my last and best link to Mother, gone without sharing all she knew.

Fourteen

SCOUT TRUNDLES OFF DOWN our driveway as soon as I let him out first thing Saturday morning, so I grab his leash and jump in the VW, collecting him just before he makes the turn into Hannah and Mick's yard. After yoga, over coffee at home, I start reading online about the Great Pyrenees breed, and am dismayed to learn that my sister gave me a lemon. I wish she'd asked – or done some reading herself. Scout's not really a lemon, but he is a dog that needs a job, a sheep's guardian used to responsibility, independent thought, and a large territory. And creatures to guard. Great. Should I get Scout his own flock? Put up a post and rail fence around the yard? Around the farm? Then I learn how high Great Pyrenees can jump. Their propensity for digging. So I need a tie-out line, at least. I call Con and ask her to buy a long, long dog line. When she shows up with one in hand later that morning, I describe Scout's outings.

"I'm sorry, Luka. I didn't mean to add to your work. What can I do to help? Do you want one of those electronic leashes? Or maybe a fence around the back yard?"

I don't know the answer. Connie's genuinely distressed, so I let my hard feelings slide away.

That day, we pack Anky's clothes for the Goodwill box. On Sunday, she browbeats me into sorting Anky's books, farm accounts, and papers in the parlour while Jordan naps – he's still waking at night with nightmares. "Let's get some things cleaned up," Con insists. "You need the help – it's a huge house. Besides, some of those books are just dust catchers. It'll be easier to keep things cleaner if we get rid of some."

"I want to keep the Audubon!"

A few minutes later, I bark my shin on the schlofbonk. Squatting to rub my protesting leg, I swivel around and shove all the books and papers aside, then heave the bench top up, revealing a storage space filled with fabric. Five neatly folded patchwork quilts emerge, one after another. I set them on the table to look more closely. Fading triangles and diamonds and strips of coral and copper and yellow and teal cotton are stitched to tiny worked squares of red flannel, bands of blue broadcloth, threadbare green ribbons and sunny plaid. Silken embroidery floss in herringbone stitches like birds' feet. Cross-stitches like safety pins. So lovely. Who made them? What did they celebrate?

"These are gorgeous," Connie says, leaning forward to look closely as she runs her hands over the hand-stitched folds of colour. "I've never seen them before. Anky must have forgotten about them." She unfolds the fabrics. "Beautiful. All hand-quilted. Turn them over, Luka. Most quilters sign their work. They might have labels on the undersides."

"I never realized you knew so much about this."

She laughs deep in her throat. "You have more to thank quilting for than you know. Quilting teaches patience, the art of not hurrying things. Focus. My therapist suggested years ago that I do something with my hands. I can teach you if you'd like. When we both have time."

"I don't know. I love looking at them, but I don't know if I want to go to all that effort."

"Says the gardener of tropical plants. Ha." Con flips over the top quilt, almost whooping with excitement. "Here! This Log Cabin has a hand-embroidered label that says, 'Matilde Tschetter Walter, 1899, for Klara's birth.' And this Double Wedding Ring was made by her as well, for Klara's wedding to Jordan Mueller in 1917. The other Jordan, Luka. And this one of Flying Geese was made by Klara and Tilly, for Anky's birth in 1918." She squints to read the fine stitches. "What about those two?"

"Anky's wedding to Oldvetter Paul, 1947, made by Marina. And this one was for Mother's birth, made by Klara, 1944." Other women's memories and lives, cascading across our laps.

"This is real history," Con says. "All these people are members of our family." She inspects the lengths of pieced fabric, peering at stitching, running fingertips over seams. "You could hang them on the walls. They're precious things, far too beautiful to risk letting Jordan use."

"We should use them. That's what they're for."

"They're irreplaceable, Luka. I wish I knew what those fabrics were cut from. It's all there – births, marriages, deaths, children – decipherable if you know the code of where and what the fabric pieces came from, just a jumble of scraps if you don't. What else did she hide away?"

Con leans forward and peers into the dark interior of the schlofbonk. "Hmmm." She scrabbles about and sits up in triumph, clutching a scribbler amid a few dust bunnies, with a yellow cardboard cover, "MCMXLIV" inscribed in emphatic black lines on its front. 1944. Beneath it, Anky's maiden name: Charlotte Walter. Inside, each page is covered in tight black rows of a familiar, close-written, angular script with a decided cant to the east and an authoritative down-stroke: Anky's writing. Clippings, photos, letters, and envelopes protrude like aging ears from the pages – not just a diary, but a record of a life. Con almost carols with glee. "Luka, we've got ourselves a goldmine."

I take the book from Con's hands. The fine script is difficult to read. "This will need close attention. Do you want to take it home to work through?"

"No. I'll be on tight deadlines after missing work for a week, and I'll feel too rushed to pay close attention. I won't have time. You need a project, you read it. Now what about the bookshelves?"

"Hang on. This notebook. Anky is so – was so private. Do you think we should burn it?"

"Are you nuts? You're the one who's been sagging around like a sack of old spuds about wanting to know more about the family. Burn it? Not on your life, Luka. You read it, and fill me in. Now, those things on the top of the bookshelves. You can reach them all."

"Just a sec." I set the notebook on the kitchen table beside Anky's finished puzzle, stroking its cover for a moment before I return to the parlour shelf. "Dad's trophies. Anky's King James." As the worn red leather Bible tilts in my hands, two pieces of paper slip out, the sheets folded and refolded, their creases wearing thin. I pick them up, unfold both. They contain spare words in barely legible scrawls. Mother's writing. I read the oldest aloud.

19 October 1965
  Hi Ma –
  Vancouver is expensive. Pls send money. Y'll be glad to know I had an A–.
  Don't wanna clutter up the world with more unwanted kids.
  Lark

An A–. I sit down abruptly. Con takes my hand and strokes the skin on the inside of my wrist. My stomach tenses with remembered stress, my own mental and emotional upheaval, the wrestling match of a decision that led to my having Jordan. Now I can't imagine life without him.

"We could have had a big brother. Or a sister," says Connie, subdued for once. "It must have been terrible for her. Abortion was still illegal. Dangerous. And probably expensive. Hard to find. Risky. She must have been scared. Luka, did you ever consider...?"

"Don't ask, Con."

"I was just going to say how brave you are to be a single mom. Braver than Mother."

"That's harsh, Con."

"No, just realistic. She shouldn't have had us." Connie's mouth twists.

I re-read the letter: 1965. What was Vancouver like back then? The Only already existed, I know that. Was the city just as dangerous? And then I remember – Mother went to live at Marina's as a teenager in 1959. This letter means that somehow, Anky and Mother reconciled in the intervening years. A few moments pass before I read the second even briefer letter out loud, surprised that my voice doesn't waver. The same handwriting.

9 November 1975
  Hi Ma –
  Coming home. Married a cowboy. Name's AJ Dekker. Train next Monday.
  L.

"Do you remember him?"

Connie squints at the sky through the open window. "He was kind. Funny. Patient. An amazing horseman."

"I remember. Those trophies." We look up at the shelf above our heads. "Do you remember the riding lessons? He spent hours with us on those horses. I wish we'd had more years with him."

"We had him. Let's be glad of that. And we were better off with Anky than we would have been with Mother," Con says, her voice level, simply stating facts. "Mothers who drink – I've met plenty."

She holds out the Bible. I take the book and rifle through the well-thumbed pages marked with half a dozen bookmarks. The Bible falls open at a garish blue bookmark embossed with a gilt cross, and I read a long list of "begats." Another bookmark embellished with a red rose marks St. Matthew and a passage about the birth of Jesus. One more flip of the pages brings me to a yellow sun marker illuminating the story of David and Goliath. Then the thin pages open to a worn brown leather bookmark lodged in Exodus.

"Con, give a listen to what Anky's underlined. 'Visiting the iniquity of the fathers upon the children, and upon the children's children, unto the third and to the fourth generation.' And here's more underlining, in Ezekiel, but it contradicts the first one: 'The son shall not bear the iniquity of the father, neither shall the father bear the iniquity of the son.'"

Ming winds around my legs and purrs as I set down the Bible and sit on the floor in front of the schlofbonk, absently stroking the cat. "Iniquity? What was Anky fretting about?"

After a minute of contemplation, Connie grows impatient. "Never mind that for now. Enough holy writ. And you keep the trophies, Luka. I have no use for them. What about the other house? The little one. I bet you haven't been in it since forever. Let's go see what she left in it."

"It's not a treasure hunt, Con," I say, vaguely offended by her enthusiasm.

"Sure it is. I have to go to work tomorrow so let's just do this now," Connie says briskly. "Got a flashlight? Gloves?"

"Give me a minute." I straighten the bookshelves and replace the Bible, then I refold the quilts and tuck them back into the schlofbonk. We traipse to the tiny house, sheltered, forgotten, unused. Rarely does a building go unused on a Saskatchewan farm; the extreme weather conspires with unendingly tough times to dictate that everything has a practical purpose. After Anky and Oltvetter Paul moved in with us, what could they have done with this small building? It's too isolated to rent, too small to serve for much other than storage.

The door's metal hasp resists, so Con breaks a length of caragana branch free from the overgrown shrub and hands it to me. The slider gives on the fourth whack. Connie pushes past me. I grab at her wrist, but she ignores me. "It's fine, Luka. Come on, don't be silly."

I recognize two rooms, woodstove, sink and icebox, cobwebs. Then Con's flashlight light catches an answering gleam on the stained wooden floor, a trapdoor with its pull-ring. Within a couple of minutes I have the ring pried up and loosened. The trapdoor gives way after three business-like tugs. I'm standing too close to the void. I ease back from the edge, but down the steep stairs Connie goes. A minute passes, vertigo rushing through me, then I clamber awkwardly after her while Connie shines the flashlight at the steps beneath my feet.

The bar of light reveals a shelf-lined room with rough cement walls, empty except for a single row of empty canning jars on one shelf, and a pair of wooden chairs poised against the south wall, a wooden box balanced across the seats. It looks like a set out of a fairy tale, the perfect stage for evil-doings in a dungeon.

Con directs the light at the box. Even through the dust and grime, I can see that it's two-toned, with a lid that sits square and snug.

The stairs, awkward coming down, are treacherous on the uphill trip, shallow risers and narrow treads combining with a steep pitch more suited to a ladder than stairs in a house. Still, I make it up and through the trapdoor without losing my grip or balance, the box secure under one arm, Con close behind.

"Pass up those chairs," I suggest. She scuttles back down, and first one, then the second, appears. We crouch, breathless in the flashlight's beam, on the kitchen floor. A slight shove releases the trapdoor. It drops into place with a muffled bang, the cellar closing off again, putting me in mind of Bluebeard, maybe, or one of Scheherazade's tales of dungeons, oubli-ettes, and forgotten women. A shivery thought, standing in the presence of the unknown.

In a few minutes, we have everything safely in my kitchen. The chairs are obviously handmade as well, and look like matches for the pair beside the parlour desk, with spindle backs and carved top rails. A few swipes with a damp cloth reveal that both chairs and box are made of dark walnut and pale maple. Gleaming surfaces. Someone lovingly sanded and polished these. The box seems an understated thing, the size of a shoe box, hand-made by a craftsman who knew his tools and his own skill.

The box opens willingly. Within lies another yellow notebook. Roman numerals mark the front cover in black ink, and the covers bulge from extra sheets of paper.

"What year is that? My Roman isn't so good," Connie says.

"It's 1943. A year earlier than the other one."

"Okay, keep it too. You do the reading and report back. I do my share of reading old documents for work. Which reminds me – choose three of those quilts for yourself and bring me the other two when you come to town next."

I'm not sorry to see Connie stride toward her SUV after supper. She is stubborn, but quick to forgive, an odd juxtaposition, considering how she's resented my long absence from the province.

"You call me whenever you need to," she says just before getting into her car, and pulls me close. "If you get lonely." She gives me a little shake. "If you need help."

"I've got Jordan," I say, "and Scout," but I squeeze her hand tightly.

As Connie drives off the yard, Jordan slips up behind me. "Why do people have to die, Mama?"

"Our bodies get tired, sprout."

"Will I die while I'm asleep?"

So here is another cause of the nightmares. Crouching eye to eye, I take his chilly fingers in mine. "No. You'll wake up every morning, safe and sound."

"Anky didn't."

"She was very old." I take off my bracelet and hold it in front of Jordan. "See these beads? They're made of amber, and they're ancient. They aren't stones, like rubies or emeralds. They're old resin from trees. Tree sap. And sometimes they have insects or shells caught inside them as they harden, so we can see the past. Anky's like that, Jordan, she's in our hearts forever and ever, with us always. And you will not die until you're as old as she was. Ninety-two," I say, forestalling the inevitable question, and slip the bracelet back on my wrist. "Now let's go run a bath."

Fifteen

WITH JORDAN ASLEEP IN BED, calm descends for the first time since Anky's death. I attribute part of it to the magic of finding her history. I gather up a glass of wine and both diaries, and settle on the couch. Cautiously, I peer into the pages. Both diaries have a collection of oddments – old letters and envelopes in a variety of hands, black and white photographs, yellowing newspaper clippings – interspersed among the handwritten pages, and a large, bulging envelope is tucked in at the end of one. I leave them all in place to read in the order of the pages.

The house stops and listens in the night air. I hold and release my breath as for a yoga pose. As a teenager, longing for what we'd lost, I made Anky pull out her albums and show me family pictures. Those pictures. Where had they gone? I jump up, rummage through the stacks of books on the table, where we arranged all the contents of Anky's parlour shelves. It just takes a few minutes to locate three thin old albums filled with photographs that I skim through. Some are snapshots, blurry and slightly out of focus; others are professional studio portraits. Anky herself as a young woman with a basket of onions; Mother as a little girl, her long legs tanned, eating carrots in the garden, hair loose in the breeze, hooded hazel eyes inward-looking, filled with secrets, that thin face and hands so fragile they looked like they'd break at a harsh word; Dad in the saddle on his red Quarter horse, a rope coiled in one hand, the other tipping his cowboy hat to Mother at his stirrup. None of all four of us.

I pull a dozen pictures from the albums and pin them on the upstairs bulletin board, then return to the couch and bend my head to the memoirs again. The house is too quiet, I suddenly realize, and wonder: where's Scout? Then I recall putting him out on his run-line ages ago.

The run-line is fully extended, heading west. Scout's collar lies on the ground, still snapped to the line. No Scout. It's getting late but a missing dog can't wait, so I text Hannah.

When I arrive at her house, she comes to the door in her pyjamas and points at the back pasture. "Coyotes," she says, and for a few moments we listen together: Scout's puppy voice is warbling up and down the register, giving a clue to the deep bass he'll eventually be. "I can help you put up a fence," she says, and adds cautiously, "or maybe you need to think about re-homing him. I know farmers who'd shoot him on sight if he shows up loose for fear that he'd run their cattle – not that he would! – but they'd never tell anyone. He'd just be gone and you'd never know where or why. Believe me, you do not want to lose a dog that way."

Back home, I flop on the couch with Scout alongside me, out like a light, oblivious as I play with those soft ears and think about fences and what they do, and about men who shoot family pets and bury their bodies. I'm starting to like this dog. I don't want that fate for him. Scout starts to snore as I open the first diary and peer at the first two cracked sepia photographs, faint writing on their lower edges. Why aren't they in one of the albums?

One caption reads "Klara's and Jordan's wedding, with Peanut, 3 July 1917." Photos of Hutterites taken before the Depression are rare. Even the Prairieleit, the Prairie People, the more liberal off-Colony Hutterites such as my family who observed the call of community but not of communal life, only allowed photographs at weddings and funerals. In this picture, a beagle puppy sleeps on Klara's lap beneath her folded hands. Her face reflects my own features, and Anky's. The young Klara's wide brow is calm and smooth, her dark eyes untroubled. The prairie waits in her skin, soft folds yet to change to meridians and grid roads, to dust, heat, drought, rock. Klara wears a small fox stole over her shoulders and double rows of uneven beads at her wrist and throat. That amber bracelet. I wear it now, the necklace vanished with Mother.

Standing beside Klara leaning back, hands in his pockets, stands Jordan, my great-grandfather. A three-piece suit hangs loosely on his lean frame, a full-blown rose in the lapel, a high round shirt collar, a necktie tied in an elaborate knot. His face is lean, almost ascetic in the purity of its lines, high cheekbones, hooded eyes. He reminds me of Mother, and my Jordan: the same set to their lips, the same eyes set in a long and narrow face. Anky used to say that Mother hid more in her face than any teenager she'd ever known. Volatile, she called her; she surely had been as a young mother – we never knew when she'd blow up. Look at her sideways and she was ready to cuff one or both of us, like a bear disturbed.

The second picture, simply labeled "Family at Klara's & Jordan's Wedding, 3 July 1917," portrays an older couple that must be Klara's parents, Yoppela and Tilly, standing beside the younger pair. Yoppela is short-legged, with a magpie's black eyes and beaky nose. Tilly is round, her cheeks and torso padded by life. She reminds me of Connie.

Once the pictures are pinned up on my bulletin board with the others, I step back to study them all, then I catch myself twirling my bracelet. Where did the matching necklace end up? Mother left the cameo in her jewellery box when she abandoned us. Connie, who'd never cared much about jewellery, fell unaccountably in love with it, so Anky gave it to her. She gave me the amber bracelet on my sixteenth birthday.

I imagine Mother in a variety of occupations – first as a waitress in a high-toned restaurant with white tablecloths and crystal glassware, then as a flight attendant, then as a hotel clerk in a sleek fitted suit. In each situation, Mother is the same gloriously gorgeous woman she was in her twenties and thirties, and in each scene, the double strand of amber hangs at her throat. She would recognize me, would throw her arms around me, would lift the necklace from her own neck and place its golden beads around mine with only a smile and a hand on my cheek.

A memory surfaces – Con and me as youngsters dressed in Mother's fancy clothes and dancing with Mother, Tony Bennett belting out "Fly Me to the Moon" a capella. "Ice cream! Let's have ice cream!" Mother suggested, lurching sideways across the parlour, a girl hanging onto each leg. A few minutes later, we all sat on the porch. With ice cream and berry stains smeared across her face, Mother looked like our big sister, not our mother, when Anky stuck her head around the corner. Mother smiled. "Want some, Ma?" No Dad anywhere in sight – he must have been at a rodeo.

Mother knew how to make good fun, and when he was home, Dad was a willing player. Whenever we played castles in the hayloft, Dad dressed up in a bed-sheet and was our willing servant. Mother was just as likely to pick flowers to braid into crowns as pull apart a bale of straw and rain handfuls of golden stalks across our pathways as we chased cats and dogs unwillingly wearing kitchen-towel capes. Dad would finally free the animals of their costumes, and we'd all collapse in the shade on the porch. He doesn't haunt me. She does.

Sixteen

I'VE JUST RETURNED to the parlour when the phone's ringing interrupts my thoughts, the diary still waiting on the table beside the couch. The Reverend Waldman's wispy voice sounds in my ear, apologizing for calling so late and asking me to visit tomorrow. To talk about Mother. He doesn't give any further reason, I wonder – why the sudden rush, calling late in the evening? Contemplating the possibilities momentarily dampens my interest in the diary, and I suddenly realize just how late it has become.

Next morning after seeing Jordan off, I call the school and the bus driver, informing them that I'll collect Jordan after school, then I pick up the diary and settle down on the couch in the parlour. Then the phone interrupts me again.

"What about the diaries? What's going on?" Connie's voice rackets like a steamroller.

"Aren't you at work? I haven't gotten to them yet. I was just settling in to start when you called. I just have a few hours – I have to go visit Reverend Waldman this afternoon."

"Coffee break. I remembered something that might be of interest to you. Anky lent me her Hutterite history books for a magazine feature I wrote a few years back about a distant relative of ours, a Hutterite woman who wrote a cookbook that became a local hit. She left the Colony as a kid and lives up in Prince Albert."

"And you never bothered telling me?"

"Why would I? You never showed any signs of being interested in anything Hutterite. It was research for work. The books are on the table with all the books we didn't get to. One is a beautiful little hand-stitched job, full of details about our family. Anky told me it was made by one of Klara's brothers, Pieter, I think. And I just remembered this – Anky called Yoppela a quick-tempered pacifist with a tendency to violence. I don't know what you expect to find, Luka, maybe those books will give you a little background. Gotta go, my column needs an edit."

After I disconnect, Scout watches as I return to the table and riffle the stacks of unsorted books. The Hutterite books are all together. I set aside the historic accounts and focus on Pieter's small hand-made book. It's Coptic-bound with embroidery silk, and the pages feel like high-grade parchment, still supple and smooth to touch. Some of the pages are flagged with bookmarks. A hand-drawn picture of a ship with three masts complete with sails as well as two funnel smokestacks is labelled in copperplate script: "*Hammonia 3, Zwischendeck, 1874.*" So she'd been a schooner before being converted to steam.

I set it and the others back on the table for later, and return to the couch. I stretch, run my hands over my ribcage, belly, breasts. For the first time, I hope that I'll have another child, a sister or brother for Jordan. Thirty isn't too old to have a baby. I wish I had brothers, too. I haven't seen much of them, but Hannah's boys seem so uncomplicated in their unity. In comparison, Connie and I snipe like spies forced to collaborate. Then I pat Scout, a furry comma on his mat in front of the fireplace, open the first notebook to its beginning entry, and start to read Anky's memories. Because it was her first language, a smattering of Hutterisch seems likely, but I trust context and don't hunt down an online dictionary. Her spare words on the page open into scenes that my imaginings embellish with the shimmering real-life essence of shape, sounds, substance, and colour.

Seventeen

21 March 1943

*Marina was cranky when I got home from work. She shouted from the
kitchen that I wasn't seven anymore, why was I dawdling before supper?
Marina was a rock. What could have be-jiggered her so?*

*Her tone changed to a croak. From somewhere deep inside. She said Ma had
called.*

*How could she? Ma didn't have a phone. I hurried into the kitchen. Marina
set down her potholders. Stroked my arm. She told me Ma was at the funeral
parlour in Goodfare. My Grandpap had died.*

*She said, sharp-like, that she'd borrowed a neighbour's car. Ma had asked
that I come. No sign of Gerard.*

MARINA'S HUSBAND Gerard was a Canadian Corps veteran who lost an
arm at the Somme in World War One. Post-war, he became a professor of
engineering at the university. Maybe Anky kept a photo of him, or of them
both. I remind myself to look through the photo albums in the parlour
later.

Marina wanted to fuss over me. I told her not to.

*She said Grandpap died working. That lots of men want that kind of end.
Then she expected me to eat. But I couldn't. She told me to wrap a slice of cake
for Ma. Then she grumbled about driving in the dark. That snow was coming.*

I wanted to go tomorrow. Marina frowned. So I just grabbed my notebook.

My stomach roiled – Grandpap in a coffin! I told her I've never seen a dead person before.

That stopped her. We all die, she said.

Grandpap and Ma had nursed a grudge between them. I've never seen them talk to each other. Ma's not the huggy kind. Not chatty either. She knows the breeding cycles of mares. The moods of stallions. Not my mood swings, not anyone's. She never spoke of my father Jordan, either. I can't think of him as my father. Just a disembodied man.

He vanished before I was born. Ma claims she last saw him saddling up to ride over to the Shevchenko quarter. Checking that the well was covered for winter. No one saw that gelding again. The homestead where Marina grew up, abandoned now. Left empty ever since Marina's father and brothers were shipped to the internment camp in the mountains. Ma says she and Jordan had hoped to buy that land. To get out from under Grandpap. Then Jordan vanished. That's all I know about him. Right after that Ma broke free. Started taking that stallion Marko to horse shows. Winning. Wearing men's clothing.

I used to draw a face I thought was his. Day after day. Over and over in my sketchbook. Told myself, I don't miss him, he never existed for me.

Grandpap took care of me while Ma took that stallion on the livestock breeding train across the province. Him and Uncle Albert. The closest I came to having a father. Ma wasn't much of a mother either – she chose her horses over me. I've been paying my own rent at Marina's ever since I got that job at Chan Lee's café.

I'm not ready to think about dying – anyone dying. Especially not Grandpap. Would Ma would mourn my death? Same way she'd mourned her stillborn fillies and colts? Like she cried for her herd when sleeping sickness wiped them out? I felt her grief from my bedroom in Saskatoon.

Grandpap wasn't much for laughing. When he did it cut both ways. The year before I moved to town, I showed him my latest sewing project. A drop-waisted sleeveless dress of royal blue. Grandpap took one look and snickered. Asked if I was fixing to wear it as a nightgown. I never forgot.

Donnervetter! Grandpap's old curse-word.

I NEED THAT HUTTERISCH dictionary after all. I learn that "Thunder weather" is the translation for "donnervetter." Great curse-word! Full of resonance and noise. Just like thunder.

No stars. Just heavy clouds. I rolled down the window. Leaned out. Cold air snapped my skin. Donnervetter! Fahrflucht! Zum Teufel! Verdammt! Pulled my head back in, ears and forehead stinging. Asked if Grandpap had liked horses as much as Ma did.

Marina didn't think so, said Ma was always horse-crazy. Horses were work animals to Grandpap. She told me that he threatened to take a horsewhip to Ma when he caught her in the paddock as a little girl. She laughed at him. But he did whip her a few times. Marina said he threatened to take his whip to her too. She just ran off home.

I wanted to know what he was like to other people.

He was a man with a black heart. She tried to smile as she said it.

But he was always kind to me! Then I remembered the blue dress. Donnervetter!

All his rules! Dogs and cats and horses were working animals too. I never saw a single pet on the farm. Marina said Grandpap lived through hard times – any animal had to earn its keep. She asked if Ma ever told me about Peanut. Then added, no, never mind.

So I asked her. She told me Peanut was a puppy Jordan gave Ma. As a wedding present. Told me Grandpap kicked it when it got underfoot, cursed it. Geu zum Teufel! Poor dog never got up.

I put my head back out the window. Into the anaesthetic cold. A necessity against the ache taking over my innards. A dead puppy. How had Ma mourned that loss?

I waited for more snow to fall. Waited for my father, always absent. When I asked Marina about him, she didn't hear.

At the funeral parlour, a closed room. A coffin with its lid raised. Long empty rows of chairs. Ma alone at the front. Her black fur coat and homburg piled across the chair behind her. Remnants of her glory days as a studhorse woman. She wore trousers, as always.

I wouldn't let the attendant take my coat. It cost the dickens. Fitted black wool, green lining and piping, vaguely military. I'd feel unguarded without it, exposed. Death could come too close, seeping through seams and pockets.

Marina led the way up the aisle. Toward the coffin and Ma. I hadn't seen Ma in months. Almost didn't recognize her. She looked far older than forty-

three. Her face drawn and pale, greying hair pulled into a rough bun. Her eyes reddened but dry. Her mouth the familiar tight line from my childhood.

Then she buckled. Marina and I caught her. The room shrank. Ma patted me on the shoulder. As if calming a young mare. The same absent-minded touch I received as a child. Ma said we should just take off Grandpap's harness and let him out to pasture.

There won't be a wake.

Ma's hand all sinews and bones. She led me up, just short of the coffin. The body was slight. He'd always been bulky. So small in the coffin. Hardly big enough to inflict all the pain he caused, Ma muttered. Then she called him an old hound. Ein alte Hunde, in Hutterisch. Bitter.

Marina whispered that she should let the past be buried. Enough harm done.

When I asked what she meant, she said never you mind. Told me to make my goodbyes.

But bruises covered one of Grandpap's cheeks, one eyelid swollen. Yellow and purple shone through caked-on powder and make-up. Marina and I both horrified, asking what happened.

Ma sounded jagged. Said Albert found him beside the barn, a scaffold buckled beside him. He wasn't breathing. He'd been acting strangely the last while. Talked wild, threatened Albert. Said the strangest things. Months of crazy behaviour. He kept talking about my father. Jordan.

She looked away when she said that. She said Grandpap refused to go to hospital. That's where people go to die, he always said. He never set foot inside a hospital.

Then Marina reminded me that it's traditional to kiss the deceased. I didn't. Couldn't. That body wasn't him. He was gone.

So we left. Ma didn't want a ride. Called Marina's offer foolishness. Left us standing beside the coffin.

I felt wings spreading beneath my shoulder blades, carrying me into the clouds. Ma coaxing unwilling fillies on a leadline. Grandpap in his workshop. Hammer clenched in his right hand, head back and shouting. The air vibrated.

TAPED ONTO THE next page is Yoppela's obituary, the tape yellow and cloudy with age.

Saskatoon Star-Phoenix, 22 March 1943 Obituaries
Walter, Jacob ("Yoppela") – At home, near Goodfare, Saskatachewan, of natural causes. Born 1872, in Hutterthal, Ukraine. Pre-deceased by his wife, Matilde, three infant sons, and grandson, Ronald. Survived by their children, Pieter (Edith), Mattias, Albert, and Klara Mueller, and grandchildren Charlotte and Peter. Mr. Walter came to Canada by steamship as a boy and settled northwest of Saskatoon. He was a carpenter and builder of repute. Trust that the Lord thy God knows thy name and thy heart. Rest in peace. Funeral and interment to be held at Goodfare Country Hutterite Chapel, 22 March 1943.

23 March 1943

Grandpap's funeral. One of the worst events of my life. The little church close to the farm, his casket open. I sat between Ma and Marina, trapped like a fly. Nowhere to escape to. Uncle Albert wore a suit. I didn't know he even owned a suit!

Every seat filled. I hadn't thought Grandpap would draw a crowd. Maybe a show of respect for an immigrant? For a man who'd made his own life by building homes in his community? And the hymns! Dirges, every one, some in Hutterisch, a traditional Hutterite funeral. The minister from a Colony somewhere in Alberta.

Ma said it was lucky the Prediger's eulogy wasn't all in High German, they usually were. Hypocrisy to have such a funeral, I told her. Ma said it's what Grandpap had asked for before he died. Out of the blue. Made me wonder, hearing that. Sure, he was a Hutterite. We all are. But he never mentioned God. Not to me. Not even when we'd ridden to church in Ma's carriage. Who was the church service really for? Not a single Hutterite Colony in the province. Just us. The Prairie Folk, each family on our own farm. And all of my family buried in the graveyard at that little country church.

Out to the graveyard. I left my gloves behind. Donnervetter! Avoided looking at the hole. Gaping open, a wound. The wind in the trees, exactly how I felt. Ma nodded. Did she feel it too? Ma turned away as the shovels were passed from hand to hand. Marina grabbed her wrist. Caught her as she slipped on the snow.

And then the lunch. Cold ham and beef and homemade buns, pickles, and platters of dainties and pies. Those women must have used up their sugar rations for the entire month. Just like Marina, always wanting to stuff me. I didn't think I could eat. I piled my plate like everyone else. Ate nothing.

Over and over I heard people saying I must be Charlotte, all grown up. They all but pinched my cheek. The women in worn dresses and cardigans, the men in ancient suits.

A hoarse whisper behind me. A woman's voice I didn't recognize calling my father Jordan bad names. A wild one, der Lutscher, eine feiger Hund. Then she added that maybe he joined the Yank army after all, who knew how deep 'thou shalt not kill' actually ran in him. She said her money was on my Grandpap. Put that youngster down a well, was her guess. Where else do you hide a body out in the dryland?

Ma turned red as a robin. She cut an imposing figure, despite being tiny. Commanded that room. She shoved her chair back. Stood up. Stared down the men and women at each table. She started to say something, stopped, marched out. Back straight, head high. A jerk of her head directed at Albert. He pursed his lips and nodded. He'd remembered something. He followed Ma. No one spoke. We all left the room. Behind us the room erupted.

Stone silence outside. Ma scrambled into the car. That bridled-and-bitted look on her face. I didn't dare ask her anything. At the farm, Ma stalked into the main house. Albert ran after her. I didn't want to go in but he made me.

She and Marina sat at the kitchen table with Albert. Albert told me go into the sitting room.

Was I a child to be exiled? So I listened at the door.

Albert, soft and raspy. Said he didn't want to say anything while Grandpap was alive. The old man would have been shunned if word got out. Ma deserved to know. That there might be truth in what was said at the funeral lunch. He told them he saw Grandpap walking home from the Shevchenko place.

What night did he mean?

Marina's sigh, barely audible. Then her clear voice. Saying some wounds never heal.

Then Albert again. He'd carried it for years, he said, time to lay it down. He'd been fencing and came back for some staples. Stopped in the main house for some coffee. Then he fetched the staples and rode back to the field. He said he met Grandpap in the lane this side of Shevchenko's yard. On foot. Blood on his hands and the front of his work coat. Grandpap said he'd killed some vermin. A big nest of vermin by the look of it, Albert said. Grandpap just nodded and walked away. He never walked anywhere he could ride.

Donnervetter! I ran into the kitchen.

*Ma's face, stark white as she cursed. Was zur Hölle! You men, she said.
Even Albert. She despised what he'd done – he'd thought he was protecting her
by not telling the truth. All this time he was protecting Grandpap. From being
shunned. Ma could barely speak. Every day the men witnessed him shunning
her, she said. On our family's yard, in our homes. All for the crime of doing
what no other woman had done before. Simply to feed and clothe her child.
Truly a terrible world, she said, a man's world. She cursed them all again. Geh
zum Teufel.*

*No one would meet Ma's eyes. I shouted for an explanation. Albert shook
his head when I cornered him. Not his story to tell, he said. Donnervetter!*

*In the car, I insisted Marina tell me the rest. She told me that I deserved to
know. She said Ma fell in love with Jordan when he showed up at the farm
on horseback. He led three horses in rope halters. Was looking for work. He'd
come from South Dakota, he claimed, from Bon Homme Colony. She said Ma
always thought he was a draft dodger. That those horses weren't his to sell.
Grandpap bought the horses and gave Jordan work.*

*Marina said that Grandpap had witnessed Jordan beating Ma soon after
she learned she was pregnant. He despised Jordan from that day on.*

She didn't speak again.

*What would it be like to have a family, a real family? With a father. And
a mother who talked, who shared. Who cared about the people around her. A
mother who hugged and kissed and fussed. I imagined scene after scene. But
the mother I imagined wasn't Klara. It was Marina. The father figure turned
away. I couldn't see his face.*

I CLOSE THE JOURNAL gently, my heart constricting, unsure I understood what I had just read. I make a quick call to Con. "Con, he must have done it."

"Who? Done what? Fill me in, Luka."

"Anky said something once that I couldn't figure out, about the original Jordan going back over the border or meeting a dry well." Then I recount the details of Anky's diary entries. "Yoppela hated Jordan for doing what he himself had routinely done – beating Klara. Klara was furious, not just because of the beatings and the murder, but because Albert lied to her about what he'd seen Yoppela do. Albert was afraid their father would be shunned or even reported to the police if word got around about Jordan's disappearance. Even as a rumour."

"For real? Wow, that's really bleak, and right out of Shakespeare – in *Titus Andronicus*, Titus kills his own son. But a man killing his son-in-law in our own family?"

"It does sound like a Greek tragedy, doesn't it? Anky wrote that a neighbour at Yoppela's funeral lunch suggested he'd put Jordan down the well, but of course there was no proof."

"So that's what Anky was referring to," Con says. "Holy smokes!"

"Then Klara all but accused her brother Albert of being a party to institutionalized sexism. She was totally shunned by Yoppela for wearing men's clothing, and for breaking the gender barrier with that stallion she showed. She didn't want to be the family maid. Widows without any income were expected to earn their keep, and keeping house was the easy fallback."

"Way ahead of her time, wasn't she? And take-no-prisoners fearless! Luka, like I said, that diary is dynamite."

"Now I understand why Anky didn't want to talk."

"Keep me posted. And lock the doors out there. Oh wait, you've got that enormous dog."

"Don't imagine trouble, Con, we're perfectly safe out here. But we have to discuss Scout. He busted loose from his tie-out line a couple of nights ago and went wandering."

"You said. He's your dog, Luka, and I might have made a mistake. You do what you think best. Get some exercise, too. Just burn that diary out of your body."

Eighteen

THE OLD WELL on the Shevchenko yard calls me. I pick a path past
Anky's garden, heading east to the adjacent quarter, to the farm that had
been Marina's childhood home. The place is deserted. My sleeve catches
and snags as I crawl between the strands of the barbed wire fence. Maybe
I made a big mistake in walking out alone. The fabric rips as I pull free
and carry on, intent on the well. Beyond the buildings, a coyote cries, and
its pack takes up the harmony, their voices uniting and wavering into the
distance.

The yard is bereft of vehicles, the house vacant and dilapidated, windows broken, walls buckled. Of the well, only the pump handle and spout
remain, protruding above several lengths of wooden planking in the
ground, the wood worn but still sound despite its age, almost covered by
dead stalks of quackgrass. The wellhead. I try to work the pump handle,
but the mechanism resists, the metal corroded with rust and age that red-
dens my hands.

Do the first Jordan's remains rest beneath the planking? That's a spooky
thought. When I wipe my hands in the grass I leave behind a smudge of
rust. Even my bracelet has traces of corrosion across its surfaces. I polish
the resin clean on my shirt-front, imagining the faces of all the women in
the diary – Anky, Klara, Marina, Mother as a child – the women in my family. But the path twists, leading back to this well, to the missing man who
reminds me of Earl. Missing men and women, the empty notes in my life.

My walk home echoes with the unsolved past. What happened to the
adult Jordan, and to Mother? These questions reverberate as I stand in my
son's empty bedroom and visualize his chest rising and falling. It doesn't

really matter if I never learn the truth of what happened to the original Jordan. And maybe I will never solve the riddle of Mother.

When I glance at my watch, I realize I'm close to late for my appointment with the reverend, and I speed north on the dusty gravel road to Goodfare. The tiny lavender house perches beside the church hall, and when I knock Waldman answers so promptly that I suspect he watched me approach through the miniscule kitchen window. The minister's faded overalls are too large, and hang over a long-sleeved plaid shirt that is practically transparent at the elbows. His hand feels like soft clay. In the stuffy living room, an ornate silver tray set with full tea service waits on the end-table between a floral couch and chair.

Waldman says, "My cleaning lady left me some coffee cake. It's very good – cinnamon, crystalized ginger, and chocolate, with an extraordinary nut crumb topping. Would you like a slice?"

He waves me to the couch, painstakingly pours, hands over a large slice of cake on a plate with a flourish, then helps himself. Leaning back in his chair, blinking behind his glasses, he rubs his fingers together as he chews, sips and chews. Even though I have plenty of time, an urgent desire wells up to pull him from his recliner. To wind the clock of his life. The chintz wallpaper closes in and begins to feel like an inverted teacup. "Reverend –"

He smiles and holds up one hand. "Nothing should compromise teatime. It keeps me sane in a quite mad world. Enjoy the cake."

He's right. I nod and swallow the last of my cake – he's right about how delicious it is – and stare at the elaborately carved cuckoo clock on the wall behind him, wondering if he lives every day at Victorian tea-time half-speed. When the wooden bird comes out and cuckoos twice, Waldman uses his fingertip to mop up the crumbs on his plate and gestures at the silver tray.

"My cleaning lady has a reputation as a baker, so I often have company at teatime. And I never thought I'd use my grandmother's tea service! Interesting, isn't it, how things make themselves useful unexpectedly. Now, about your mother." He steeples his fingers together and leans back into the depths of the chair. "I thought we should have this little visit as soon as possible. There's been some chatter amongst the ladies of my congregation about your mother, and about who should tell you. I thought it best if I did."

"Tell me what, exactly?"

"All in good time. She and I were in grade nine together, and we both rode the school bus. Jordan rides it now, doesn't he? So you understand how important discipline and quiet is on the bus, especially in winter, when the driver must concentrate on our gravel roads. Your mother, God rest her, had a terrible time that year." His tenor drops an octave. "You may already know that she was banned from riding the school bus during the winter of grade nine. She had tantrums, you see, and the bus driver couldn't convince her to stay in her seat. Then one day, she came up behind him and put her hands over his eyes – like so – and he drove the bus right into a ditch. In mid-winter."

"Oh no! I halfway expected to hear stories of adolescent puppy love," I confess. "Was anyone hurt?"

"No, no. Fortunately, we were right beside a farmyard, if it had been out on the stretches some of those roads run, halfway to nowhere, or if the bus had rolled, there could have been serious trouble – I recollect it being bone-chillingly cold that day. As it was, we all got off the bus unharmed and walked to the neighbour's house, but Lark never set foot on that bus again." Waldman leans forward. "You do understand that your mother upset a number of people, and news travels. People remember. I wasn't sure if your grandmother ever told you of this, I know how private she was, so I guessed she hadn't. It seemed to me that hearing this story from me might make it easier to bear."

He pauses. I wonder how to get him to continue. Then he resumes speaking without any prompting, and I ease my shoulders into the squishy couch. "I have some wonderful memories of Lark, too, from before the accident. She was a generous girl, and sometimes she shared her school lunch with me. Times were tight. My father worked at the potash mine, Mom had lost her job, so sometimes my lunch was a little – shall we say Spartan. Your grandmother, as you know, was a wonderful baker, and always packed a remarkable amount of food for Lark. Did she do the same for you, too? Yes? Love through nourishment. Well, I have particularly fond memories of her apple kuchen getting me through afternoon classes, thanks to Lark."

"Was she ostracized at school?"

"She didn't come back to school, Luka. Charlotte sent her to Saskatoon, and I don't recall seeing her in Goodfare again as a teenager. In fact, I didn't see her again until she came to town with her new husband some years later. She never did come to church."

The reverend sits back in his chair, fingers steepled together, humming to himself. I am flummoxed, and can't think of a single thing to ask. A few minutes pass. He finally stops humming and propels himself out of his chair, finally arriving on his feet, a heron unfolding.

"Now, I have a sermon to begin – I am a very slow writer! – so I won't keep you. And please, take some cake for you and your boy. Ella gives me entire cakes! Much more than I can ever eat myself." He clasps my hands in his soft palms, then vanishes with the cake into the kitchen. A few moments later he returns, holding a large waxed paper package tied with string. "God bless."

A heavy blanket of disbelief settles over me as I roll up Main Street and park, then walk into the café to wait for the end of school. The amber at my wrist rattles as I drum my fingertips on the tabletop. Mother's face slips in and out of focus. I imagine her on the school bus as a teenager, then on Vancouver's trolleys as an adult. What streets? What roads? Where is she now?

The grey-haired waitress at the counter catches my eye and raises the coffee pot inquiringly. The clink of the spoon on the ceramic as I stir my brew creates a hypnotic pattern that mimics the sound of tires on a gravel road. This old café reminds me of The Only in Vancouver, gone. I wave the waitress back repeatedly and guzzle several cups of coffee, drop my quarters in the juke box, and drown my thoughts in Johnny Cash and June Carter, goin' to hell in Jackson. Three o'clock comes quickly, and Jordan is waiting on the curb in front of the school. When we reach home, he eats an enormous slice of coffee cake and I slip into the parlour and call Connie.

The bus accident is news to her, but her response is pragmatic: no one was hurt; it happened years ago; Anky would have mentioned it if she felt the need. To me, the accident feels more immediate, a gateway into something visceral and desperate, something physical. It reminds me of the references to murder in Anky's diary. How the potential for violence bubbles in everyone. What triggers that volcanic flow? What contains it? Character alone? Upbringing? Familial blood? What's embedded in my boy? In me? Physical fear is unfamiliar to me. Even at her worst, Mother never lifted a hand to either of us, and although Dad was a tough-as-nails rodeo rider, he was a meringue, soft and tender on the inside, and Anky too, for all her gruffness. I have no urge to terrorize or lay hands on any human or animal in anger. How would I look at myself in the mirror without cringing if I did? Scout, for instance. I bend down and smooth his coat. How can I keep him safely at home?

When I call Hannah, the question simply falls from my mouth. "Did your mother ride the school bus with Mother?"

"Yes," Hannah responds without asking for clarification. I bet Waldman called her – he's the type who likes to keep people in the loop. "But people got over what your mother did, Luka."

"Maybe."

"You should ask Pauline."

"We've spoken," I snap.

"I know this isn't what you wanted to hear. You come for coffee whenever you get a chance, okay? We'll talk. Don't let your mother's life take over yours."

Guilt nips at my heels when I hang up. It's old news, and not Hannah's mom's fault. Or Hannah's. Or Mother's. There's no guilt to assign. I begin to wonder if Mother's illness was inherited. But from whom? More reading might tell me, but I don't get back to the diary until after Jordan has gone to bed later that evening.

Nineteen

19 April 1943

At lunch I was pouring Postum for Vic when the doorbell chimed. A woman came into the café. Her clothes! A snazzy red pillbox hat and red wool overcoat. Red hair loose beneath the hat, a cat's pointy face. She took the only open stool. Beside Vic's favourite spot at the end of the counter.

Vic stared. His hook knocked his mug right off the counter. His face turned red as beets – she'd just unbelted her coat. A fitted suit, red, too. Then she tossed her hair. Crossed her legs. Taut calves, fur-trimmed boots.

I laughed. Set a fresh cup for Vic. He was an old guy. Lost his left hand in the Boer War, a widower for at least ten years. But men never lose interest. I waved the pot in the woman's direction. Set it down when she shook her head.

I told her the lunch special. Brushed at my uniform. Crumbs and stains on my apron.

She asked for salad. Her voice a little girl's. Like Shirley Temple? No, not bubbly enough. Judy Garland? Elizabeth Taylor? But that thick accent. Irish? Same eyes as Taylor's, deep blue, almost violet. Hair like spun copper. A stunner, but a tough stunner – when she caught Vic staring, she let fly. Told him to stop gawking. Called him an oul' fella. Vic went brighter red. Turned his back.

I told her there were no greens this week, asked if she wanted coleslaw with the pork chop.

She just wanted the mash and coleslaw. Vegetables. No meat. No gravy.

Lit her cigarette, said deadly when I brought her plate. I never heard anyone talk like that before.

A fifty-cent tip under her plate. Promenaded down the aisle. Vic dropped his mug.

Muttered a curse in Serbian. The woman turned. Caught me looking.
I pocketed the tip, felt uncomfortable. What kind of woman dresses in red, top
to toes? Some dish. But something else caught me – that woman acted like she
was someone worth knowing. Someone valuable. Not a sense I have. Wish I did.

20 April 1943

That woman came back this morning, early. No one else about. I couldn't
help gawking. Felt a fool to think my new coat was fashionable. It can't hold a
candle to dolman sleeves with caped shoulders in black and scarlet wool.
A long swing that fell below the knees. She threw that coat across an empty
stool like it was nothing. Sat down and spun around. Yellow wool dress, fabric
ruffle over her breasts. Clinging. Skirt flipped over her knees as she spun like a
kid. Round and round.

She apologized about yesterday. Smiled so wide I could count each tooth.
Her teeth not as immaculate as the rest of her. Stained. Chipped. She said she
didn't mean to be a holy Joe. Didn't mean to cause a ruckus.

I told her Vic just didn't know what to make of her outfit.

She said oul' fellas always did that. Asked what was fiercely good to eat.
Pointed toward the shelf. All it held was half a cake and a plateful of scones.
Asked if any of that baked stuff was worth a dekko. I had no idea what she
meant. A look, she said. Any of it worth a look.

I told her the victory cake was pretty good toasted. That the scones were
nice too, but no butter, right? So they didn't quite taste like scones were
supposed to.

She told me to crack on, called me doll. Asked if the eggs were powdered.
Course, I said. Then she said she'd be so glad when this war was over,
desperate it was. Ordered eggs, scrambled. Toasted victory cake. But no
Postum, said she hated the taste of molasses. Asked if we had any coffee. Made
a face when I said no of course not, no one has coffee, damn war. Herb tea then,
she said.

I told her Ma calls it Kreiter tee. That those words made me think of rocks,
not something worth drinking. Don't know why I said that. She asked what
language, and I told her Hutterisch. Like Yiddish.

Then I remembered my job. Told her she could hang the coat on the hook by
the door.

She was no twenty-year-old like I first thought. Thirty, maybe thirty-five.

Tiny crows-feet at the outer corners of her eyes. Wrinkles downward from her nose. Her hands had me wondering. Smooth nails, buffed to a sheen I've never bothered to work on. Money and time. That's what made nails like that. Seemed like she had plenty of each.

Chan Lee's bell rang. I set her plate on the counter. She called me doll again, said thanks, bleedin' deadly.

The bell over the door chimed. Vic. He veered like a rabbit running for cover. Took a table at the far end of the café, his back turned.

Breakfast kept me jumping. But each trip down the counter aisle I wondered. What work paid that well? She had no rings, unmarried. Maybe she'd been born into money. Maybe her sweetheart taught at the flying school. Maybe she designed fashions in Toronto or New York – I pictured snazzy dresses and fancy hats.

The daydream burst. She stopped me, one hand on my forearm. I jumped a foot. Hot tea slopped from the mug I held. Over my wrist. Onto her cuff. She winced.

Chan Lee was gonna kill me. Donnervetter!

But she apologized. Called her dress an old rag. Said she'd had it for donkeys' years, nothing to worry about. Ten minutes later, she waved me over. Introduced herself as Tessa. Read my nametag. Too fancy a name for her, she said and laughed. Said she'd call me Lottie.

10 May 1943

Tessa in for lunch every day, weeks on end. Vic got over blushing. He still can't look her straight on. The cook always puts extra vegetables on her plate. Odd that Tessa never eats any meat. She cracks jokes about cattle manure every time I pour her dandelion tea. The tip jar behind the counter fills with change whenever she's here. Not just from Tessa. The men along the counter and in the booths all anxious that Tessa see them as generous.

Today she came by just as I finished work. Asked if I had time for a stroll in the sun. Down Twentieth and over to the river, to the Traffic Bridge. Discussed things in Europe.

I told her I was glad I didn't have brothers. Losing one of my cousins at Dieppe last year was bad enough.

Brutal, that, she said. Her accent thicker, harder to follow. She told me about her Da who emigrated from Ireland. She said he told stories about lads who went to Belfast from Doolin and the islands and got killed when Ireland was partitioned.

I didn't know what she was talking about. She explained about the Irish fighting in the twenties, after the War of Independence. Damn fool Irishmen, she said. Ousted the bloody Brits, then blew each other up over religion. A right bunch of bowsers, she said. Asked if I went to church.

I told her I liked to sleep late on Sundays. That I boarded with Marina and Gerard. They were both churchgoers, but didn't mind me staying home. I told her Ma sent me to town to live with them years ago, for high school.

Tessa scrunched up her nose. Wrinkles suddenly around her mouth. She looked as old as Ma. She asked if I knew lots of lads. A pretty little thing like you, she said, maybe I had a fella away at the front, a flier, maybe. She said there were dozens of flyboys in this town, and they all wanted to go on a tear before they went off. She didn't believe me when I said I'd never gone out with a flyboy.

Marina never discouraged young men. But none come calling. I don't know many people my own age. A book always seems better company. Or pen and paper, or paint brushes. And now most of the men gone off to war.

She shocked me when she said her Da beat her regular. That she'd run away dozens of times. I lied, told her my father died young. Don't know why I lied. But Tessa's pity would bite worse than sympathy.

When Tessa told me she found a benefactor, I wanted to ask more. Something made it clear I shouldn't. I told her about my family's farm. That if I was back home, I'd be out there weeding. Or milking the cows. She teased me, said it's 1943, doll, I shouldn't wait tables all my life. Or marry a farmer. Plenty other choices, she said. That she might be able to help me find something else to do to put a few quid in the kitty.

Another job? Doing what? Mostly I don't mind working at the café. Except for when Chan Lee gets cranky after losing at mah jong.

25 May 1943

We went to Gone With the Wind at the Roxy. I didn't like it, but Tessa was keen on Scarlett. Said she knew what a man was for, a little action under the sheets. I had stared and shaken my head. But my belly warmed up at the idea.

AN ENVELOPE IS TUCKED between the next pages, lilac-coloured paper crowded with florid lettering and curlicues, Tessa's name in the top left corner. Who was this Tessa, this Irishwoman? What would a fancy prancer like her want with my practical-minded everyday Anky?

2 June 1943

Hey Lottie!

I'm going to Manitou Springs for the weekend. A couple of days of fun will make me feel like a new girl, and I have a new dress. Come? My treat. We'll take the train to Watrous Friday evening. Pack something snazzy to wear dancing and we'll go to Danceland!

Hey, what did you think of that Kraft Dinner I brought you to try? It's so fierce brand new! Just trying to broaden your horizons, doll.

Don't worry about your boss. If he won't give you the day off, just don't show up. What's he gonna do, kill you? It's a junk-hole joint, Lottie, he won't care. You can find a better job than that, easy. We'll get started on that project right after Manitou Springs. You'll be brilliant. See you at the train station by five! I'll have your ticket.

Tessa

I FLIP OPEN MY LAPTOP and Google Danceland, then spend twenty minutes ogling a clean-lined white stucco hangar overlooking a lake an hour's drive east of Saskatoon. A dancehall in the centre of the province seems somehow misplaced to me, but apparently it was the bomb at the time. An external rainbow sign, "DANCELAND," arcs the entire width of the building. Internally, more splendour – gleaming maple floor, elevated stage, and a spectacular vaulted ceiling with large drop-ball lights and exposed trusses festooned with ribbons.

When I learn that Danceland was built with the same type of floating hardwood floor as the Commodore Ballroom in downtown Vancouver, I email Cherie. "Remember the dance floor at the Commodore, how springy it was? I'm reading my Anky's diary. She's just about to go dancing at Danceland on Manitou Lake, way back in the day, 1943! Oh, she's going to have a ball on that dance floor! How cool is that?" Both buildings have burlap-wrapped coiled horsehair bundles beneath a floating maple floor; the bundles compress beneath the weight of dancers to give the floor the wonderful spring I remember from dancing at the Commodore.

5 June 1943

A train! I hadn't ridden a train since I was six and Ma took me to the east coast. Ma sold a bunch of horses and I got to see the circus.

Marina gave me a hard stare when I asked to borrow the suitcase. Wanted to know if I knew what I was doing. Wanted to know about my new friend Tessa. Wanted to know why I haven't brought her home for a meal. She asked if it was Tessa I was ashamed of, or her and Gerard. Then she warned me to be careful. Black souls wear white shirts, her favourite saying.

I'd never be ashamed of Marina. Tessa, though? Great fun. Truly. But not a girl I could introduce to Marina and Gerard. Marina would die of mortification. The things Tessa says! She's crude in a way that even Ma never was. Despite her years as a studhorse woman. Marina would find some Ukrainian saying or word for her. I would understand the meaning even if I didn't know the exact translation.

I arrived at the train station in a tizzy, direct from work. Hat and hair flying loose. Marina's suitcase thumping against my legs. Tessa on the platform beyond the fence of the station, waving with her cigarette. Yelling at me to fly, to get going. Train engines hissed and belched steam. Hurry, hurry, the train was rolling. The conductor waved his flag. We scrambled up the steps, Tessa first. Flopped in the first empty seats we found.

The conductor took a close look at us and our tickets. Told us to move along, that this was a first class carriage. Second class was in the next three cars toward the rear.

Tessa's shoulders and back went rigid. She led me through the car's narrow central aisle. Into the vestibule between the cars. Fumed about the clever dosser, what a nasty piece of work. Give a man a uniform, she said, and he turns into a right and proper arse. Then a tight smile, her teeth barely visible. A warning that we'd best find seats. This train was the bleedin' beach express, she said. Bound to be thick with screaming sprogs and cranky mams. The joys of motherhood when the lads go away to fight the Hun. The trip was a couple of hours. If we stood all the way we'd feel knackered when we got there.

Tessa was right. Twenty minutes to get three cars back. I lost track of the number of times I muttered excuse me. Dozens of sweaty bodies. Short-tempered women and crying children. Bulging suitcases and bulky baby carriages. Lunch hampers. Finally we found two empty seats and stowed the luggage.

The train picked up speed. Rumbled over the river and headed east. The carriage felt luxurious. Tessa sat knotted in her seat, scowling. I didn't resent the conductor for ousting us from first class. He just had a job to do. Considered the disappearing river and the train tracks unfolding. The two so briefly meeting.

A crowd hemmed us in. Children in grubby play clothes. Mothers perched precariously in the aisle seats to contain them. The children watched me unpack cold fried chicken from the café. Tessa produced cucumber sandwiches. She stuck out her tongue at the kids. Bit into her sandwich with gusto. The children stared at me. Sulky faces turned expectant. I counted heads and insufficient chicken. Kept my chicken to myself. Smiled and shrugged in the children's direction. Tessa unearthed a flask of gin. We took nips whenever the mothers' attention shifted. When children ran to the far end of the car.

Tessa caught my eye, waved at the window, said it was a bit of a bog out here. Just like back home. Wanted to know if it looked like the land where my people were.

I nodded. Watched the farmland fences unspool. Thought of how women were. Last autumn, Marina gave garden beets and onions to a migrant worker in ragged clothes. Turned her back on a Broadway shopkeeper badmouthing his competitor's inferior fabric and badly made buttons. But I don't understand her. What gives women like Marina their sense of balance? Their ability to recognize safe routes and risks? Does that awareness arrive with age? Not a knack I have. I want to believe that goodness will triumph. But it seems unlikely.

Tessa looked like a lady. Her day-dress showed a hint of cleavage. Her hair caught back with gold barrettes. She always looked as if she'd just stepped out of a powder room. And me with sweat on my face no matter what dresses or shoes I chose. How to feel as cool and self-possessed as Tessa? Not slightly harried? Not coming-apart-at-the-seams?

A uniformed flier sat with his back to us a few rows away. Tessa waved the flask. Made a sour face. She said flyboys were bowzers, you'd think they never collected any wages, how tight they hung onto a nickel. A shower of bleedin' savages, they were. Another nip of gin. Her voice slurred. Such nickel nursers, she said, the fuss they made over the cost of movie tickets, a quarter each. Tight as a duck's arse, all of 'em, she said, like boyos on their first date. That town was too desperate for her, she said.

An ugly grimace. She patted her hair, said she was turning thirty next month. Flounced a bit, preening. Said a girl had to look out for herself. No more silly servicemen for her. But they were fine for a girl like me.

She said she wanted a dekko at my get-up. Almost sounded complimentary when she said that I didn't dress like a bogger. When I told her I'd brought a dress she said I could change when we settled in at the hotel. Said she was going to move to a big city and I should visit her. She was going to find herself a rich businessman. Met plenty in Toronto, she said, what a dead town, plenty of money, but no fun. She waved the flask. Took another sip of gin, added she might go to Vancouver, or Seattle.

The young mother of two of the sleeping children scowled at Tessa. Tessa smirked and carried on. Talked about Moose Jaw. Said it was small, but men there knew how to have a good time. She asked if I'd brought a swimsuit. Said, we just have to get you exposed.

All these deep urges. A yearning I can't explain away. Where would I be at thirty? At forty? Doing what, with whom? Impossible to imagine. This war. Would it end soon? Would I ever marry?

Marriage doesn't seem likely. The men who visit the café are old, like Vic. Or rowdy teenaged braggarts. No Hutterite farmer for me. No farmer, definitely not. But how long will the war last? Will any soldiers come back? In what shape? Damaged, like Marina's Gerard? He can't tolerate loud noises. And his arm... On bad nights I hear him moaning. Then he and Marina come downstairs late, both looking peaked. Marina with a set to her mouth that I rarely see otherwise. At least he has a wife who loves him. According to Marina, marriage offers men and women an oasis. Tessa just scoffs.

Tessa closed her eyes. The children and their mothers slept. I pulled out my notebook. Scribbled. Started a drawing of a pelican I'd seen by the weir as we left town. Then set down the pen. Gazed at their smooth faces. Wondered what Tessa saw in me. I wanted to ask but couldn't. Our differences such a huge gap. I was painting again in my spare time. Watercolours, inspired by walks beside the river. Lots of birds from my walks beside the river. Kept the finished pieces in my bedroom, couldn't show even Marina. But my books! I took them everywhere. Tessa made rude comments about my reading. Asked if I was fixing to be a bluestocking. I never answered. I'd learned from Ma, silence had its uses. Tessa burns hot, a live wire, exhausting to be around. What does it feel like? Just once, to live like Tessa. To be a girl men look at with admiration. With desire.

I mean to sit down after this weekend out with Tessa. To ask Marina some serious questions about life, men, marriage. And come fall, concentrate on painting. Take some art classes. A woman with paint across her hands and a bagful of paintbrushes had stopped by the café last week. I had surprised myself, asked if she was a painter. She nodded. Told me she was heading to the university. Introduced herself as Wynona Mulcaster. Asked if I was a painter. I couldn't answer. Wanted to say yes.

Twenty

THE DIARY WAITS while I brew a pot of tea. I carry it to the parlour and stretch out on the couch. I want to find a magical way to tell this young unprotected Anky that the war would last another two years, that thousands more men would die before their sorry remnants would make their way home, a ragtag army of damaged victors. I want to warn her that Tessa's intentions couldn't possibly be pristine, that trust in her was like putting trust in a flighty bird bound to fly away. To honour her instincts, and paint.

Tessa shook me awake. Hot. Bedraggled, groggy. Too much gin. A glass of lemonade and a damp cloth, please. But no. She said she had some things to tell me. Her voice took an odd tone. Strained. She wanted to explain what to expect at Danceland. Not all fun and games. Work. She asked me if I knew what she meant. No. Flummoxed, brain still fuzzy. No.

She lowered her voice, said that she worked at another café farther west along Twentieth Street. Not slinging hash. That she told people she was a lady of leisure.

I didn't understand. She shook her head in amazement. Told me I was some bit of fluff. Then spelled it out. She was a working girl. Still foggy – took a moment before I twigged. A –. Tessa shushed me. Whispered again. A tart, she said. She told me that she sat in the banquette at the front of the café, by the window. And waited for gentlemen callers. At Danceland, she said, she worked for Mister Ayres. She appraised me, her eyes cold. Promised to introduce me. So I could see how the other half lived. She swore it was an

easier living than that café I worked in. Fun, really, to chat a bit and have
a pint with a lad first. The rest, well, it was just business. Just another ride.
Men were all the same. She laughed. Seemed to enjoy my shock. Told me that
tarting never goes out of style. That I'd have to dress differently, easy enough
to fix. She patted her bag under her knee. Said she'd brought along a dress that
should fit. That I could pay her back. She peered at my feet. My shoes. Said
they'd do. Asked if I was game.

I said no. What made her think I might be? I looked away, out the window.
The ground rushed past. Fence posts passing so quickly, dizzyingly fast.
Leading somewhere. The speed frightened me. On the window, a small fly
buzzed. Its circles getting wider and wider. I imagined myself in one of Tessa's
dresses, breasts showing, high heels. Felt dizzy. From excitement or disgust?

She told me to think about it. That we had a bit of time before we arrived.
She swore she wouldn't feel offended. That she'd still come drink that rotten
herb tea I served at that joint I worked at. She leaned close. Tapped my
forehead between my eyes. Told me I was fooling myself, thinking I'd make a
good life and a rich living as a waitress. Jam on your egg, she said. The boys
weren't gonna march home anytime soon. She nudged me, her elbow sharp.
Who'd want a shot-up laddie who comes home the worse for wear? I thought of
Gerard again.

She fluffed her hair. Whispered. Not for everyone, shaggin' the lads for
money, there were rules, she said. Precautions. Making him wear a rubber, for
one. She gave me a little push. Told me to freshen up in the bean jack and have
a bit of a think. Another push, harder.

I tiptoed down the aisle. Thought again of Gerard. 'A little worse for wear'
doesn't describe his life short an arm. Even buttoning his shirt is impossible
alone. The personal things Marina has to do for him. Wouldn't Marina have
plenty to say! The very idea. Selling myself for money. And Tessa's language.
A prostitute! What did she call it? A tart! I could never tell Marina the truth
about her. What scathing expression would Marina use to describe her? What
if I did invite Tessa home for supper? If Tessa accidentally let that information
slip? But it would never be accidental. Tessa would want to shock Marina.

Never been to a dance. Never had a sweetheart. I'd only considered what
Tessa called 'a ride' in theoretical terms. Never the actual mechanics. And
a rubber? How exactly was it put on? What kept the rubber in place? I'd
seen erections on Ma's stallions. From a respectable distance behind a fence.
Whatever would Marina say?

A whore. It echoed in that tiny bathroom. All the Victorian novels I'd read with ruined women! Things hadn't changed. Nowadays, a woman who sold herself was still an outcast. Shunned. Still damaged goods. Was that what I wanted? What about painting? Would I see the world differently? Paint differently? Feel differently? If I become a whore? Would I carry myself like Tessa? Would men look at me differently? With the heat I'd seen, even in old Vic's eyes? So many questions from such an impossible situation!

In the mirror, no sign of wrinkles except my clothing. I'd never look as sophisticated as Tessa. Those dresses! Then there were her comments about men. Her casual attitude toward money. It all made sense. Still, how could she? Sex with any man with the means? I couldn't. I couldn't simply stay and dance. I had to go home.

The train whistle blew, one sharp blast. What to tell Marina? A pinprick of curiosity slowly woke. The war had taken all the likely men. This might be my only chance to find out about it. About sex. Ma had never discussed her work as a studhorse woman. It was Marina who'd taught me how to care for myself. Her face peering over my shoulder. Her carefully coiffed silver hair and impeccable eyebrows. What if I fell pregnant? No. I couldn't, simple as that.

Tessa's glare sharp as her elbow when I returned. I looked away. Out the window. The fence and its posts beside the track blurred. The train took a curve. Behind me, tracks back the way we'd come. The fence ahead suddenly came into sharp focus. I couldn't. No. I had to go home.

Tessa shook me, told me not to be daft. That I should come along and we'd have fun dancing. Just dancing. Nothin' more. No worries, she promised me. She leaned close. No gin on her breath, only the strong aroma of peppermint.

Twenty-one

I WAKE AT THREE A.M. on the couch, my head buzzing. After I tiptoe upstairs for my robe, I turn on the reading lamp in the parlour, return to the couch, resume reading.

5 June 1943

No taxis at the cabstand. We sat down on the bench. I pulled out my notebook. Tessa smoked, picked lint off her dress. Fidgeted. A few minutes later, a black Ford Model A rolled up. A man leaned out of the driver's window. Offered us a lift.

He swung out of his car when Tessa said we were going to Danceland. A mock salute and a grin. His teeth stained yellow, his fingers too. Air Force wedgie cap, starched and immaculate uniform. She told him we were staying at Martin's Tourist Hotel. That the mineral baths were good for a girl's skin. He laughed, said her skin looked fine. Tessa raised one eyebrow. Smiled at the airman without showing her chipped teeth. He asked if he could take us to our hotel. Tessa directed him to Danceland first.

How could she be so bold?

He introduced himself as Terrence. Terry. Tessa nudged me. Slid through the open door onto the rear bench. Terry held the front passenger door wide. Asked our names. Told us he'd driven all the way from Calgary with his buddy. He wanted me to hop up front where he could get a good look.

I scurried into the back seat, my face red. A twenty-minute drive to Manitou Springs. Terry watched us in his rearview mirror. His eyes small and dark, like beads. Platinum-blond hair and sunburnt ears. I thought of jug handles. Stifled the giggle.

*When he asked where we were from, Tessa flirted. Said she could murder a
pint of plain. Asked if he danced. Called him boyo. Did he jitterbug or rhumba?
She glanced up at the mirror through her eyelashes.*

*I cringed and pulled away. Tessa was so obvious, so pushy. So forward.
I didn't want to witness this.*

*We stopped in front of an arched building shaped like an airplane hangar.
The single word, Danceland, in capital letters, a rainbow against the sky.*

*Tessa clambered past the suitcases. Told me to grab her purse. Told Terry to
wait. That he and his buddy needed jitney tickets to dance with us.*

He grinned, brandished his Brownie. Snapped a photo.

*Tessa pushed the screen door open, yarded me behind her. Stepped into the
dancehall. Led me into the building. I asked what a jitney ticket was. Pulled
my arm away when she snapped at me. Looked about the building. A wooden
floor edged with vertical columns. A soaring roof cut an arc above us. White
lights in globes dangling from the trusses. A stage, musical instruments,
microphones.*

*Tessa told me not to gawk. That the whole world knew about this place but
me. Called me an eejit. This joint was where the rest of the world whooped
it up, she explained. Not kindly. She said that the dance-floor was famous
– something about floating metal and horsehair, that its spring was what
brought the dancers. The Canadian Carlsbad, they call it. She sniffed, said
she'd go to the real Carlsbad in Germany. If the right fella took it into his mind
to ask her when this war finally ended.*

*She led me along the edge of the shining floor. Pointed out the window to
the canoes. Said I'd make a few extra bucks if some guy took me out on the lake
in a canoe to listen to the band under the stars. And a little bump in the boat.*

I told her again that I'd just dance. Stepped onto the floor.

*A raspy baritone voice in my ear ordered me off. Steel fingers pinched my
arm. Yarded me back to the tables. He was short, my height. Wide. Balding.
Reminded me of a badger, if a badger ever wore a suit. Sleek white eyebrows,
an unsmiling face, rough grey stubble. Not a badger. A weasel in winter. He
looked past me to Tessa, greeted her by name. She called him Mister Ayres.
Right, I'd forgotten. The boss. He turned back to me, eyes flicking over my face.
My body.*

*The urge to curtsey. Instead, I extended my hand. Ayres stared at it, touched
his palm to mine, the skin just kissing. I pulled my hand back, rubbed it against
my skirt. Couldn't rid myself of the dampness of his palm.*

Tessa tugged me onto a chair. Berated me in a whisper.

Ayres touched right hand to forehead. A mocking salute. He pulled me to my feet. Twirled me in a pirouette, his sweaty hands spongy. Every time I met his eyes he was staring. Gave me a thorough once-over, dress to shoes to hair. His fingers tightened before he released my hand. He was halfway across the dance-floor before I collapsed onto a chair again. Shaking. Was it revulsion? Or the sheer propulsion of that pirouette that caught me in the gut?

I choked on my words as I told her that he was a scary guy. Tessa giggled. Said she called him Black Jack, never to his face. She claimed he was a straight-up fella, good in a jam despite his manners. He'd helped her out a few times in Moose Jaw, when she was working down there. Her little-girl voice brittle at the edges.

She hauled me out the door, back to Terry waiting by his car.

Into the hotel lobby after Terry dropped us off. I asked Tessa to tell me more about that little man.

Tessa glanced around. The hotel lobby was crowded. Lowered her voice. She chided me for calling him that. Admitted he did look a bit gammy, but he'd right and proper hate hearing that, she said. She warned me that I didn't want Mister Ayres hating me. She had an arrangement with him. When I asked her what she meant, she snapped at me and called me simple. Then relented. Told me that he took a cut of everything. Told me to look for a man with a long string of tickets dangling from his pocket. Told me to stay on Mister Ayres' good side, whatever he wanted.

I tried to argue. I wasn't –

Tessa steamrollered me. Told me I was missing out on a good bet, easy dough for anything beyond straight-up shagging.

When I asked her what she meant by beyond straight-up shagging, she called me green. Told me to use my imagination. Things men and women do in bed.

She led me to the registration desk. Her squeaky voice acquired a snappish brevity that astonished me. The clerk, equally frosty. He dropped a key on the counter. Said the room bill had been settled in advance. Tessa told him to send up two cold suppers immediately, no meat, no garlic. To have a cab waiting in an hour.

She led me toward the stairs. Told me again not to gawk. And to grab my bag. She pulled me past the elevator as I jabbed the call button. Told me to never take the elevator, climbing stairs was good for the legs.

I watched the elevator rise, a latticed black box with a gilded cage. Pictured myself in it, wearing a gold lamé dress like I'd seen in the movies. And a man who looked like Clark Gable standing beside me. Beyond straight-up shagging. Whatever did that mean? I couldn't imagine. Thought about dancing on that amazing floor. I'd never taken lessons. Never gone to a tea dance. Danceland woke something in me. Despite Mister Ayres and his straining seams. He scared me.

I took Tessa's arm. But she snapped at me. I dropped my hand. She sounded like Ma.

Room service! Smoked goldeye! All the way from Winnipeg! Pie! And cheddar cheese! No real cheese since the war started.

Tessa told me to not rabbit on. Not to eat the stuffed onion or my breath would reek. And no afters either, pie would make me fat and my clothes wouldn't hang right. She told me to get dressed and we'd have a lesson so I could get around the floor without tripping.

She sounded more and more like my boss. Less like my friend. I wanted the Saskatoon pie. But I pushed the tray away.

When I emerged from the bathroom in my grey linen dress Tessa had changed, too. Wore a red sleeveless dress that haunted her curves and made her skin look like porcelain. She struck a pose. What a looker. Her bossiness seemed less crucial. Her approval all-important.

Tessa sniffed and said my deadly outfit was fit for lunch with my gran. She stuck out her tongue. Pulled a bundle of pink froth from her red suitcase. Told me I looked some desperate. To put on the pink dress. Told me ya catch more bees with honey, honey. To strip it off like a good lass. That I'd not got anything she hadn't seen before. She was vulgar. Cruel. I pulled the froth over my head. Tessa patted and straightened the lace along the hem. Told me to have a dekko.

In the mirror. Who was that woman? Silvery lace ruffle along my throat. Bare shoulders, arms, legs. The tops of my breasts. A little racy. I tugged at the dress. It didn't budge.

Tessa ignored my anxiety. Brushed my hair and put in two silver barrettes. Then a little lipstick. She twirled me in front of the mirror. Told me I was ready for dance lessons. She let go and turned on the radio. Grabbed my arm again. Swung me around. Right! Under. Around. Two three four. Again. Told me to kip it this time. To count to myself, no, not out loud. To loosen up and let those gams go. I was laughing and breathless when Tessa released me. I warmed up to her again when she complimented me.

She told me that men were decent blokes, for the most part. That Mister Ayres weeded out the manky ones and the plonkers. Asked me straight if I'd ever – Laughed when I blushed. I pulled back as she adjusted my neckline, her hands deft.

Easy money, she said. Told me to show them boobies. Stick out my arse and wiggle. A bit of skirt and honey for the bees, she said. Then tugged me down the stairs to a waiting cab.

At Danceland Terry found us within minutes. A taller sandy-haired man hovered at his elbow. Rail-thin wrists and ankles stuck out of his uniform.

Tessa tossed back her hair. She nudged me. Told me to stop daydreaming. Terry draped his arm over her shoulders. Introduced me to Simon. Announced the rule: no talking about the war. Tonight was all about tonight, and being at Danceland with a pair of lovelies.

Simon's hand sweaty on mine as he tugged me into the line of dancers at the edge of the floor. The band was tuning up. He fidgeted. His hand across my forearm, fingers tattooing my skin. Other hand fiddled with the tickets in his pocket. Tapped his toe, a rapid-fire rhythm that made me want to tap my toes too. I surged forward. Simon pulled me back. Told me not to hurry. That Ayres had to come by. Said pennies to pounds they'd play Cole Porter.

The band swung into a dance beat. Simon gloated – he was right, it was 'Anything Goes.' He chattered in my ear – sweet piano, better sax. Told me the name of the orchestra, the owner's house band. The name of the lead singer. He thought she was pretty good, he'd heard her before. Would they play Gershwin? Did I like 'Someone to Watch Over Me'? Did I like the Duke? 'Take the A Train'?

Ayres stopped in front of us. His eyes slid over me. Stopped at my hemline, my breasts. My dress like water over my skin.

Better, he said in my ear. Held out his hand, palm up. Simon passed over a pair of tickets. Led me to a gap in the middle of the room. We waited. I watched Ayres stroll around the perimeter of the dance floor. He stopped in front of each couple. Every woman got the same raking examination. I shivered, my skin suddenly clammy.

Simon started to sing along with the band. Now god knows, anything goes... His voice a light tenor, musical and bright. He asked me about my scent, was it lilac? Nice. The bandleader raised his hand. Simon tugged my arm. We danced. He talked shop nonstop. His captain was a fool, his CO no better. The squadron scheduled to fly to England in three weeks. Nowhere near combat-ready.

The room whirled. The floor surged, waves of energy.

I found my balance. Asked Simon what he did in the squadron. He told me he was the navigator for an Avro Lancaster bomber. He rattled on about his fool of a CO. The idiotic prime minister. The fiasco at Dieppe. His expectation of night runs across the Channel.

I felt light-headed. Stopped listening. This was real dancing! Wait until I told Marina! Even the thought of Marina didn't dampen my excitement. Why had I never danced before? Why had it taken meeting Tessa to learn about Danceland? What was wrong with my life? The music flowed through my body. I stopped thinking and moved. My feet and torso followed Simon's around the floor. I laughed when the song ended. Didn't step out of his arms,

He made nice compliments. Offered me a cool drink. Returned moments later with lemonade. Led me outside.

We walked along the boardwalk. The moon sailed high above the lake. Simon pulled a hip flask from his pocket. Tipped some liquid into our glasses.

Gin, he admitted. He grinned. Asked if I'd ever gone swimming here. Pretty nice, he said, pointed out the water slide. Suggested we take a dip, maybe, later. When I said I'd left my swimsuit in the hotel, he ran his fingers down my arm. Told me that I didn't need a suit.

I stumbled saying it. That I was not like Tessa.

He shrugged, said of course not, that Tessa was a real looker. Caught himself. Added that I was pretty too.

I tried again, told him that I was just there to dance.

Simon scowled. Then seemed to think better of it. Held out his flask. When I refused, he grabbed my hand. Said we should dance if I was just there to dance. The band had resumed playing.

Ayres met us at the door. His knowing look. What did he think we'd done? I wanted to grab him by the lapels and wipe the smirk from his face. Instead, I straightened my spine.

Simon handed over the tickets. We stepped onto the floor. This time I relaxed. It was what sailing must feel like. We spun through a turn. His hand slipped down the small of my back to just above my buttocks. At the end of the dance he led me outdoors. Offered another drink. A canoe ride.

He talked. He paddled. I leaned back and relaxed. It was like being rocked. I lay in the canoe, stared up at the sky. Stars everywhere. Simon at the far end, watching me. Talking, talking, talking, his voice climbing. I could barely hear the band. His voice didn't falter. He stopped paddling. Unbuttoned his trousers and started to rub himself. Appalled, I looked away.

Simon laughed. A high-pitched sound like metal on metal. Told me to get on my knees and take him in my mouth.

I said no. No!

He asked me just what did I do? He grounded the canoe. Scrambled over the crossbraces. Kissed me, his pants still unbuttoned. Put his hands on my breasts. Something foreign, a man's hands. He lifted me out. Carried me through the water. Tessa's dress drenched. Onshore he grabbed the top of the dress. It ripped, shredding as the threads gave way.

His voice climbed. Urged me to let him. That he knew I wanted to. It was time, he said, that dress, that dancing. He ground his body against me.

I begged him to stop. He met my eyes for half a second. I swore that he heard me. Was about to free my arms. Then something turned off behind his eyes. He didn't let me go. Instead, he leaned forward and lifted the dress.

He shoved his hand between my legs. Fingers pushed underwear aside. Prying. I flailed and started to scream. He clamped his free hand over my mouth, his fingers shaking. Hushed me. Warned me. His breathing turned into a racing engine. The staccato beating of his heart. His breathless panting. Another scream couldn't get past his hand on my mouth.

Afterwards, Simon crawled off me. Rolled to one side. Lay motionless, his eyes closed. A few minutes later he sat up. Adjusted his clothing absentmindedly. Stared blankly at me. Apologized repeatedly.

I shuddered. He tugged at my dress. Half-carried me along the lakeside in silence. The muscles in his arms shaking. My own muscles trembled, relaxed, shuddered shut. How did muscles know what to do, and when?

Then I spotted Tessa by the jetty. She had two men with her. I couldn't look away. She was moaning, her skirt hitched high. A ripple through my abdomen shocked me. How could I possibly feel excited?

Simon said we'd take Terry's car. I huddled on the seat while he cranked the starter lever. Tried to ignore the burning between my thighs. He ground the gearshift. In front of the hotel, he held out a handful of bills. I didn't touch the money. He got out of the car. Pulled me out. Crammed the cash into my handbag. Whispered that I'd earned it. He hoped he hadn't didn't hurt me. Hadn't meant... He'd just... lost control. It happened to him sometimes.

I kept my head down. He got back into the car and drove off.

No key. I clutched the ripped dress closed. The desk clerk behind the desk leered. His eyes on me through the elevator's open wire cage all the way up.

Twenty minutes in the room. Washed, washed again, then again. Stuffed my clothes and Tessa's dress into Marina's valise and ran downstairs. A cab idled at the curb.

6 June 1943, 4 AM

The train station had one light. No trains for hours, no people either. Even the stationmaster was gone. A sign in the window said he'd be back at 5:30 AM. I huddled on a bench, clutched pen and notebook. No choice but to wait. I couldn't stay in the hotel room. Couldn't face the possibility of Tessa coming back. Never wanted to see Danceland again. Or Tessa.

Such a fool. I thought we were friends. But Tessa betrayed me, and now this. Because of her. I could never tell anyone. I had to write the truth. Purge it from my body before I froze inside.

I kept the cash. God forgive me. I'll need it if the worst happens. I should have fought harder. Bitten his hand so I could scream until my lungs burst. Kicked him. Drawn blood. All the things I didn't do leapt out of the shadows and taunted me. My own fault.

My body and mind no longer bound together. Two separate animals. It might have hurt less if I'd relaxed. But he forced me. I remembered staring at the sky. His hand over my mouth. Men and women have done this thing together every single day of every year since time began. Surely it shouldn't cause pain. His actions betrayed the very idea of love. What I heard coming from that man were not the sounds of love. He'd twisted and thrust and shuddered like an animal. All the time he shook, as if ill. My mouth and insides. Lakeside and lake water. Sediment. Silt. Muck.

I wanted Marina. I wanted all to be well. That almost made me laugh. I'd come to Danceland a virgin, and now I wasn't. If I become pregnant, then what? Could I ever love a baby begun this way? I was lost. Oh, I wanted my mother. I wanted Marina.

On the train a waft of lilac. My insides rebelled. I ran out to the vestibule and leaned over the rail. Heaved. Prayed to be rid of the self-loathing clamped like a leech onto my heart.

ANKY'S SADNESS FINALLY makes sense. That she was able to make even a brief record of events is remarkable. Is it a good sign? I wipe away my tears and peer at the clock: not yet four A.M. I turn back to the diary, praying the worst is over.

Twenty-two

6 June 1943

 The train rolled into Saskatoon under steady rain. Crossed the trestle. I remembered standing on the Traffic Bridge with Tessa. Wondered now about the river that flowed beneath me. How rapidly a new channel cut through banks. Winter swamped and overthrown, currents in full spate.

 Ten minutes at the streetcar stop. A car pulled over beside me. Marina and Gerard, out for a rare weekend outing in their neighbour's car. Marina was surprised to see me. Told me they were on their way to – Interrupted herself to ask what was wrong.

 I lied. Kept my voice steady. Climbed in. A million miles separated me from my aching body, drifting farther away with each breath.

 Marina admonished me to be gentle with the car. She asked if I'd met someone at Danceland. A handsome airman, perhaps?

 I said a small and bitter prayer. Turned to face my foster-mother. My smile tight and strained. Asked how she'd guessed.

 Marina laughed. Told me that your head is not only for putting a hat on. She was glad to hear I'd had a little excitement. And she was partial to fliers. She put her hand on Gerard's shoulder.

 They took me to Early's to look at the new supply of rose bushes, then looked at the new college on the university grounds. Finished at the Bessborough. At the hotel the gargoyles on the roof leered like the desk clerk.

 During lunch I ignored my salad completely. Puddled my soup. Smiled at the waiter when he fussed. Kept my mind firmly on describing Danceland and the hotel. Even managed to volunteer descriptions of Mister Ayres and Simon. Tessa I didn't mention at all. I told them I'd learned to do the Lindy hop. That the music was jazz, swing, a Saskatoon singer and band, Clarice somebody?

Gerard scratched his thin hair, considering. Asked if it was Claribel Hicks.

Marina inquired if I'd be seeing the flier again. Not likely, I told her. My fingers whitened. Told them he was being shipped overseas soon. Marina wanted me to contact the air school. Invite him for lemonade.

At my emphatic no, Gerard intervened. Told her to leave be. That everyone's entitled to a few secrets. He thought I'd tell Marina the rest soon enough.

We returned to the car. Marina threaded her arm through mine. In an undertone she advised me not to fret. That we all meet people we won't see again. The ones we can't forget cause the problems. She patted my arm and opened the car door. Invited me to talk whenever I felt ready.

My composure slipped. So close to tears. I wanted to forget Simon more than anything. But why hadn't Marina asked me about Tessa? I bit my lip and left the subject alone.

At home I ran a bath. Immersed myself in bubbles and soap. Stayed in the tub for what felt like hours. Marina rattled the doorknob several times. The hot water didn't ease me. I replayed the final moments with Simon. He thought that a few words and the added insult of money would undo the damage? Tessa was right about one thing: men were shallow.

Crawled out of the tub. Retreated to my bedroom without examining my skin. Without touching myself any more than necessary. Stumbled over the suitcase just inside the door. I opened it. Pulled out the ripped dress with its silvery lace. Laid it on the bed and regarded it. My arms clutched my towelled midriff. I gathered up the dress and wept. Damaged, spoiled, ruined, shamed.

12 June 1943

I took the streetcar to work as usual on Monday. To do otherwise would have caused a fuss. The last thing I wanted. I couldn't decide who I hated more – Simon, Tessa, Mister Ayres. Or myself, for being so easily duped, so foolish.

Tessa didn't show up. A relief and disappointment. I rehearsed again what I'd say.

Almost a week. At night the weight of the entire world slopes in. Simon's voice and hands and body inescapable. I can't eat. Can't sleep. Spend my free time in the bathroom. Wondering – how will I know? Other than the obvious, what clues? I could ask no one. Except Tessa.

I threw out my lilac eau de cologne and soap, all my lilac-infused sachets.

14 June 1943

The dream again: a long-nailed woman in red, red nails. A man, his hands, touching everywhere. Exploding suns, shooting fire in jagged streaks. Blood on my legs and hands. I woke gasping, nails cutting crescents in my palms. Four nights in a row I've dreamt it.

ANKY'S DREAM IS unnerving. What would my shrink have made of it? My own visceral response is clear enough: I don't need to pull out my dream dictionary to come up with anger, playing with fire, the weight of the world, moral judgment, guilt, suppressed rage, all the primal hot buttons.

15 June 1943

Tessa walked into the café. Sat down on a counter stool. Folded her hands on her lap, calm as you please. Her skin looked coarse and thick. Wrinkles showed through the clumps of powder, her eyeliner smudged in the morning light. The only other person at the counter was Vic. I knew that Chan Lee would run out, cleaver in hand, if I screamed.

She said Simon had told her what happened. She sounded normal. Normal! As if nothing had changed. According to Tessa, Simon could barely stand up. She wanted to know what I'd done to him. To him! Finally she lowered her voice. Muttered that he'd confessed to forcing me. She wanted to know if I had any bruises down there. As if she had a right to know. She stood up. Leaned across the counter. Her hands tight on my shoulders. On my chin, turning my face this way and that.

I jerked free. Vic looked up but didn't interfere.

Tessa shrugged. Said I looked fine-o. That Simon said he was so sorry, that I was ever so sweet. That I said no. That he lost control. She looked at me, her face twisting. She reminded me that she'd warned me. Said not to get all holy Joe on her.

I told her to leave. That she had no right to speak to me. Tessa laughed. Down the counter, Vic stared. She lowered her voice. Snorted that I was just a farmer's daughter. So righteous. That I had nothing that every other woman didn't have. She called me a nobody, just another box. She said I should cop on to myself. That I had no skills. I wanted to slap her. But she was right.

What else could I do? She was sneering as she whispered, asking me if I'd sell real estate. More cheap breakfasts? Or go back to being a culchie out on my mother's farm. Her voice slid in. Spread through my belly and ribcage. I could barely breathe. Each rib closed tightly. Around my lungs, my heart. Reproving my foolishness.

Then she opened her purse. Pulled out her wallet. She laughed as she waved a wad of bills in front of my face. Her laughter, hoarse as a crow's. She told me that the ruined dress had set her back. Claimed I owed her money. She reminded me that Mister Ayres weeded out the rough players. That this was just a little accident. A little time to heal and the old box would be good to go.

She grabbed my wrist. I twisted free. The temptation to slap her grew. She preened. Told me to look closely at her. That this was how a tart lived and spent money. Her nice clothes. She didn't need to marry a flippin' farmer, she said, and I didn't either. Not that one would want me now. She snapped her fingers. Laid the money on the counter. Took out her cigarettes. Offered me one.

I looked down. A heap of small bills on the counter. My fingers reached out. Hovered over the cash. Left it lying. Finally I pulled a cigarette from Tessa's pack.

Tessa held out a lit match. She made kissing sounds. I wanted to knock her over. Told me not to cry. That she'd been turning tricks since she was twelve. Her Ma was gone by then, she said. Her Ma used to lie in bed with a baby at her boob and tell Tessa and her brothers about the selkies, coming to land as women, lying with the men, then disappearing. That's what she told herself she was, a selkie. Love them and leave them, Men are liars. She told me to never trust a man.

I didn't know what a selkie was but I refused to ask. Coughed as I smoked. The smoke in my lungs almost ignited. Donnervetter! I wanted to pound Simon with my fists. Him and that shark in a suit, Mister Ayres. But mostly Tessa.

Why was she still sitting there? She wouldn't stop talking. On and on about Simon. If he'd used a safe. A rubber. What? She looked at me in derision. Said that I was no gobshite, not to try so hard to sound like one. A condom, you eejit, she said. When I shook my head, she said she'd get in touch with someone. To let her know if my monthlies didn't come calling. She knew someone in Moose Jaw who knew someone. Her bright smile didn't reach her eyes. She said that it was nixer work, cash only. No tax payable. That I'd make a terrific tart.

When I shouted at her, Vic set down his coffee cup with a thump.

Tessa gestured at the cash on the counter. Told me to take the money.

I shouted again, told her to leave.

Vic half-rose. Glowered. Tessa strolled down the aisle. Stopped directly in front of him. Smiled again, all her teeth showing like a cat hissing. Swung around and strolled out of the café.

Every nerve rubbed raw. I rested my forehead on the counter. Collected my breath. Straightened. I grabbed the cash, stuffed it into my apron pocket. Said something to Vic, some lie. At home I hid Tessa's money – about $100! – with Simon's in the top shelf of my dresser.

21 June 1943

Things bad at work. I dropped a blue plate loaded with scrambled eggs and bacon. Chan Lee snapped at me. The third plate this week. I have to pay attention.

I dreamed of Danceland's rainbow. Of Simon. The rip and rupture of my inner membranes. Fluids flowing down my thighs. Woke feeling suffocated and panicky, alone in her dark room. Wondering if I'd screamed.

During the daytime, I replay the entire scene over and over. From the moment we stepped onto the dance floor. Searching for one small incident to re-imagine that would change the course of events. All those unspoken no's. If I'd not boarded the train. Declined the pink dress. Refused the lemonade. Turned down the second dance, the gin. Avoided the lake and the canoe. Surely I said no. Shouted it, screamed. The word chokes me now, hanging in the air around me.

Another week. Chan Lee in the kitchen doorway, hands on hips. Warning me.

The situation worse at home. This morning Marina peered at my untouched toast. Said I shouldn't bark at Gerard like I did last night. I apologized. She asked if I wanted to go for a walk by the river. Even Gerard said I hadn't been myself since I went to Danceland.

I told him he couldn't fix things. Stormed out. Slammed the bedroom door. Then regretted my inability to hold my tongue. But my tongue won't be held for much longer. I sat on the bed, rocking, wishing for time to rewind itself. My monthlies officially late.

I slipped out of the house. No one noticed as I swung the front door closed. The streetcar heading downtown was empty. The driver looked up once into his rear-view mirror. Turned his attention back to the road. What did he think of a young woman travelling alone on a Saturday afternoon? I could barely see the far bank of the river. Squinted at the bank that I'd left behind. My entire life re-defined by one moment. Everything after Simon is new country. If I'd changed so greatly, has the landscape as well? I want my life back.

A block before the Twenty-first Street and First Avenue stop, the streetcar screeched to a halt. The driver told me that the street was blocked up ahead. Some big celebration. Could be a while. Did I want to wait or get off?

I disembarked. Headed north on Avenue A. People thronged around me, pushing and shoving. I tucked in my elbows and ignored the jostles and bumps. Edged deeper into the crowd. Finally arrived at the cordon that divided the street from a milling sea of men. All wearing familiar wedgies and dress uniforms.

I tugged at the sleeve of a middle-aged woman. Her upswept hair reminded me of Marina's. The woman swung around. Told me it was a military tattoo. The squadron on parade. Pipes and drums. Even a flyover. She held up a newspaper. Hadn't I read about it? Her son was going off, she said.

The people around me shifted. Panic welled through my bloodstream, urging me to run. Then a red-haired woman stepped in front of me. What would either of us say? I steeled myself. Wordlessly tapped her shoulder.

But it wasn't Tessa. She shifted a pace, clearing my view of the airmen. A whistle blew. The men snapped into lines. The lines tightened, the drums rolled, the pipes and whistles started a jaunty tune. They marched forward. I scanned each man's face as they passed. Row after row of strangers. Legs out, arms swinging, natty jackets, gleaming boots, perfectly creased trousers. My breath took off again, ragged and stuttering.

I saw him in the last row of marching men. Waking after nightmares, I'd imagined throwing stones at him. Imagined screaming, shouting obscenities, marking him as I'd been marked. Now he marched toward me, his high forehead topped with that inane wedgie. Going, going, gone. My knees buckled. I found myself sitting on the curb, crying.

The Tessa lookalike comforted me. Handed me a handkerchief. Asked me if one of the men was mine.

I shook my head. Gathered my breath, wiped my nose. Simon's back grew smaller and smaller. By the time he moved out of sight, I'd pulled myself together. Stood up. Held out the handkerchief. The woman patted my shoulder. Told me to keep it. Plenty of fish in the sea, she said.

Hearing one of Marina's favourite expressions stopped me cold. I smiled at the woman, jaws and cheeks feeling unhinged. Like some crazy puppet. Then I walked toward Twentieth Street in search of Tessa. I needed the name of her shady doctor.

Hours later. I hadn't found Tessa. Marina was asleep on the deck. Her feet up on a wooden crate that held her gardening tools. A small envelope fell out of the package she held. A seed packet. My throat closed in recognition. Something within me had started an inevitable turn toward the sun. I dropped the seed packet in Marina's lap. Sat down beside her.

It wasn't long. The words came easily.

Marina immediately asked if it was the flier, if he was gone. I nodded. But it wasn't like she thought. She guessed about Tessa's involvement too.

A blue jay flew into the yard, scolding. So I spoke up. Told her about Simon. That he forced me.

She wrapped her arms around me. It didn't help. I clenched my hands. Studied the clouds, the blue spruces dividing them. Willed myself to not break down. I begged her to not tell anyone. How calm I felt. As if simply telling Marina solved everything. I begged her to make it all right. I asked if there was – a doctor. Someone I could go see. I told her that Tessa said she knew someone.

Marina went silent. Asked if that meant what she thought it meant. At my half-nod, she gathered both my hands. Held them snugly as she told me that the idea was too dangerous to even consider. That we couldn't ask Doctor Macleod. I'd have to go to Toronto, or maybe Vancouver. A long, long train trip, she said. Especially for a girl who – She broke off. Asked me how Tessa could possibly know someone.

I looked at the seed packet in Marina's lap. I wanted to shelter on her lap again, shielded from whatever might come. Steeled myself. Finally told her Tessa was a prostitute.

Marina spluttered something in Ukrainian. Had to stop and draw a breath before she asked if Tessa had planned this. To take advantage so shamelessly. She shook me gently. Told me not to cry, that it wasn't my fault. She said we'd think of something. Asked if she should tell Ma. I didn't know how to say no.

She asked if the airman knew. At my headshake, she said that silence might be for the best. Asked how I felt.

My laughter sounded sour. I felt better, surprisingly. Not quite so alone. I couldn't imagine what I was going to do.

She stumbled over the next question – if I needed some salve or ointment. I couldn't look at her. Then she asked if I could love this child.

I shrugged and stood up. Said no. But maybe I could find her a real mother.

I CLOSE THE DIARY and silently climb the stairs to bed. It takes a long time to go to sleep.

When I wake at seven, I avoid looking at the diary where it lies on my bedside table. Instead, I stand in front of the bulletin board, staring at the photographs of Anky. That broad brow and calm eyes hide so much pain.

Yoga and adult companionship are what I need. After moving my body, feeding Jordan and putting him on the bus, I walk toward Hannah's driveway, Scout romping around me. Then a halt while I call Connie.

"Con, I was right. Anky was raped. In 1943, at Danceland. By an Air Force flier."

"So that means...?"

"Yes. Mother." I study my feet, then gaze up at the grey sky. Flecks of freezing rain fall like small crystals, catching on my face in speckles that melt and vanish. "I almost called you in the middle of the night after I read about it. And even though it happened decades ago, to another woman, I feel like it was me, like I was there." I can't tell her that I feel violated, that my body aches in sympathy. "I get it now, why Anky was so sad."

There's nothing I want to tell Hannah. I just need to sit beside her. Hannah picks up on my mood and asks no questions.

Back home after our visit, I carry my lunch into the parlour and settle in to read more of the diary. Scout watches me, playtime in his eyes, and I soothe him with petting. "Later, Scout. It's quiet time."

Twenty-Three

26 July 1943

Marina asked me if I wanted to go away to a home for unwed mothers. The 'visiting her aunt' story. I was shocked that Marina would even ask. But she called it just one more thing to rule out. Nine months with adoption as the outcome? No. The shame.

I'm not going to one of Tessa's terrifying doctors. The idea! Worse than a butcher! Gives me the shakes. What a relief that I hadn't found Tessa. I could've landed in worse straits. That doesn't bear thinking about. I can't run away. Where to? How many other women's lives has Tessa ruined? I hope she – well, I don't know what I wish for Tessa. I hope I never see her again. That will do.

Simon marched away. He didn't come looking for me. Did he think about me? About what he did to me? Did he feel any shame? If he'd known me. If I'd been a girl from his childhood, from his neighbourhood in Calgary. Not some woman he'd just met at Danceland. If he had to face me every day. What would he have done then? He'd behaved so oddly. So tightly strung. Couldn't stop talking. Couldn't keep still. And afterwards... his clock wound down to full stop.

8 August 1943

We hatched a plan. Not much of one. We don't have many choices. Part of me wants to read Simon's name in the newspaper as dead. Or missing in action. So coldblooded. Then I did see his name. In the list of those shot down or missing or wounded: "Aviator Simon Mitchell of Calgary, late of the RCAF's 406 Squadron, shot down over the English Channel on his first mission, and is missing in action."

I read it to Marina. Then re-read the paragraph. Just the two of us sat at the breakfast table – Gerard still in bed, a bad night.

Suddenly Marina lit up. She held up her left hand. Wiggled her fingers. Her idea was to hide the truth in plain sight. She'd go to a jeweler's shop and buy a ring. A plain wedding band. We'd tell everyone I got married right before he left for Europe and died. Then I'd go back to the farm and live with Ma.

One sentence that will change my entire life. As drastic as Simon's assault. Pretend to be married? And then live as a widow before I'd even been a wife? On top of being a mother? A single mother? My whole life, unravelling faster than I can catch and re-knit it.

When I wondered if I should tell Ma, Marina told me not to be a hypocrite. That I shouldn't be blind to what Ma is and isn't. She hasn't loved anything or anyone except her horses since Jordan.

Truth: I want Marina to be my mother. If I am to bear a child and raise it alone, please God, let it be under Marina's roof. I nearly said so. Marina read my face. She said it wouldn't be right. Told me she loves me as her own. But she has Gerard to care for. His health not up to having a baby in the house. Plus they couldn't afford to keep me and a child. Then she told me I'd need my own mother. Even if I don't know it yet.

So. The plan is I will to wear a lie of a wedding band. Go home. Have my baby alone. And Simon, floating somewhere in the English Channel. Another casualty of war. So sorry. I don't hate him enough to wish that on him.

17 August 1943

I just couldn't take Simon's name. I couldn't bear it. We had to look for a dead Canadian soldier with a plain name. A name that would blend into records and newspapers. Someone with no surviving family. A ghoulish search. Several weeks' worth of newspapers. Long lists of men dead or missing in action. I felt like a grave-robber. So many dead! So many names to choose from!

How would a bereaved widow feel? How am I to act? What is normal? When the war conspires with my bad luck? Heaps disaster at my door? When I am just pretending? All the world in this war. While it rages, I need to live a lie. To mourn Simon. How? Stay in my room? Emerge tragically pale-faced and silent? Melancholy? Weeping? Hysterical? Angry? Stop eating to chide myself for my loss?

Donnervetter! Lava burns my throat every day. Ignites at the slightest provocation. I do my best to swallow it. Sit hushed at meals or conversations with Marina and Gerard. I'm not done with this anger. With Simon. With pretending. Sadness is almost impossible, except when I consider the child. Then I weep. I have no room for God in my life anymore. How could I love the child?

Marina bought the ring. I put it on my left hand. Cruel mimicry of all those real brides left alone by war. I agreed to Marina's marriage scheme. But it hadn't occurred to me – I would need to act as if mourning the death of the man who attacked me. When I washed the dishes after supper, the ring on my hand flashed. Reminded me of my immense lie. Of my belly, growing though not yet obvious. Already I feel confined within a smaller space as this child grows. My organs lean too closely on one another. I have nightmares. How will I respond when I see his child's face? What if she looks like him? I am the only parent she'll have. If I am addressed as Mrs. Simon Mitchell... oh, donnervetter! I will fly into a rage of biblical proportions. Fierce enough to rival even Grandpap on his worst days. And if my child resembles Simon? How to endure that? All those overlooked questions. That moment of mad acceptance.

20 August 1943

We found a name. My husband was the late Bill Jones, flight sergeant, dead flier. An only child, born and raised in Toronto, parents also deceased. I am the widow Mrs. Charlotte Jones. My child to be named Jones as well. The lie is uttered, made into truth. It can't be undone.

24 August 1943

Marina took me to the farm in the Buick to tell Ma. She was out in the barn grooming her mare, Albert said when we arrived. When Ma walked in I thought I'd leave it to Marina to say. But the words just fell from my mouth. I'm going to have a baby.

Marina squeezed my hand hard. Took over: Bill Jones. A flier. Flew to England. Shot down and gone. She raised my hand. The ring's glint. The honourable thing, done first.

Ma finally said I should take the small house. That Albert was the farm's Weinzedel – the steward. He'd add a storm-porch and a deck, and a new outhouse out back. She said I'd do better'n most of those city girls, all those young widows facing life without their men. Plenty enough with this war.

Her matter-of-factness left me wondering. Maybe she didn't believe me. But I couldn't ask. No one inquired when this marriage took place. Why I hadn't invited them. This choice was no choice. A flight from fear that hamstrung my life.

1 September 1943

When Marina delivered me and my few possessions to the farm Ma greeted us with a surprising offer. She said I could breakfast with her and Albert. She said she remembered being a young mother on her own. Not something she'd wish on anyone, least of all her own kin. No one was going to put me out. This was my home.

I was touched. Then Marina cleared her throat and jingled the car keys. I implored her to come visit. My fingers clenched the suitcase. The same one that accompanied me to Danceland.

Of course, she said, but gas rationing. She gave me another yellow notebook. Said motherhood had its own voice. She'd brought her camera. Albert took a picture of us together. And that was that. A minute later, I walked around the corner of the caraganas and into the small house.

A fire in the stove. A wave of warm air.

Albert pointed out the metal pails on the washstand in the storm porch. No running water. I'd forgotten. A cord of poplar stacked on the east side of the house. Kindling and a hatchet in the basket beside the stove.

He was about to hang the door on a new privy out back. Was working on the deck and porch that Ma had promised. And a bassinet. Bad enough I got married in a hurry without family around, he said. And my husband gone so quick, and me in the family way. Told me to let him know what I needed. Of course I started to cry.

He studied the trunk. Polished its brass fittings with the cuff of his shirtsleeve. Told me ask Ma about the treadle sewing machine. That she'd already started a baby quilt. Said he was just glad to see me safe back home. He picked up his jacket. His back to me. I barely heard his mutter – when would I apply for widow's benefits from the Air Force?

I almost choked. Widow's benefits? I had no documents, no evidence. Just a fake ring and a babe growing under my ribcage. So I told him the next in a

growing string of lies. That the marriage license had accidentally gone with
Bill in the flurry of his last-minute packing to get overseas. That it must have
gone down in the Channel with him and the flaming Lancaster.

I wasn't the only girl in that boat, he said. At least we tied the knot before
he left. Wouldn't do to be holding the bag alone. Then he went off to feed the
chickens.

In the bedroom, two beds, one double, the other a shlofbonk with storage
space beneath the hinged seat. The same narrow couch-bed I'd slept in as
a child. I heaved the mattress back and lifted the seat. What did I expect?
Nothing. But I found something wonderful. A pair of wooden bays lay at the
far back behind a stack of towels and bed linen. Albert had carved and painted
them for me when I was small. I re-settled the mattress. Buffed the horses
on my skirt. Set the pair nose to nose on the pillow. Smoothed the yellow and
green quilts that covered the bulky duck-down comforters on each bed. A red
striped wool blanket neatly folded at the foot of the double bed. A familiar
chest of drawers. A tiny roll-top desk. Two spindle-back chairs. All the wood
surfaces sanded and oiled to a dull gleam. All hand-made by Grandpap before
Ma's wedding. So she once told me. Strange, how knowledge was so limited, so
filtered by others' memories.

ANKY'S WORDS ECHO my own frustration. How I must rely on her
memories, and the recollections of Reverend Waldman, Marina, even
Pauline, to reconstruct her life. And my mother's life. Just shimmering
hints of the rainbow filtering through the darkness.

Where are those horses? I remember playing with them as a child, but
haven't seen them since. Anky would've kept them. I sling a chair in front
of the bookshelves in the parlour, climb up, stand on tiptoes, running my
hands along the very back atop the deep bookcases. My hands bump into
two somethings behind a stack of paperbacks we missed, somethings
smooth and hard. Why hadn't I found these earlier? The horses touch
down lightly on Klara's s roll-top desk after I polish them on my clothes
as Anky had done. Before reading the diaries, it never occurred to me to
question the provenance of the furniture in my childhood home. Turns
out I'm surrounded by family heirlooms. Quilts, horses, furniture, amber
bracelet, this house. The past isn't dead, no matter how Mother insisted.

My pleasure abruptly subsides. A flood of loss seeps in, as cold and real as high tide in English Bay. So many losses. What do the Buddhists say? Life is suffering? Life is loss?

But not all is lost. These memoirs connect me to Anky, her spare words a bond to her past. And these horses are a link to Albert, my great-uncle, a man I've only met on paper but know as kind, generous, fiercely loyal. His careful hands wrought their manes and tails, their sharply defined muzzles and fine-boned legs. My boy will play with these old toys just as Anky did, as I did. Feeling a little less grey, I pick up Anky's journal and recline on the couch.

Shocking to find a coal oil lantern on the desk. I'm used to electricity and running water. All those years in Marina's house. The literal dark realities of farm life had escaped me. Just as I'd overlooked the realities of life as a war widow.

I hauled the desk and chairs into the kitchen. Sorted and stacked and re-folded clothes. My mind filled with images of my childhood. Playing on the wooden swing. Chasing old Toby the collie. Standing on one side of the fence while Ma fussed over her horses in the paddock.

Sunset. The walls turned orange in the lamplight. Put my clothes into the schlofbonk. Lined up the books. Straightened the papers. Closed the desk's roll-top on my paints and brushes. A rummage through the cupboards turned up tea, pot, knitted cozy, fresh biscuits, a loaf of bread, butter, honey.

Wood-smoke still smelled like home, somehow. In spite of ten years in Marina's lovely civilized city palace. I'd forgotten how much I loved this tiny house. I am going to miss town life. And Marina. What have I gotten myself into?

No bathtub, no phone, no electricity. Butter and milk down the well or immersed in the watering trough, or in the icebox. Using the icebox means trips to the icehouse to chip pieces of ice out from the sawdust. Cooking over wood flames means lighting a fire in the morning and keeping it going all day. Or eating bread and jam for lunch and supper. Reading by lantern-light. Filling those buckets at the well. Hauling and heating water for cooking, for washing, for laundry. For sponge baths in front of the stove. Dashing to the privy in the middle of the night. (I need a chamber pot!) So much effort just to survive. I once asked Marina if she ever missed living on the farm. How she'd laughed! Daily farm life is a stone that must be thrown again and again, she said. Chores will keep my hands and mind busy. No brooding. Except about this baby.

I want to tell my baby this: forgive me, you'll have no father, only me. Can I set aside my fears? My anger? Donnervetter! My own father vanished, maybe murdered. Was that why Ma turned into a cold, cold woman? Am I any different? If it's a boy I'm going to see Simon in him. So I'll imagine a different father to tell the baby about. The kind of man I would have chosen. If choice had been left in my hands. Maybe I'll make up stories about my own father. The invisible Jordan, the father I never met.

2 September 1943

I rose at first light. Shivered as I lit a fire. I'd forgotten to stoke the woodstove last night. In the firebox, a photograph caught alight. Simon's face from the news clipping before me once more. Donnervetter! The last time! Then the fire kindled, crackling and popping. The picture withered. Vanished into the flames.

Outside to the privy. Barefoot. Need warmer clothing. Cool wooden seat. The crying of Canada geese. Their mournful voices infected me with a nameless ache. By the time the birds return, I'll be holding a baby. Back into the kitchen. Mint tea. Socks, sweater, trousers, boots, jacket. Diary and a pencil in my pocket.

The latest farm dog waited outside the door. Tall and leggy, black-and-tan. A raccoon-like mask and a wide grin. He rose, stretched, bowed. Headed off down the driveway. I laughed, curtsied, followed. The dog glanced back. Slid under the wire. Took off at a jog through the field. I set the empty teacup on top of the fencepost. Dog waited at a slough lined with cattails. Looked at me expectantly when I caught up.

I scratched his ears, rubbed his spine. What did he want me to see?

Blackened trees clustered at the slough's east end, dying or dead but still standing. Evidence of a past brushfire. The north side of the slough still vividly green. A few birds, including several geese, on the water. The birds waited. The dog whined, wriggling slightly under my hand. Then the geese flew off. Their wings thundered. Smaller birds in their wake. I pulled out my notebook and pencil. Sketched until the dog whined again.

Breakfast. Walked to Ma's house. The dog lay down on the porch. His front paws touched the lower step.

Inside, the smell of bacon and fresh bread. Suddenly I was famished. Ma at the table with her elbows planted, contemplating the teapot. Albert immersed in a book. Ma poured a cup of nettle tea for me without a word. Albert looked up. Smiled. I told him I'd met a dog outside my door. Bandit, he said. A softy. Did I want him? The dog never took to guard duty for the cattle. Sang back to the coyotes instead of running them to ground, but he was good company. Quietly took a waiting bowl to the dog.

When he returned he offered to bring me some gizzards for Bandit when he butchered next. He confessed that he made pretty good dog cookies from them, I stifled my laughter.

Ma said Albert was the softy. He'd wanted a dog to sleep in his room when he was seven, Grandpap wouldn't hear of it. My uncle? Really?

It occurred to me that Chan Lee might want to buy some chickens. Or a side of beef. Albert agreed to stop in with a couple of birds the next time he went to town. Promised to bring a few to me, too, for canning. He looked pointedly at Ma. Was she going to get around to slicing that bread soon or should he?

Ma frowned. Told him to keep his hands off her good knives. Her grace as she sliced bread and served up bacon. I'd never noticed how fluidly she moved. A bowl of butter on the table. A plate heaped high with bacon. A basket of sliced bread. Heads bowed briefly. I ate a stack of crisp bacon slices. Several thick pieces of crusty bread, butter melting into each. So good! Of course, homemade. Ma reminded me that I'm eating for two. Her flickering smile. She recalled being teased when she was carrying me. My uncles told her she ate like a threshing crew.

Albert grinned. Said Ma had taken after them with a horsewhip. He raised his eyebrows at me. Ma always was feisty, he said. It went with wearing hand-me-down trousers. Girls back then wore dresses. Seemed to keep them in check.

I laughed. Wished I had a brother. When I asked if they had a bird book, Ma said no, but she had a few good horse husbandry and training books. If I was interested.

Albert offered to bring more paper and paints from town. To give me something to occupy myself when I wasn't busy making baby clothes. He offered to help name the birds, too. None of that fancy Latin stuff. What locals call them.

WHEN I FLIP AHEAD in the diary, pencil drawings of birds fill page after page. They progress from clumsy to sure-handed, some rough and obviously unfinished, some quick sketches, others rendered in full with shading and careful detail. After examining a dozen pages of sketches, I open the bulging envelope stuffed with watercolours glued to the back cover of the diary, their raw edges suggesting that each page had been carefully cut free from the book before being painted. Pages are smudged in colours like a wet sky after an afternoon thunderstorm, growing more assured until the birds almost lift off the pages, sheet after sheet of feathered flying. Almost thirty paintings, each meticulously labeled, dated, and signed "C. Jones," Anky's ambiguous new name. Names are written beneath each in Anky's authoritative script: cinnamon teal, chickadee, killdeer, coot, bufflehead, avocet, yellowlegs, blue heron. Even the great horned owl I know only as a giant shadow floating past me in the early dusk makes an appearance.

I know these birds from my own walks along the edges of the slough. Since returning to the farm, I can no longer say, "Just ducks," when a flight of water birds flushes. I've learned to recognize the broad snout of a northern shoveller, the blue bill of a ruddy duck, the elaborate Mardi Gras mask of a horned grebe, the stubby body of a snow goose, the call of a Canada goose, the distinctive voices of sand hill cranes and whistling swans. And like the birds, like Anky, like the stubbornly enduring lady's slippers, I came back.

Is the essence of belonging, of home, to be found in one familiar spot, returning in peace or mute acceptance, or even in desperate love? Maybe it means finding myself drawn back without any clear sense of why beyond duty, then looking around one day and recognizing the dust motes as part of my DNA, part of the skin I shed and re-grow, part of the bones that propel me through the day, drawn from the soil and conjured into motion by the air and sunlight. It's pure magic that surprises me, how I am attached to this place. How I returned like the birds, another gardener called back to the soil. On my desk I fumble through my forgotten sketches of vegetable beds and orchards. Maybe there is something here for me.

I call Connie and leave a message about Anky's artwork. Then, eager to talk, but really wanting to tell Earl, I call Hannah instead and leave a message reporting my find. She calls back a couple of hours later.

"If you think the paintings are good enough, take a few to the curator at the Mendel," she suggests. "Or one of the smaller galleries. Ask about a showing. The fact that they were stored out of the light all these years should have kept their colours strong."

"She'd have liked that, her art hanging in a gallery. Did you ever see Anky paint?"

"Never saw any evidence, no easel, or canvases or paints. Maybe she quit when she started to raise you two. Lots of work, that. Y'know, I could write up a bit of a blurb in Hutterisch and English about each bird for you, as part of the show if the gallery bites. Might help differentiate, to set Charlotte up as a local artist with a slant, I mean."

"You speak Hutterisch?"

"Sure. Don't you?"

"Anky never taught me. And Mother didn't know the language."

"Ah, that's too bad, my girl."

"Will you teach me?"

"Whyever not?"

I feel the wings of my community settle in around me as I burrow a nest into the couch and resume reading.

13 September 1943

I sat on the porch with Albert. Bandit at my feet. It's been a long week. The summer air cool. Fall coming. I'd risen early the past four days to help Ma cook for the threshing crew. Pacifist Hutterite men, older, mostly, and a few boys too young to enlist. But they all ate as if they were in their prime.

A LIST OF RECIPE titles follows: Katufel Totschelen. Rascha Zwieboch. Brötchen. Albert's Samstich Wurscht. Bobak. Russischer Vorsch. Schwarz-Weiss Gebäck. Gutheit. Gurken. Kartffelsalat. Wurstsalat. Krautsalat. Saufgurken. Zucker Pie. Mogn Krapfen. Zauner Krapfen. Rote Grütze. Lebkuchen. Apfel Henelich. Apfelstrudel. Apfel Kuchen.

I stop to think. Didn't Con mention a cousin who was a Hutterite food writer? I ransack the shelves for her book, then my stomach starts to growl as I look back and forth from Anky's diary to the cookbook, finding correlating recipes in English with Anky's Hutterisch names. Anky and Klara made potato pancakes with cream sauce, crisp buns. They sliced Albert's garlic sausage, then baked biscuits with chunks of sausage, and cooked vegetable-heavy Russian-style borscht, garden salads with sour cream and honey, pickles, spice cookies, fruit soup, poppyseed pockets, apple pie, and turnovers.

When I reach Anky's final entry, apple kuchen, my eyes tear up. I am crying in earnest by the time I reach the kitchen and start peeling apples. By the time Jordan arrives home from school, my best re-creation of Anky's caramel apple kuchen with streusel sits on the counter.

"Oh yum!" he shouts. "What's that? Can we eat it now?" We make short work of enormous slices, then he listens intently as I tell him about learning to cook with my grandmother. "Teach me, Mama," he says when I stop. "Then we can remember Anky every day."

When I tuck him into bed that night, something Jordan does reminds me of my own long-gone nightly ritual with Anky. He reaches up with slender fingers to tickle my chin, strokes the bridge of my nose, tugs one ear. "You're a good Mama," he says sleepily. "Can we have some of that yummy apple thing for breakfast?" My heart bursts as I return to the parlour to resume reading about Anky's harvest.

18 September 1943

All week I cooked and washed dishes. Tomorrow the threshing crew heads to the next farm. Albert will go with them.

Earlier this morning, Ma and I worked side by side in Ma's kitchen. Half a dozen empty pie tins on the table. Bandit at my feet. Waiting for apple peelings.

Ma asked if she'd ever told me about her boss mare, Lily. The rolling pin in her hands kept time. Round after round of pastry. When Lily had come in season, Ma thought she'd be the one to teach her new young stud, Duke, a thing or two. Duke was shy.

I blushed. Ma noticed. Teased me that the baby under my apron proved my late husband wasn't as shy as Duke. The heat spread down my neck. Ma laughed so hard she stumbled slightly. Bumped into me. Raised apron to eyes to catch tears of laughter. She'd raised a prude! Verdammt!

I told her I wasn't used to discussing it.

Ma laughed again. I knew she was thinking about the upbringing I'd had. All those years of her breeding horses. Surely I saw the great plan of Nature, she said. Birth, death, then birth again. She brushed flour off my cheek. Trimmed a circle of pastry. Laid it in the next pie plate. Admitted she never saw it at my age either, when she lost her virginity. And her husband.

I slid the bowl of apple slices along the table. It stopped right in front of her. She divided the slices among the pastry rounds. I barely heard when she said that she'd been too hard on me. That Marina doubtless did better. I melted.

After supper a dozen men from neighbouring farms strolled across the yard. Waved at Albert and me on the steps. Albert half-raised a hand in greeting. Told me he'd taken chickens to Chan Lee. Said he wanted a side of beef too, next time he butchered. He stood up, seemed smaller. Ruffled my hair, said it was time to get along. The crew was leaving in the morning, and he wanted to say his thanks. A good crop, he said. That new-fangled machine, that fancy combine. Worked harder than all the horses and threshing machines put together. He said that not even Ma had workhorses anymore. Just her fat lazy saddle mare. That those machines were worth thinking on. He wandered toward the bunkhouse.

I stretched aching back and arms. Tomorrow I could sleep late. Maybe resume sewing baby clothes.

One of the men veered from his path. Stopped at the foot of the stairs. A salute – fingers to straw hat, perched at a cocky angle. A thicket of ash-blond hair. Fair skin. Introduced himself as Paul Wipf. I nodded. I'd recognized him earlier. His crooked shoulder, heavy limp, badly set nose. A boyhood fall from the rafters of the Goodfare skating rink.

He said I looked different. That he thought I'd never come back from the city. He peered at my hands. Asked if I was married. Who the lucky guy was, if he was here. I shook my head.

Paul fidgeted with his hat. Took it off. Round and round in his hands. Said it must be the war, then. Whatever else he meant to say died in the evening light. He scuffed his boots in the dust. Twisted his hat brim. Patted Bandit. Finally nodded and limped away. His face flaming. He was a Hutterite too, I recalled. Exempted from military service. Not for being a conscientious objector, but because of his limp. I retreated to the house. But the stifling air brought me back outside. The last thing I wanted was male attention.

22 October 1943

Out walking, a trio of white-tail deer in the field. Bandit beside me, head up, watching. As if he wanted to greet them. I dared not tell Albert, or we'd eat venison all winter. Who could kill such lovely creatures? A while later,

I spotted Ma in the old Shevchenko yard. Something told me to hold Bandit's collar. Hushed him with one of Albert's grisly dog cookies. Ma squatted beside the pump handle. Gently set down what she had concealed in her skirt. A bouquet tied with a ribbon – the last of the season's petunias. Then she walked back to the house. I followed with Bandit. Kept my distance.

Were the flowers a remembrance for Marina's menfolk, long gone to the internment camp? Totally befuddled. Then a sharp memory: a neighbour at Grandpap's funeral saying he must have put Jordan down a well. My grandfather, drowning my father! Then Albert in the kitchen while I eavesdropped from the parlour, saying he saw Grandpap. And afterwards, Marina's admissions as the two of us rode home in the car.

I can't ask Ma. Not even with this new gentleness between us.

23 October 1943

A solitary goose above me in the morning chill. I heard it calling all day. Has its mate left?

14 November 1943

Each morning, I put out grain for the goose beside the slough. This afternoon the explosion of a gun. Two hours later, Albert appeared at my door. A dressed goose over his shoulder. My shock must have shown when he held out the carcass.

He muttered that he thought that was why I was feeding it. Struggled to hide the bird behind his back.

I didn't tell him I fed it because it was so like me.

27 November 1943

The land froze over. Birds flew away in small flocks, two dozen, one dozen, a handful of coots. I tossed a stone onto the slough's ice. It rattled and rang. Beyond it, a late-departing goose watched, curious.

I heard in my head the morning prayer of my childhood: May the peace of the Lord, the love of God, and the community of His Holy Spirit be with us all in this morning hour.

I turned toward my house, Bandit beside me. The baby inside me moved.

A rolling turn that left me gasping. My body no longer my own, occupied by a stranger.

31 December 1943

When Marina visited she brought the photo of the two of us that Albert had taken. And many books.

After she left, Albert brought me a sealed envelope. Addressed to me at Chan Lee's café. Inside, another photograph. Tessa and me, the rainbow of Danceland visible behind us. A note in Tessa's hand: "Lottie – a keepsake of Danceland for you. Slainte."

Donnervetter! Outrage flared in my belly. I threw note and photo on the table. Then my babe moved in response. Surely she suffices as a keepsake! I burned the note. Resolved to burn the detestable photo as well. But I kept it. As a warning.

My heart in an uproar, hatred welling up again and pounding in my chest. I thought of Ma at the breakfast table. How calm she seemed. I crave that settled sense. Of belonging, of being where I fit best. Here? I can't tell.

So I turned to the package from Marina. Novels, blankets, clothes for me and the baby. Another precious little Beatrix Potter book, Appley Dapply's Nursery Rhymes.

I looked again at Tessa's picture. Donnervetter! I hate that woman! Picked it up. Ripped it in half, right through the rainbow. Horrified to realize I'd torn the picture of Marina and me as well. I sniffled. Wrapped my arms around my midriff. Stuffed away all the pieces of both pictures to deal with later.

19 January 1944

Seeing Marina brought back thoughts of the Saskatchewan River flowing through Saskatoon. The bridge across it. That water must have frozen solid. Steam rising from its open cracks. I am the steam. A ghost waiting to take substance with the spring. This child will bring me back to earth.

What I still like about the prairie winter: Light in late afternoon. The way snow burns my tongue. Immense sky that leaves no room for lying or equivocating. Hoarfrost like jewelry on tree branches. Smell of woodsmoke. Stars, the northern lights. The coyotes' songs echoing like glass about to crack. The dog answering. The way my feet find the path. As if I never strayed. Waiting.

Twenty-four

AS EXECUTRIX, Con went through Anky's will the week after she died. No surprises, she said, we own the farm jointly. When she calls one early November evening, she attempts to manoeuvre me into moving to town.

"Why not move?" She sounds like an exasperated teacher. "It's easier. Your kid can go to a decent school until next spring if you still plan to go back to the coast. You won't be isolated. You can get a good job, or you could start a horticulture consulting company or a landscaping business. That would give you a good living."

"Course we're going back to the coast. What made you think we wouldn't?"

"Nothing, nothing," she says quickly. "I just don't want to have to worry about you two alone out there. I've done my share of that." She draws a deep breath. "Okay, here's my idea. I've figured out what we'll do. You stay on. Take full and outright ownership of the farm."

"What?"

"It makes sense, Luka. You told me how you felt when you found those paintings of Anky's. You belong there. On the farm. I have my house already. We can split the cash so you'll have a cushion and start-up funds for this garden you've been talking about, you do it here, not in BC. And you won't have to get a job in the interim."

"I wasn't planning on staying past this spring."

"I know. Just think, Luka. It's only reasonable, given what you want to do. You'll never be able to afford building or buying a greenhouse and garden in the Lower Mainland, never mind in Vancouver. And like I said, I don't want to have to worry about you. Yes?"

"I have to think about it."

"Good. It's settled then."

"Con, I said I have to think about it." I'm tempted to throw in an Anky-style "Donnervetter!" but it wouldn't help.

"Okay, okay. I'll handle the banking and transfer of funds after I see the lawyer. Now – Anky had some savings and life insurance, and there's a death benefit as well. You and I are joint beneficiaries." I go faint, wondering how Anky managed to save for her grand-daughters' future on her limited income. The moment passes and I hear Con's voice again.

"Are you all right money-wise for now? Do you need cash? What do you think you'll do?"

"I don't know, Con." I must sound like a fool.

"You said you wanted a market garden. Why don't you make it so?"

After the call ends, the farm feels empty all over again. Jordan and Scout are close by, but their presence only exacerbates Anky's absence.

The situation slowly sinks in. We can stay. Here on the farm, where Anky raised us, where Mother still wanders. How would I manage? I know nothing about the finer details of life in an old house in the country during the wintertime – how to care for a septic tank, keep the driveway plowed, tend a well so the pipes don't freeze, plus all the things I don't even know I'll need to know. Then I remember Hannah and Mick, a stone's throw away. They helped Anky, they'd help me. And Suzanne and Earl. I have friends.

I go online, buoyed by the thought of unexpected largesse. I didn't expect any money, never thought Anky would have paid insurance premiums all those years. What to do? Stay? Go? I make lists, then impulsively order seeds and look at greenhouse schematics. Then I look at the pie-in-the-sky notes I made when I first arrived, details for raised beds and orchards and planters, new greenhouses, a market garden. I email the farmer's market and request a stall for the spring. Just in case. I can always cancel. Then I return to my grandmother's brief life-notes. By morning my impulsive acts will be forgotten in a blur of fatigue and heartache.

2 March 1944

The old doctor in Saskatoon said I was healthy as a horse. His whiskers twitched every time he said anything that might be considered salacious. Poor timid man. Attendant to the needs of the body and so uncomfortable with it! I bet Ma never flinched when she helped her mares deliver their foals. She insists she'll make an admirable midwife. I believe her. Ma's spent months working on a baby quilt. Won't show it to me. Bad luck, she said. Too late for that, said I. She troops over to check on me several times a day. They've tied a guide-rope from my house to theirs. Albert rigged a bell to ring if I can't get there alone.

I am sick of it all. Hate it all. Can't find a comfortable position for reading. Fitzgerald and Hemingway will have to wait. Childbirth doesn't frighten me. Having a child – this child – does. I have to find a home for it. Someone who can love it. Maybe Marina knows someone. Maybe Marina?

ANKY'S FACE RISES before me, but Anky as a young woman approaching the throes of childbirth. Would I want anyone to read my journal entries about Jordan's birth? I haven't looked at those pages since I scribbled them, but I'm sure they're tempestuous, full of fear and loneliness as I faced labour and parenthood with only Cherie to hold my hand. That isolation and uncertainty. I don't know if it will ever fade. Even the quilts we found in the schlofbonk have faded with time. And the ink on these pages, fading in spots. But her life! Such vivid images, the rainbow of Anky's life unfolding in brief slashing words.

I open the diary and read her single phrase on the page: "The child is a girl but I cannot love her."

It isn't hard to imagine Anky's voice and visualize her, to fill in the unspoken and unwritten world between my grandmother's words.

12 March 1944

I woke before dawn. In labour. Boots and coat, fur hat and gloves. Bandit snuffling.

The cold air sucked my lungs empty. A low-slung half-moon. So many stars. Half a dozen times I stopped. Bent double. Cursed, glad of Albert's rope. Bandit whined. So this was it. Waiting at an end.

Within minutes, at Ma's house.

Ma told me to breathe. Make noise if I needed to, no one to hear. Walk, she said. She sent Albert to put on the kettle.

I lost track of time. Shuffled up and down the length of her bedroom. Felled by a contraction, up again. Finally couldn't get back on my feet. Ma immediately beside me with a chair.

I wanted to shout. Couldn't. Told her I don't want this baby.

She said there's only one way out.

I hope it's born dead! I shouted the words. Ma didn't recoil in disgust or horror. I'd only thought them.

When Ma finally said push, I did. Leaned on the chair, Ma on her knees beside me. Pushed until I couldn't anymore. Ma caught the baby. She proved a good midwife. Clean sheets. A sponge bath.

She leaned over me, asking what I'd said. I repeated that I wanted to hear the geese arrive. She told me to hush now. Held out the baby. Told me to take her, that she was perfect. I said over and over that I didn't want her. Over and over she tried to put her in my arms. I never asked to have this baby.

I turned away. The door closed. Every part of me ached. I was never meant to be a mother. Closed my eyes. Tried to block out the world. Wanted numbness to settle in.

Ma came back. Pestered me again. She held out the bundle. I told her to give her to Marina. She's always wanted babies. Ma sighed. Said she couldn't, that Marina couldn't either. Finally she said she'd get Albert to fetch some milk. She still had a bottle from when one of her mares died in labour. But just one bottle, she said. The baby needed me, she said. I needed the baby. That I'd be in pain in a day or two if I wouldn't suckle my baby.

Not my baby. Never my baby.

When she came back, Ma opened the curtains. It was a new day. She smiled at me, told me I was a mother now. That there was nothing else I could do.

Every door slammed shut in front of me. This helpless creature staking its claim. Ma waited. I had no choices left. I held out my arms. Ma tucked the baby in position. Helped me open my nightgown.

I don't love this creature. Maybe I never will. It doesn't look like me at all. I can't see Simon in that tiny face either. A relief. But what if the baby proves more his than mine?

I named her Lark Kestrel. I pray she'll fly fierce and free.

22 May 1944

Marina came to visit. We met in Ma's kitchen for tea.

She set down a tote bag before kissing me and taking the baby. Winter driving, she said. Sighed and rolled her eyes in apology for the delay. She peered closely at me. Offered to tend Lark while I napped. Ma and Albert both at my elbow. Too close for me to speak frankly. I made do with lifting my eyebrows. But needed to speak. Leaned closer to my godmother. Asked her to keep the baby.

Of course she said no. Then rummaged in the bag. Held out some baby clothes and the post. She left too soon. I was thunderstruck to unwrap a full-colour Audubon book, a gift from my uncle Pieter.

7 September 1944

I'm never alone. It used to be so simple – put on boots and jacket, Bandit would escort me out the door. Now, I spend twenty minutes bundling up the baby. I carry her in a sling that Ma sewed. I can see how this is going to play out. In a month, a sled from Albert. Come spring, she'll walk. Then run. Motherhood has taken over. I tend Lark, cook, wash her and her clothes, feed her. I've never been needed so utterly.

Lark looks up at me while at my breast. I want to love her back. I do, I mean to. Then I see Simon's face. And crash-land, back to insufficient sleep, endless work, Lark's needs. Do all babies need so much? Overwhelming. I haven't read anything since before Lark was born. No painting. I haven't even opened that Audubon book. If I wasn't so exhausted, I'd feel empty.

Ma said that I should have a Lukelah. A baby nurse. Maybe at Marina's house. Not possible here. Ma and Albert do what they can to help. And Bandit sleeps beside Lark's bassinet. In the middle of washing clothes or cooking, I catch myself straining. To hear her breathing.

One afternoon last week, I walked into the bedroom. Bent close to watch her chest move. What if? If I. If I just. It would take such a small effort. And then I hated the fact that I'd even thought such a thing. In my guilt, I stroked her face. Woke her. Albert came in soon after with a load of firewood. I shouted at him like a fishwife.

HALF A DOZEN ENVELOPES, neatly slit open with folded papers within, fall from the diary when I turn the page. The first envelope, covered with swirling handwriting, has a Saskatoon return address in the upper corner. The rest, typed, bear wings that flank a stylized cross with "ROYAL CANADIAN AIR FORCE" embossed at the top of the envelope above an

Ottawa address. After I sort them chronologically, I set them aside and turn to the diary for an explanation.

22 December 1944

Albert brought me some rare post from town. I never get letters. And who would I write to? Marina? Tessa? Telling her to come take the baby and give me back my life? He handed me two letters. Stood in front of the stove, snow melting from his boots and overcoat. Looked at me. Exactly the same look Bandit uses when he expects the scrapings from my plate. I told him to at least take his wet boots off. Then he spotted Lark and swept her up in a giant hug. All my annoyance vanished. He loves her so unabashedly. The way I want to.

Marina's letter first. Love and holiday cheer. The promise of a visit come spring. As I opened the second envelope a folded piece of paper fluttered out. A cheque. The amount made me sit down. The letter itself, in formal military language. Addressed to Mrs. William Jones. Widow of the late William Jones of the RCAF. The first time I'd seen that name in print. Me. That's me.

RCAF, Ottawa, Ontario
December 5, 1944
Mrs. William Jones
General Delivery,
Goodfare, Saskatchewan

Dear Mrs. Jones,
Distribution can now be made of the monies held here at credit to the Service Estate of your late husband. The total available to this Branch for distribution is $273.25, being made up as shown in the following statement:

Cash in effects $22.75
Balance of Deferred Pay. $160.00
War Service Gratuity. $75.00
First installation, monthly widow's/dependents' pension. . . . $15.50
Total. $273.25

Your claim for widow's and dependent offspring's pension benefits has been duly processed. You are entitled to this money as the sole

Beneficiary as evidenced by your submission of relevant documents. Further pension cheques will be issued monthly, and shall continue for your lifetime even in the event of a remarriage.

Enclosed in this missive please find a cheque from Treasury in the above amount. Please complete and return to this Branch the enclosed receipt after this letter and cheque have reached you. Receipts will not be required for subsequent monthly cheques.

Yours faithfully,
F. R. Tourney, Colonel, Director of Estates

A MILITARY SPOUSAL pension! This must be the source of the death benefit Con mentioned. It went right past me at the time. She had all of Anky's papers, and must have notified the Air Force when she died.

Who set them onto me? That made my heart pound even harder. Then Bandit whined and Albert coughed and shuffled.

I shouted at him. Widow's benefits? What did he know about this? Yelled at him to take off those damnable boots.

He was smiling. Smiling! Admitted that he had a hand in it. That if he'd left matters to me, Lark and I would be starving under that new bridge in Saskatoon. Set Lark down with a slight thud. Patted her. Pulled off his boots with the bootjack. Told me to climb down off my high horse. His voice calm. Time someone took charge of what was going on around here, and he was the man to do it.

I saw red. What do he mean, he was the man to do it? My fishwife voice again. Did it never occur to him that I had my own good reasons for not applying for that pension?

He waved me off. Picked up Lark to calm her. Said none of that concerned him. That in the absence of a husband, a government pension seemed the best bet to keep us fed. He told me he went into town to the War Office last month. Filed my claim. Took a bit of finagling, as they weren't used to uncles doing such things for nieces. But he admitted he had a bit of help. You need to eat, he said, and let's not hear any more about it. There's nothing wrong with accepting a little help. He put Lark in my arms. Blew his nose loudly and left.

A little help! Well. I needed a cup of tea. What had Albert done? What skulduggery did he resort to? What lies did he tell? How was this possible? What documents could he produce to make my case? None existed. And what did he mean by 'having a little help'? Whose help? Did Ma know? Did he bamboozle Marina?

But the cheque. Like Ma said, what's done is done. Albert's finagling aside, this income means I'm a free woman. I could rent a small house in Saskatoon. Maybe it will stretch far enough to hire a Lukelah. But no more morning walks beside the slough with Bandit? Not seeing the birds? Their lift-off into the air? No silence filling the landscape? That hum that keeps time for me all day, gone?

No. I'm staying. My uncle knows me too well. But the consequences! Someone – no, not just someone: the government! – knows of my existence, and the name I took.

What am I to do with the money?

30 March 1945

A bad dream. Hands grasping. Rainbow shattering. The whistle and crash of a plane. No sleep. Am I a thief?

12 May 1945

All these Air Force letters. They remind me of that poor man and his death overseas. First a letter telling me that Bill's boots and overcoat had been donated to one of his squadron members. How morbid to walk in a dead man's boots and live in the shadow of his overcoat! And me in his shadow as well. Using the short form of his name. And his surname. As if I had the right! In the next letter, the Air Force reported no evidence of where his plane went down. Just the fact that it was a Stirling Mark 3 bomber. Next letter, he'd been found. With his crew and the wreckage. And another – all the bodies now buried in a military cemetery in Hamburg, Germany. Cemetery to be beautified with trees and flowers after the war ends. Offered sympathy again. Dear God, let that be the end of the letters. My guilt is deep enough.

19 May 1945

The money preys on me. I lay sleepless last night, feeling like a fraud. What was that Ukrainian word Marina used about Tessa? I need those cheques. That is no fraud. It makes me laugh, hearing myself. All charlatans doubtless say the same thing. Justifying their actions. But I keep cashing them. Stash the money in the breadbox. What am I going to do with it to justify its acquisition?

29 June 1945

Paul Wipf appeared on my porch after breakfast. Hair slicked back, overalls tidy, even his hands mostly clean. Two kittens tucked inside his overalls, orange ears peeking out, white paws nestled under their chins. Lark held out her hands, shrieking. Poor Paul blushed, red as tomatoes. He asked if I wanted them, that they were weaned.

I laughed, oh I laughed. Haven't laughed so hard in years. So I invited him in.

His face went bright. He stepped right inside and sat down quickly. Maybe he thought I'd change my mind and send him packing. I knew I'd done the right thing when Lark perched on his knee, a kitten under each elbow. Not a smiley girl. Solemn most days. Long and leggy as one of Ma's colts. But she sat on his knee. Cozied up to Paul as if she'd known him all her life. The chamomile tea went fast. More, and some date squares. Paul polished them off too, fed the crumbs to Bandit.

He finally said that Lark didn't look like me. He stroked her hair. Impossible to keep her tidy. Every day she crawls about with Bandit. She always looks a little grubby around the edges. At least she doesn't complain when I mop her up.

I hated saying she looked like her father. The words brought back Simon. His nonstop chatter as we spun on the dance floor at Danceland. His grunts as he lay on top of me. My lies about Lark's parentage.

Paul asked if he was coming back.

When I said he was dead he didn't sound sorry. Grinned at Lark as he tickled her under the chin. After he left, Lark and Bandit sat on the floor staring at the door. If they could talk, I know what they'd say. I'm not interested. The idea makes me nauseous.

22 July 1945

I raised my voice to Lark yesterday. She retreated like those kittens. As always, Albert stepped in. Picked her up, stared at me with accusations in his eyes. He was in my house almost every day last week. Like most weeks. Hauling wood for the stove. Polishing something or other. Underfoot like the damn dog.

18 August 1945

Paul dropped by again. I was surprised by how pleased I felt to see him. Albert was sharpening his axe beside the stove. Just gathered his whetstone and axe and left.

Paul took Lark out of her high chair. Sat down at the kitchen table with her on his knee. Asked if I'd like to go to the victory celebration in Saskatoon. Pulled a scrap of newsprint from his overalls. He handed me the clipping. Said he'd pick up Lark and me in the truck.

21 September 1945

This morning the sky a pure blue. Bird weather. Snow geese flying south. The mist settled half an hour later. Down the path toward the slough with Lark. Bandit came trotting by with a dead duckling in his mouth. It reeked, covered in muck and grime. Who knew how long it had lain in the mud? I took the duckling. Gave Bandit a cookie instead. Told him that the wee animal didn't deserve chewing up. It had to go back to God.

I flung it into the slough. Far as I could. With a prayer. Felt like someone out of the legends. The Maid of the Mist flinging King Arthur's sword into mystery and myth. I realized that I meant what I'd said – the duckling came from God. So I still believe in a God. My denials have been habit, coupled with hurt. I am again Geistlich – my faith has returned. But donnervetter! How could God allow such a thing as happened to me?

22 October 1945

Paul finally asked the question. Showed up while I mended Lark's sweater and she played with the kittens. Then we sat on the front porch swing. A world between us. Lark at our feet.

He courted me all fall. Brought squashes and onions. A handful of wild sage and yarrow blooms from the meadow. Never met my eyes as he handed over his offerings. He and his brother Pete live in a farmhouse a few miles north on the Goodfare road. Pete inherited the farm. It worries me, thinking of the land I'll inherit when Ma and Albert die. Will Lark want it after me?

The idea of his touch made my stomach tighten and heave with outright fear. The thought of him inside me. Well, I could never bring myself to let him. Could I? I didn't have the courage to tell him why. He'd shun me for certain. So I put him off. Said I had to think about it.

He kicked the ground at his feet. Said he was no flier. No war hero. Just a farmer.

This lie never ends. He's a good man. I can never be a real wife to him. Lark loves him. Is that enough?

26 October 1945

A market garden. I'll start a market garden with that filthy money. Sell my vegetables to the war widows. The ghost of that flier can sleep, and I'll feel peace.

29 October 1945

A mild day as I dug a new garden bed with Ma. Lark in the dust beside the carrot patch. Shaking her wooden horses into gallops through the air.

Paul showed up. Told Lark they do better if you give them carrots. Tugged one of the last carrots from the soil. Bandit sat up. Looked expectant. Paul wiped the carrot on his trousers and handed it to Lark. Pulled another and tossed it to Bandit. Nodded to Ma.

He told me he'd packed lemonade and coffee and sausages and such. A picnic at the slough? It was plenty damp this year, a fire should be safe enough. He had blankets to keep the small one warm, he said. She could help him cut willow sticks to roast the sausages. He smiled, picked her up. Asked if I was coming. Called me Lottie.

My fishwife voice as I told him not to call me that.

He drew back. Said that Charlotte was a mouthful. That I seemed the Lottie type. Maybe he'd call me Char. He swung Lark up onto his shoulders. Walked ahead to his truck. Hauled out a metal picnic box. He didn't look back. At his whistle, Bandit obediently fell in at his heel.

Ma's eyes on me. I snapped at her, asked why everyone was in such a hurry to marry me off.

She took that soothing-the-mare tone. Thought I'd appreciate the company. Raising babies can exhaust a woman, and she and Albert weren't going to live forever.

I left her the hoe to finish.

Bad dreams still bother me. I've told no one. What to say? Bad dreams are no reason to stay single. And then hearing Tessa's nickname for me! Rattled my bones. I still see her so clearly! Could paint every line and curve of her face.

Should I accept Paul's offer? Lark and Bandit trust him. Why is a decent man unmarried? So many men died in the war. Is he one of those 'bachelor uncles'? Sad-eyed single men who subsist on beans and toast. Waiting on invitations from married sisters for Christmas and Thanksgiving feasts. Marking their social doings around coffee row at the café every morning. But I have my own questionable habits. A cross-grained, sharp-tongued widow, they'll call me if I say no. The widow lady with the paintings. With the dog and the daughter. No better than a bachelor uncle.

Paul had a fire burning. He'd cut green willow twigs, sat cross-legged whittling their ends. Lark gurgled at the sky. Bandit beside her. I sat down some distance away. Many will call me a fool for saying no. I balk at the idea of lying beside him. His weight and skin against me.

3 November 1945

Nightmares again. The roof opening to the sky, the heavens crashing.

19 November 1945

Marina appeared in that ancient borrowed Buick, a guardian angel in turquoise and silver. Marched into my kitchen as if it belonged to her. Her nose twitched. She threw open both windows. Said I looked like I could use a good airing too. Invited me to a day in the lap of the city. Tea in town.

We took Lark to Ma and Albert. In the car I told Marina that Paul had asked me a question. Her attention on the heavy car wavered. It slewed through a deep patch of sand. I told her that he asked me to marry him.

Marina looked at me sharply. Shifted her attention back to the road. Magpies on the shoulder by the remnants of a coyote carcass. Flew up with noisy complaints. Returned to the carcass after we passed. Her voice noncommittal as she said that Lark needed a father.

I must have wailed the words – that I don't love him. And I don't know if –

Marina conceded that it did make things a tad difficult. A nice cup of tea, perhaps, while we thought it over. She drove to the Bessborough. Inside the hotel lobby, a rack of newspapers on the front desk. Headlines about rationing. The war is over. But nothing seems to have changed.

Deep armchairs next to a window in the hotel's café. Dandelion tea poured and pound cake on our plates. Marina patted my hand. Mourned the ongoing absence of a nice cup of coffee. A smile in her eyes as she urged me to tell her about Paul. I told her what I knew. Talking triggered the panic. I couldn't speak past that choking, heart trip-hammering, breath like a straining plow horse's. Marina noticed. Who wouldn't? She patted my arm. Poured more tea. Waited. I felt so fearful. Thought the nightmares had lessened until just a few days ago. But thinking of Tessa –

Outside the window, a red-haired woman in a grey overcoat. She stopped to adjust her bootstrap. Straightened. Our eyes met. No. Not Tessa. Just a middle-aged woman with fading red hair.

I can't marry him.

18 December 1945

Paul showed up a week before Christmas. I admire his tenacity. He brought a small box. Lark on the floor beside the stove playing with her wooden horses. Peered at him and held out her arms. Paul picked her up and set her on his lap.

I invited him to stay for freshly baked pie. Mint tea.

Told me he'd brought Lark a Slinky. A crooked half-smile as he swung the door open twenty minutes and two slices of pie later. He wished me a happy Christmas. Reminded me that if I changed my mind, a fella was just a few minutes away.

The package rattled. I unfolded the cardboard. Pulled out the Slinky. And a small white box fastened with a red ribbon. Inside, a gold-enameled pin, a white goose flying above a blue forget-me-not.

I closed the box. Put it under the tree. My decision unchanged.

The Star-Phoenix, 12 April 1946.

"Victory Garden to grow food for war widows and families."

A local widow has started a truck garden aimed at providing produce for widows of fallen soldiers, as well as for returned soldiers and their families. Mrs. Charlotte Jones of Goodfare, whose husband Bill, a navigator, went down in an RCAF Stirling early in the war effort, has announced that she will plant vegetables to offer for sale, to military widows first and to military families second. Mrs. Jones' uncle, Mr. Albert Walter, will provide delivery services. Mrs. Jones is the daughter of the well-known breeder and studhorse woman, Mrs. Klara Mueller of Goodfare. Mrs. Jones has hopes of enticing other local market gardeners into the formation of a civic farmers' market.

Twenty-five

"MAMA! SOMEONE'S HERE!"

Jacketless late one afternoon in the first week of November, I unload groceries from my new-to-us truck with one eye on the sky, wondering how much longer the fine weather will hold as Earl's pickup rolls onto the yard. Earl leans out of the window and smiles. Claudine is in the back seat, Lennox's blocky head beside hers.

"Hey, you bought a truck! Sure sign of settling down, Luka," Earl says.

"It's all about the dog my sister gave us, Earl. That's all."

"Okay. Told you I'd call. Give us the nickel tour?"

Jordan leads Claudine around the back yard, the dogs romping under the trees. Jordan leaps for the old swing, misses, tumbles to the ground, shouting at the top of his lungs, "I'm going to have a slide and a new swing! Can I get a fort and climbing bars too, Mama?"

Earl raises his eyebrows. "Really? So you *are* staying?"

I fumble for an answer. "Umm. Like I said. I haven't really made up my mind. It's just a slide and swing. To give Jordan something to do."

"I can put up a swing for you, Luka."

"Don't be silly! I can't ask you to do that."

"Well, you didn't ask. I'm offering. I put myself through university working construction, and I made Claudine a climbing gym when I started dating Suzanne." His face tightens. "Sorry. I don't mean that to sound –"

It isn't funny but I try to laugh anyhow, a sound like a croak.

"I'll check on lumber prices and get back to you lickety-split on what it'll cost. Right?"

"I don't think so, Earl. That's too much to ask of a friend."

"It's not a big deal. Cut it out, will ya?" He sounds surly, then reads my frown and backtracks. "Sorry, Luka. I offered, I said. Think of it as business. You'll pay me a fair wage. It's not about the money. I just want to make your life easier."

My nose stays out of joint as we drink cocoa at the kitchen table. The pups sleep, flat on their sides, worn out after their romp. Jordan sits beside Claudine, asking soccer questions and chattering nonstop. Earl and I barely speak. When Jordan finishes his cocoa, I point Claudine toward the soccer ball.

Earl and I stroll to the meadow and inspect the lady's slippers. Then shouts and laughter draw us to the greenhouse. Claudine, with Jordan balanced on her shoulders, deftly dribbles the soccer ball around a slalom course of empty ceramic pots, Scout and Lennox leaping and wrestling at her heels.

"Your dog is sweet," Claudine says, coming to a halt in front of me.

"He's on the shit list," Jordan says. Claudine giggles as she sets him down. "Well, that's what Mama says," he adds.

"What's he done?"

"He runs away."

Claudine looks up sharply, and I can see apprehension in her eyes. I rush to reassure her. "No, I never hit him, Claudine, don't worry."

"What does he do all day at home?"

"Hangs around."

"He's bored. He needs a job." At my nods, she asks, "Are you going to get him his own goat? We could probably give you a goat or two. We have lots."

Earl starts to laugh. "Hold on a minute. Your mother and I won't be too keen on you giving away the farm. I'm sure Luka has a plan." He glances at me, then down at his watch. "But it's a good idea. What about a fence around your back yard? We could build it together. Think about it. Okay, we gotta fly, Claude, I promised your mom we'd be back before five."

That evening, I am lost in a muddle as I order plans for Jordan's playground. Should I let Earl take on the assembly? It feels like too much to ask. Especially when I have such complex and indefinable feelings for him I download the swing's plans, then I twist my brain inside out, and go to bed feeling uncomfortable. How would Mother respond to this charming man who is so like the cowboy she married?

Next day, I decide to forge ahead on my own, and print the schematic and assembly instructions. At the lumberyard, a bored young man in ponytail and scuffed workboots builds a small pyramid of lumber and hardware. "Drive your truck around and I'll help you load it," he says nonchalantly, popping his mouthful of chewing gum between every second word. As we load, I am relieved that I bit the bullet and bought the truck last week.

At home, I rummage around for tools, eventually finding Anky's hammer, circular saw, drill and drill bits, and a variety of screwdrivers in the shed at the south end of the yard. Three hours later, sweating and swearing, I stomp inside, leaving the plans and tools askew in a heap amid half-sawn two-by-sixes and a scattering of wood screws and lag bolts. I'd bought a more ambitious set than I originally settled on and the plans confuse me – diagrams and jargon-laden instructions that might make sense to a real carpenter but read like a foreign language to me. When I warn Jordan to say clear of the mess after he gets home, his face puckers but he doesn't argue.

EARL DRIVES ONTO the yard the next day while Jordan is at school. Leaves skirl around us as we tour the yard, Scout barking from inside the house. Earl's lips purse as he studies the mess of wood and metal framing littered with tools.

"I thought I'd come give you a hand."

Embarrassment tightens my throat. "I've had to take a break."

"I sure am sorry you didn't wait for me to build it for you. Want help?" He looks up at the sky. "Snow's comin'. I can get this done in a day or two. No big deal. Let me help." I shake my head, stung and humiliated. "Why not? Luka, what's this about?"

I don't know how to separate my feelings into sensible order: I can't accept his help – he's Suzanne's husband and I want him; I can accept his help – he's my best friend from way back. So I just stand there like a dolt, cursing my foolishness.

"Well. It's a kit, right? Must have cost you the earth. I hate to see one of my best friends drop so much dough. Not when I know how little it costs to build."

"I have the money, not the skills."

"Don't you get it? *I* have the skills. And I'm willing to do it for you." His face is taut as we walk back to the house. "At least let me assemble it for you. A waste of good money."

"And what are you so peeved about? It's my money to spend."

"It's not about the money, Luka. I thought we were friends. I just want to help," Earl mutters, talking downward toward his clenched hands. "I've got no right. I don't mean anything by it." Back at his truck, he looks pointedly at his watch. "Gotta go."

"Fine."

As he drives off, all my frustration and guilt churns into a vat of heat. So that's that. Alienating a friend with my bumbling foot-in-mouth disease, from silly to sublimely ridiculous. Anky never talked about money in front of anyone, but she had a way of disarming people despite her bluntness. That's a skill I haven't learned. I wish she were here. Every time my guts flare with temper, everyone around me feels the heat. Reticence and fire – maybe I am more like Yoppela than I like to admit. But I can't open my mouth to apologize.

My sense of the conflict magnifies as the day passes and I resume my struggle with the kit's complicated instructions. What now? Even on a good day, I can't tell Earl how I feel. Then I begin to wonder if I've misread all of Earl's comments and actions since my return. Back in the house for a cuppa, I look at the photos of my family on the bulletin board, suddenly resentful. Family patterns imprint indelibly. If I even try to tell my kid I love him, I trip over my own tongue. How can I teach myself to speak my mind?

In a fit of pique, I yank off my amber bracelet and fling it across the bedroom. The wire snaps, beads scattering across the floor like wild mice. Scout, asleep on the floor at my feet, jumps to his feet in surprise. I spend the next few minutes on my knees like a penitent, retrieving the amber, Scout snuffling at my neck and shoulders. Another half-hour passes as I painstakingly restring the beads on a new wire I dig out of my toolbox where it sits abandoned in the yard. "My own bad temper," I tell Scout as I re-clasp the bracelet on my wrist. "I should practice patience by talking to you."

ON FRIDAY at puppy school, Claudine has Lennox all to herself.

"Is Earl okay?" I ask as she fusses over Scout.

"His uncle in Ontario died. Cancer. Dad flew out for the funeral last night. He was pretty shook up." Claudine looks at me curiously. "You like my step-dad, eh? He's a good dude. But, like, married."

"We're friends, Claudine. I've known him all my life. Seeing him reminds me of being a kid your age. It's cool that he's writing a book, don't you think?"

She nods, seems reassured. "He won't show it to anyone. Not even Mom. Hey, did you think about a goat for Scout? I can ask Mom for you. Dogs and goats make good buddies."

I laugh. "I haven't had a chance. Do you really think it will solve the problem?"

"Sure. Why not?"

I don't want to admit to this sleek and self-assured teenager that a gap has opened, a gap of my own making. A gap of pride. Was this how Mother felt each time Dad hit the road? Why she picked fights?

Next morning, Scout and I visit Hannah without telling her about the fiasco in my yard, then come home to drink coffee in the parlour, soaking up the fading sunshine. I ignore all thought of the swing and slide lying in pieces in the grass despite the looming chance of snow. I sidetrack instead into the easier topic of contemplating seeds I could order for an early start in Anky's greenhouse. Life passes so quickly – arugula, chard, mustard greens, kale, pak choy, kids – despite our self-imposed boundaries. The fetters of my family's unspoken rules. My rejection of Earl's offers of help. My reluctance to talk about money. They all twist into a double-stranded bracelet of barbed wire tightening around my foolish pride.

I am stretching out my hand for my cell phone just as it chirps.

"Luka? Can Suzanne and I buy you and your kid a piece of pumpkin pie?" Earl's voice sounds thin.

I can't help it – I giggle. "Well, it is almost pumpkin pie season. Funny, I was just about to call and apologize."

"You've got nothing to apologize for."

"I do. My bad manners, for one. My ingratitude, for another. I needed an excuse to call."

"Let's not play games, Luka. I lost my temper. I'm the one who should be sorry. I was rude. Overbearing. And probably patronizing too."

"It was me. My old tapes. You'd think I never spent any time talking to a shrink. Things I've learned about dealing with people just slip away some-times. I should have been more upfront about what I can and can't do." My heart runs its marathon again. I gasp it out to the finish line. "Come for brunch – you and Suzanne. I bet she's never set foot on the place. Don't worry about the pie. And Earl, I'm sorry about your uncle."

"Losing him hurt." A pause, then his voice resumes, barely audible. "I have to feed the animals first. Don't sweat brunch. Just coffee, okay? Be an hour."

Twenty-six

SUZANNE CLIMBS OUT of the truck with a pie plate in one hand. Earl lugs a small blue toolbox.

"This farm is some sweet gig. You must be busting your buttons to be here," Suzanne says pensively, gazing around at the yard, then she hands me the pie, squats, and rubs Scout's ears. "So here's the runaway who needs his own goat. And is that the swing-set-to-be?" she asks, pointing at my rubble on the grass. All I can manage is a nod. Earl sets down his toolbox on the steps and moves among my abandoned project, bending now and then to examine pieces of wood.

"Claudine still hangs out on the gym set Earl built for her," Suzanne says. She stands up and looks quizzically at me. "You could let Earl put things to right, couldn't you? Maybe as a memento of days gone by? As an act of friendship?"

"I don't know, Suzanne. I already told Earl it feels like too much to ask."

"I get it. Well, give it a think."

Over coffee in the kitchen, I can't eat my pie. Jordan rescues me, slipping into the kitchen, his pyjamas flapping behind him. "Hey, Mama, are you eating pie? For breakfast? Can I have some?" Then he notices we have guests and hushes, one arm around my neck, the other hand on Scout's head.

Earl introduces Suzanne to Jordan. "She made the cheese your Mom gets at the market."

"I don't like it."

"Jordan!" I snap. "That's pretty rude. What have I told you?"

Suzanne intervenes. "He's being honest. Just like his mother."

"Mom says I should say things are not to my taste when I don't like them," Jordan says. "I forgot. Your cheese wasn't to my taste, Suzanne." Obligation to politeness discharged, he swings back to Earl. "Did you come to help build my swing?"

"Only if your Mom says I can." Earl stifles his laughter in his shirt-sleeve under the pretext of a cough.

"All right, I surrender. Go ahead, Earl." I try to keep it light, but I feel weighted down with something more complicated than I am willing to acknowledge.

Suzanne asks me to show her the house while Jordan vacuums up his cereal and then a slice of pie. Earl waves us on, settling in with his coffee and a second slice. We tour the house, chatting quietly about Earl's writing project, Anky, cheese, dogs.

Ten minutes later, the two males walk out the door, Earl's head bent to listen as Jordan describes his plans for converting his new play structure into a Fortress of Invincibility. I watch as Earl gives Jordan his blue tool-box to carry, then he gathers up all my tools and my toolbox. They haul all the tools into the back yard, then he vanishes – with Jordan – into his truck cab and drives down the driveway.

"Well, that settles that," Suzanne says, laughing. "He's off to enlist your son in the Mexican army. Either that or find the Franklin expedition to the North Pole. In either case, he won't be back until he's completed his mission. He's pretty generous, Earl is. You must have learned that when you dated him, yeah?" Her fine-boned hand touches down on my wrist as lightly as a sparrow. "He's a good guy, and Claude's crazy about him. But there's no spark between us. Never was. He was the good guy I married when I needed someone. Truth to tell, I'm feeling a little... restless. Preoccupied. We're discussing if we should separate. You know. But there's Claude."

No spark? I have to keep my head turned away from her so she won't see the jolt of electricity that surges through me. Even if she separates from him, he's still off-limits. Still attached. I can't tell if she's noticed my body's flare-up, but she sounds calm as she continues. "I hope you and I can be friends. It's a big world and we all need a friend. Now tell me you've decided to stay here in Saskatchewan. A dog, a swing set. Looks to me like you've made up your mind."

"No, I really haven't," I say quickly. "It's just life. Things just gallop ahead of me sometimes. Like Con getting me this dog. Then I needed to get a truck because I have a big dog. But my apartment is sublet for a few more months, and Jordan's enrolled in school, and we've got Scout. Speaking of, hey, what do you know about fences?"

An hour later, Earl has not returned, so I drive Suzanne home to tend to her nannies. He's not there either, so I return to my kitchen and sit staring out at the yard. My applecart is completely overturned yet again, confusion mingling with elation, both centered around the woman who sat opposite me, cracking jokes, sharing her pie and her life, drinking my coffee. I never met Marlon's wife, nor the wives of the other men I slept with. They never felt real. Suzanne is unshakably real. I like her. I want her as my friend. With that, the remnants of my resistance about the swing set shrivels and blows away. But Earl – I tell myself again that he's still married. Still off limits. Separation is still a bond.

THREE HOURS LATER, Earl's truck reappears. Earl steps out and unloads two large toolboxes on casters. He and my grinning son manoeuvre first one, then the other, into the greenhouse. I leave them to their work, but eventually my curiosity gets the better of me.

"Show your Mom, Jordan," Earl says when Scout and I step into the greenhouse. Jordan grins as he wheels over a red toolbox. The box is full, all my hand tools organized. Earl gestures at the wall. Electrical cords, saws, and drills hang on pegs in rows.

"Your young hooligan is pretty cool," Earl says quietly to me after I stutter my thanks. "I'll teach him, and you too, if you want, how to make good use of those tools – they were Charlotte's? Now I've got a few hours I can put in on that gym. You want to help, Jordan?" Jordan's nod is enthusiastic. Earl kicks the blue toolbox, a match for the smaller one he and Suzanne arrived with. "These are mine. You mind, Luka?"

"No, I don't mind. I just don't know what to say."

"Just 'thanks' is enough." His grin holds no shadows.

I retreat to the house. Patience, I tell myself, recalling Anky's words – patience is how the heart develops its muscles. It galls me that I need to learn patience with myself most of all.

Jordan bursts into the kitchen, Scout behind him, thirty minutes later. "Mama!"

"Is everything okay, sprout?"

He nodded and throws his arms around me. "I just needed a snack." He grabs an apple. "Why do you call me sprout, Mama?"

"Because you're growing so fast."

"When I'm a big man, will I still be me? Will I be a boy inside?"

"You'll always be exactly you, Jordan, sweet and wonderful. And there are millions of kinds of men."

"Well, I want to grow up into the kind that pats dogs, and eats ice cream, and fixes things, and smells good. Some men smell funny. Earl doesn't, though. He smells good. Like peppermint and hay. Earl says that love is when someone does things for someone else that they don't like to do. What don't you like to do?" His face is sticky with apple.

"I don't like... hmmm. I don't like ironing."

"What's ironing? Do I like ironing?"

"I doubt it. Ironing is taking wrinkles out of things."

"How?"

"Steam. An ironing board." And patience. Anky's old ironing board stands upstairs, stacked high with books on gardening and transplanting and seed catalogues and two unfinished sun costumes for the solstice party Hannah invited us to.

But Jordan's recharged. He leaps outside.

I settle down to Anky's diary in the parlour, looking at two photographs tucked between its front pages. The two photos could almost be pictures of different children; both are indisputably of Anky and her mother, Klara. One is of Klara as a serious young mother holding a smiling toddler – Anky – bundled in layers of clothing on a wind-swept sand dune. The other shows Klara as a frowning horsewoman, stern and forbidding, more of Yoppela than Tilly in her features, standing in front of a gabled barn beside a muscular Percheron stallion and a short-coupled serious child with a wild mop of hair – Anky again. Other than the diary's two pictures from Klara's and Jordan's wedding that I first saw on the evening after Anky's funeral, and now posted on the board, there are no more pictures of Jordan, and none of Marna's husband, Gerard.

Up on the board go the new images, where I turn again to Klara's and Jordan's wedding-day portrait – Jordan as a preoccupied young man, head tilted back, almost sneering, pale shuttered eyes appraising whatever lay beyond the camera lens, his heavy-lidded eyes disconcertingly like my own. What did those eyes hide? Did someone hurt him? Yoppela? With his sudden temper and reputation for violence, it seems likely that Yoppela was behind Jordan's disappearance. Then back to Jordan, an inevitable loop: did Jordan ever plan to stay and make a life with Klara? Maybe she was a diversion, met by chance. Yoppela stares at me from the wall, his raptor face contorted with the effort of forming a half-smile for the camera. No answers there.

Noises from the kitchen wake me from a sound sleep. I find Jordan standing on a chair in front of the cupboard, rummaging. He looks around, abashed, when I clear my throat.

"Earl had to go. He said to come eat something sweet quick like a bunny to get my blood sugars up. What's blood sugars, Mama?" He's found the chocolate chips, and his speech is muddy. "He said to say talk soon."

My phone chirps a minute later, Earl texting an explanation of his abrupt departure, a replay of Jordan's words: "Time to feed the stock, toolbox in the greenhouse, gym almost completed, talk soon, kinda wiped out and need a bit of space, all good, thank you."

As messages go, it's cryptic but on point.

I email an update to Con. When I go to bed a few hours later, Yoppela's bitter face haunts my dreams. If Hutterite Colonies had existed in Saskatchewan at the turn of the century, if my ancestors had not settled on individual farms but lived communally – none of this would have happened.

Twenty-seven

TWO DAYS LATER I come home from a visit to Hannah to find the gym completed. Swing, climbing bars, slide, fort. My new toolbox is indeed in the greenhouse, and the lumber offcuts – precious few: the schematic was unbearably accurate in its usage, with no room for errors by neophytes like me – are all stacked tidily beside the slide.

I start dancing. Scout bows and gambols in response. "Wowee, look at what Earl made, Scout! It's beautiful!" Scout scrambles up the steps and I snap photographs, sit down on the swing, and send several images to Earl, with big 'thank yous' emblazoned on the screen.

JORDAN AND I are intent on celebratory sticky rice and pork dumplings that evening at a busy dim sum café on Eighth Street when I spot Earl, walking out of the bookstore on the far side of the parking lot.

"I'll be right back. Stay put!" I say to Jordan, and dash through the door. "Earl!" It takes no effort to convince him to join us. I am so glad to see him that I don't bother trying to analyze whether lust or something deeper drives how I feel as he pulls a chair close and sets a bag of books at his feet.

"You don't have to feed me as well as pay me, Luka. I'm glad to get the gym built. Jordan here helped out big-time. It means a lot to be able to help you."

"Anky had one of these things, remember, Jordan?" I say and spin the central lazy Susan, bringing the dumplings closer to Jordan's bowl. "It's up on the high shelf in the kitchen. Let's bring it out and use it. Here, you want to share this last dumpling? No? Earl?" Earl nods and nabs the dumpling.

"Take some rice, too. Of course she called it a spinner because she avoided the word 'lazy', as if it would rub off on her if she so much as used the word."

"Do you always duck comments about how people feel? No, never mind. No lazy women in your family, Luka. That's a truth. You and your gran could outwork half the men I know."

The noisy room's tables are full. The singsong blanket of Cantonese muffles any sense of the outside world. At the adjacent table, a gathering of ten adults and several young children make a loud clatter as they set down glasses and teacups and chopsticks and pass around teapots and bowls, everyone loudly speaking at the same time. How would it feel to belong to such a clan? That kind of family – a large, talkative, noisy family that eats and argues and forgives in public, noisily, unlike my reserved clan – that's the type I wish I was born into. My pork dumpling suddenly tastes sour.

As we walk out of the café half an hour later, Earl drops his voice. "I've been writing, Luka. I'll call you soon?"

I can't get any words out. Jordan, bouncing up and down beside me, says it for me. "Yes, Earl! Come see us!"

THE NEXT AFTERNOON, my world closes in. Snow begins falling, the wind picks up, and Jordan develops a fever. He doesn't look up as I carry in two cups, his voice muffled by the duvet.

"Do you like Earl, Mama?"

"Do *you* like Earl, sprout?"

"He's fun. Can he live with us?"

"Earl has his own family. He's our friend, Jordan."

"You do like him though, don't you?"

"Yes. But –"

"You always say there's no room for buts, Mama."

"Drink your tea, sprout."

Jordan pushes away the cup. It clatters onto the bedside table. "I wish I had a daddy. All the other kids know who their daddy is."

"Your daddy is wonderful."

"You always say that. I want him. I do."

I tuck the duvet up under his chin, and touch his forehead. "Maybe your daddy can come visit sometime. Okay? Now go to sleep, sprout. You'll feel better soon. I'll be right here."

I shove aside the cushions and tuck into the armchair beside Jordan's bed, sipping my tea. Jordan's questions have caught me off-guard, although he dropped a clue in July when het met Earl at the threshing bee. But how to clarify my feelings for Earl? It's messy. Not as clear-cut as writing a list of pros and cons, this business of attraction and liking and anxiety. If I composed such a list, how would it read? Pro: undeniable sexual attraction; kindness to Jordan; generosity; wit and humour; willingness to work hard; loyalty; gentleness with animals; intelligence; wide-ranging interests. Against: sexual attraction; a tinge of envy at his easy kindness to Jordan; discomfort with his taking over my building project; an uneasy worry that after all, maybe he just wants a quick roll. And then there's Suzanne's news. Surely that changes things. Or does it? This whole thing seems too rooted in sexual attraction for trustworthiness. Not even to assuage Jordan's sense of loss will I take a risk that might end in loss and suffering for my boy.

There. The decision made, as simple as that.

Snowflakes collect on the deck and new play set outside. My cell phone chirps. I kiss Jordan, scramble over Scout, tiptoe out of the room.

Connie's voice, rapid-fire as ever. "Have you made plans for Christmas? I want you both to spend it with me."

"What about Neal?"

"I told you. We're divorcing."

"Come here instead. We'll string popcorn and cranberries. Dip candles. Play games. Remember how we used to play charades with Dad? Scout's getting big, and Jordan would love to show you his gym. They'll give you something else to think about besides dealing with a divorce, Con."

"I told you, I'm fine. But you sound a little – I don't know – off."

"None of your business."

"Now you sound like a teenager."

"Stay out of it, all right?"

"I was just trying to help."

"Well, help somebody else," I snap.

"Luka, what's gotten into you? Who else am I going to help? I've only got you."

"I don't know, Con. I just can't get a grip, and Jordan's sick, and I need a fence for Scout, and I feel like I've made a huge mistake coming here. And it's snowing."

"Okay. One thing at a time. Let's solve the fence problem."

We talk for ten minutes, and I tell her about Great Pyrenees' jumping abilities, their climbing, digging, and other nefarious methods they use to get out of fenced yards. "A six foot palisade is what we need. With a coyote roller on the top so Scout can't climb over it. It's all about being able to roam," I say.

"A coyote roller? No, never mind, I don't really want to know. The ground's frozen. Too late to dig fencepost holes. What can you do until spring? I mean if you stay," she adds quickly.

"Well, the run line, I guess."

"Okay then. Kiss the sprout for me."

The phone rings again ten minutes later. I almost don't pick up, thinking that Connie has come up with a riposte. But it isn't Con.

"Luka?" Earl's tenor. "I'm across the road, having coffee at Hannah and Mick's. Hannah said that Jordan's sick. Need anything?"

All my distress coalesces, a spiral of grief and confusion that chases from gut to throat. "No, but thanks, Earl." Even in my ears, my voice sounds distant.

"You sure? You don't need chicken noodle soup for the kid? What about some unabashedly adult company?" A long moment passes before his curt voice cuts the cord. "All right then. See ya."

I stare at the phone in my hand, wishing I still felt the clarity that guided my initial impulse to perhaps stay in Saskatchewan, then I fling the phone across the room.

WHEN JORDAN RECOVERS, we brave the snowy roads to Saskatoon and buy used snowshoes in two sizes. We work on learning to use them on our daily trips to and from the bus stop. Jordan doesn't ask again about his father, and I try to avoid thoughts of Earl.

I think about the meaning of gardens, peruse seed catalogues, wonder if I should have sown onions, leeks, garlic. If I dig deep enough, what will I learn? Beneath seethe the perennial questions: Where is Mother? Is she alive? Or dead? Will I ever hear back from that Vancouver detective? In frustration, I turn back to reading the thin lines of Anky's diary, and re-create her life.

Twenty-eight

19 May 1946

Today I sowed the first seeds for my Victory Garden. Seeding independence beyond the government's handout. Redemption from the shade of Bill Jones. Lark helped for a few minutes. But she was wild with the seeds. When she tired, she sat down on the damp ground. Soaked her clothing. Stared at the sky, unmoving for fifteen minutes. Her face utterly rapt. What did she see? Angels? She's nothing like anyone I've ever known. Her blood from another spring.

23 June 1946

Paul found me in the garden. Invited me to Saskatoon for ice cream. A celebration for seeding being done, he said. When I hesitated, he asked who else he was going to eat ice cream with. I did want to go to town, I told him. But to make my first delivery to my market garden customers. He laughed. Said he'd save Albert the gas. Told me to throw my basket in back.

I insisted we stop in and see that Lark was behaving for Ma. These spring mornings, so gorgeous out, I said. Paul soberly studied me in a way that made me squirm. Gorgeous. He repeated the word twice.

Wee spent the morning in Nutana, Marina's neighbourhood across the river. Delivered radishes, green onions, garlic scapes, even a few peas and lettuces. The second-last set of radishes and salad greens handed over to yet another widow with sad eyes and a toddler tugging at her skirt. I drew a breath. Directed Paul to the house on Temperance Street.

He looked up at the canopy of leaves as he parked. Took the basket from me. Asked me if I'd care for a tree or two in my yard, he could pick a pair and haul it home. I was laughing as we approached the house.

Marina called Paul by name from the porch. She fussed. O she fussed. Made eyes at my vegetables, then at Paul. I'd seen him blush before, but not like this. Full radish-top from collar to hairline. She ushered us in. Called all breathless for Gerard. Sent me racing up to the top floor for her special cordial glasses. Then to the cellar for peaches. When she said that peaches are what God had in mind when he invented kissing, Paul almost dropped his sandwich. What would she blurt out next? A mistake, a gigantic mistake. And Marina usually so tactful. Another trip to the cellar for leftover ice cream.

When I returned with the ice cream, Paul was talking through a mouthful of peaches. Telling Marina about the Slinky he gave Lark for Christmas. How Bandit ran barking from it the first time it cascaded down the porch steps. Then returned. Picked it up in his mouth and carried it to me.

Marina observed that he must be a regular visitor to my home, maybe he already knew the way to the stove from the door. She sounded smug. Paul, red-faced again, admitted he was trying to be.

Marina played her ace. She told him that I have a stubborn streak. That Paul should take comfort in knowing that the hare didn't win the race. She patted his forearm, invited him to talk about himself. The conversation slowed. Paul shrugged. Said he was a farmer. When Marina asked what he did for fun, Paul seemed puzzled. Then admitted to going fishing, but didn't have much time for fun. No, not fishing with me, we both answered. Marina, stymied, rarely lost for words. Turned to me and asked about Lark and the garden.

Gerard leaned on his one good elbow across the table. A half-grin as he raised his eyebrows at his wife, then at me. Quizzed Paul about his preferred fishing spots.

We left with Paul's hands full of jars. Peaches and chokecherries and plums in syrup. Marina's farewell gift. Paul asked what happened to Gerard's arm. Looked dismayed when I told him about the Somme. Then he wanted to know about Marina's last-minute whisper to me. About faith.

I was too exhausted to reply. Nature couldn't compare with Marina's energy. She had whispered to me that my daughter would be difficult to raise alone. That she needed a daddy. A gentle man. What I needed, too. That, and a bit of faith.

I took a deep breath. Re-counted the risks and benefits of saying yes. Of saying no. Glanced sideways at Paul, his calloused hands firm on the steering wheel. Shivered. Told him she'd said nothing that mattered. Paul nodded and wrestled the truck into gear.

A BLACK AND WHITE picture of two adults and a child is taped in the center of the next page, the details in meticulous block-letter print on the photo's bottom edge: "Paul, Charlotte & Lark, 1947." I squint to get a better look at Mother and Anky, both unsmiling. Anky, seated, tidy as always, her broad face composed and dark eyes settled, mouth tightly closed, is dressed in a pale skirt and jacket, a pin on her lapel, a clutch of lilies fastened to her cuff, her hair braided and coiled like a coronet. At her throat is the cameo, one of the necklaces I untangled as a child. Oltvetter Paul, standing at Anky's side, is a tall, bulky man, palpably uncomfortable in a black suit at least a size too small, his hair a pale tangle as he leans down toward his bride. The child, long-legged and lean, could be my Jordan as she stands like a captive fawn beside her mother, one hand on Anky's forearm, poised as if ready to run away, squinting beneath a sailor's cap that doesn't contain her flyaway hair.

This is only the second snapshot I've seen of Mother as a child, her stance already recognizable, her wariness unmistakable and heartbreaking. A wild blend of pleasure and grief carves a track deep behind my ribs. I set the photo aside for placement on the bulletin board, and return to the diary, but I've already guessed the occasion.

19 September 1947

Marina confessed she spent the past year making our wedding quilt in secret. Not knowing whether I would or would not. Another act of faith. The quilt was finished. I finally said yes. Marina gave me a necklace too. A gorgeous cameo. I doubted I'd find many occasions to wear it as a market gardener.

Paul kept asking. Kept coming by. After months of debate and argument with myself, I simply gave up. My daughter's need for a father outweighed my fears. I'll never feel anything but liking and respect for him. Maybe that's better in the long run. He's gentle with cats and children and dogs. A good sign, surely.

We married in the little church several miles from the farm. Uncle Pieter did the honours. Paul smiled as I walked toward him. I was preoccupied with Lark, two paces ahead. Marina had bought her a charming sailor suit, blue and white and pink. Its ridiculous cap wouldn't stay put. Lark behaved herself. A relief. She clutched that cap as we marched down the aisle. Albert's hands cool and dry as he handed me over. My own sweated and shook. I could barely hear Paul's voice as we spoke our vows.

As we left the church, I glanced at the graveyard. Where my grandparents lay. How had Grandpap treated his wife? Ankela Tilly had died before the question occurred to me as worth asking.

Where were Ma and Marina? I wanted them both. Spotted them standing by the door. Albert and Gerard between them, Albert with Lark on his hip. Ma looked drab. Still fitted the trousers and faded morning coat she'd worn in her heyday as a studhorse woman. Marina stylish in a tailored straight skirt and peplum jacket. Her hair upswept from her high cheeks. For the hundredth time, I wished she were my mother.

Marina and Gerard hosted the wedding supper. Several people photographed Paul and me beside the garden fence. Lark plucked at the rosebush tangled in the rails.

Paul downed a quick whisky with Gerard and Albert in the house. I caught a worried look from Marina, plain to read as a newspaper. But he drank nothing else.

I could barely eat Marina's good roast beef and perogies. Paul in the chair across the table. He kept looking at me. An intense stare that lowered his eyebrows and gave his face a heavy, almost sullen, cast. Marina saw it, too.

She caught my arm before we headed out. Lark clung to her hand. Her face covered with smears of icing. Marina wished me a happy marriage. And a gentle night on our honeymoon at the Bessborough. Lightly touched my hair, a coil of braids. How my mother used to wear her hair, she told me, so regal. Mostly she wanted to know if I'd told Paul. She thought best not, some things a woman must bear herself. She whispered that Gerard had ordered a nice bottle of bubbly for us. A relaxer. I tried to smile. Drunkards know no danger, my Tato claimed, she whispered. Her hand on my arm a brief reassurance. Stay calm and relax.

20 September 1947

Well. I survived. I spent as long as I dared in the bathroom. Changed into a plain nightgown and robe. Left on the cameo for luck. Pictured myself putting on everyday clothes and leaving. Just walking out the hotel door. But when I got to 'What then?' I stalled. Could only visualize going back to the farm. And the farm inevitably led back to Paul.

I tried not to think about what would come next. Anxiety swamped me. So close to panic that I could barely breathe. My hands shook as I uncorked the champagne. The wine bubbled and frothed over the lip of the bottle.

Paul still wore his jacket and tie. The clink as I set my glass on the tabletop. At his inquiring look, I told him it was champagne. A gift from Marina and Gerard. My voice brittle. I pointed at the chair opposite. Far enough away that he didn't pose a threat. I looked him straight in the face. I said we don't have to rush. He flushed. My suspicions most likely true. He was a virgin. He won't really know what to expect from me. Or from the act itself.

We didn't speak. Drank the entire bottle. Paul took his like medicine, shooting it down his throat as if he needed to swallow it without tasting. The wine's bubbles grew in me. Into light and air. I felt weightless as he took my hand. Led me to bed.

Partway through, I started to laugh, just this side of hysteria. Tiny coughs that felt like hiccups and sounded like a dog's yipping. Then tears. I choked back any sound. Turned my face away. Mourned a loss I could never voice. Something forever denied. He buried his face in my neck. I tried not to flinch, but did. He ended the same way Simon had. A muffled cry just before he drew away. The sheet stuck under his hip. His face reddened again as he pried it free so I could cover myself. He shifted his body so we didn't touch.

A few minutes later, his voice husky, he asked if there was any of that fancy wine left. A fella gets thirsty.

Twenty-nine

19 September 1949

*Our second anniversary supper. Roast pork and onion pie, chocolate cake,
nothing fancy, nothing new. Paul's not big on change. How easily he's fit into
our lives. He works steadily each day beside Albert. Tends the fields, feeds the
cattle. Albert hangs about less since the wedding. And Ma – she bought a new
saddlehorse.*

*Ma and Albert made us switch houses when they married. Albert insisted
he preferred sleeping on a cot beside the stove in the little house. Said it wasn't
right for Miss Lark to not have her own bed in her own room. It only made
sense. It no longer feels odd to be in the main house as a resident instead of a
guest.*

*I am glad of the privacy. Paul's unfailing interest in my body is still a nightly
event. My monthlies late again. He has often said how much he'd love to watch
his own baby daughter grow into a girl – in his words – as cute as Miss Lark
on her good days.*

*Today, Lark did not have a good day. She scowled and scraped her knife
along her plate at supper. Paul silent at the far end of the table. He rarely
interferes when I discipline her. But both love it whenever she goes with him on
the tractor into the field. She comes back calmer somehow.*

*I asked Lark to take a plate of cake to Albert and Ma. Lark stuck out her
lip but took the plate at one look from Paul. She returned with Ma close behind.*

Ma looked at me eye to eye. Said my daughter had done something.

*Paul asked lazily if it was something good. Ma ignored him. Something she
took to doing once he'd settled into his role as Albert's right hand. Talks only
to me now. Said Lark brought her a basket full of stones she'd gathered and*

washed. Pretty things, she said they made her feel safe. Ma asked me why a child would need to feel safe. I had no answer.

7 June 1950

Another false hope. Still I don't conceive. My doctor can't tell me why. This inability. A thing Simon stole from me. Far easier that than blaming God or fate. My sympathies for Marina, childless for so many years.

Paul recently stopped his monthly inquiry into the state of my health. But his interest in me at bedtime hasn't waned. My body doesn't waken to his touch. I am compliant but dispassionate. I ache to feel passion. The blame for our colourless coupling lies with me. I wish I loved him.

12 July 1951

Men swarmed all over the farm for days on end, helping Paul and Albert string wires. Power has arrived. My pension money from Bill Jones let me change our lives completely. So I thanked him under my breath when I first lit my daughter's room. Bathed her in warm water from the tap. Wrung out her clothes in the new machine. I won't hang my head again.

Come fall Lark will start school. She'll take the bus into Goodfare. My days will change. What should I do once the market garden season has wrapped up and the garden is put to bed? I thought I'd investigate some bird books. Especially the Audubon Uncle Pieter gave me when Lark was born. Study wings, bone structure, beaks and bills and bottom bobs and such. How do other painters paint their birds?

19 April 1954

I finally figured out why Albert never married. He loved Marina all along. It was him who carved those initials, M.S. – Marina Shevchenko – into the newel post.

Albert himself gave it away. He joined us for a cup of coffee and was emptying his pockets after a morning in the field. He pulled out a photograph, much folded. Laid it on the counter beside the wash-basin. Lark, the scamp, grabbed it. Careened into the kitchen, where she unfolded it.

She looked at me puzzled. Said it was just Baba Marina. Threw the photograph on the table. A long silence. Paul didn't know where to turn his gaze.

Albert's face stricken. He glowed, then looked haunted. Stared down at his damp hands, motionless on the towel. Retrieved the picture. Muttered that we shouldn't tell her.

So glad he loved. Marina was a worthy choice for him, even though. Even though.

I worry. He's sixty, getting old for strenuous doings. But he loves Lark. Dotes on her. Still stares me down when I lose my temper. Still hops on and off the tractor like a boy. Just grins whenever I bring up his age. Jokes that all I need to do if he keels over is get him into the truck and into the hospital in town. Old Tommy D. will have him right as rain in no time and at no charge, compliments of the good folks of the CCF. Albert votes CCF. We all do.

14 July 1958

Marina came for tea on the porch in the shade yesterday. Lark ran up. Chattering ten to the mile about absolutely nothing. Shrieked like a wild monkey. I told Marina how she'd gone on a binge a few days ago. Raced about the house for the entire afternoon and the next. Scrubbed everything that looked even halfway close to dirty. Headed out to the garden and weeded like a maniac.

I confessed that I had no help. Paul withdrew once Lark became a young lady. I don't know what to do. Marina wrinkled her forehead. Without a word to either of us, Lark threw herself in a chair beside her.

I am exhausted by Lark's rackets from one extreme to the other. Which version will come to breakfast tomorrow? My sweet girl? Or a wild demon spinning into high gear? Or a withdrawn mouse who needs coaxing to do more than sit on her tuffet? Beyond my understanding. Guilt corrodes me whenever I leave Lark alone in her room.

I told Marina I wanted to paint Lark's portrait before she got any older. The unspoken: before she got worse. Marina sent me for my paints. Lark was quiet.

I returned with paints and easel. Found Lark sitting on the porch steps with her head in Marina's lap. I painted while Marina talked about life in Saskatoon.

21 September 1958

Lark spent a weekend in town with Marina and Gerard to see Hitchcock's new movie, Vertigo. Marina was concerned when she brought Lark home. Said she spoke little all weekend, and at times seemed completely wound up. Like a top that could not control its spin.

19 October 1958

The trip to town to see Marina was ruined. Not by Lark. By Tessa. I'm so relieved that Marina wasn't with us.

I knew her right away. Those Elizabeth Taylor eyes. Still handsome. An ivory suit snug over a bosom more ample than I remembered. Tight skirt to her knees. High heels, legs as taut as ever. She marched toward Lark and me on Broadway. I'd parked in front of McQuarrie's to collect Marina's tea. When I saw Tessa I turned away, clutching Lark's hand. Lark pulled free.

Tessa's voice was the same. A squeaky child's pitch. Then she grabbed Lark's wrist. I screeched at Tessa to not touch her. Tessa dropped Lark's wrist. Seized mine. She told me, don't be a silly bonzer, Lottie. How I hated that name in her mouth. She wanted me to introduce my girl. Stared at Lark. Avid. Nice, she said, no farmgirl's legs, this one.

I jerked my hand free. Poor Lark looked baffled. I tugged her behind my own body. To shield her. Shouted. I practically shoved Lark through the door into McQuarrie's. My breath suddenly thick in my throat. Through the window Tessa smiled, shrugged, walked up Broadway. Indifferent to damage. Donnervetter! How dare that woman!

My daughter dithered over the tea samples, innocent, untouched. My body reminded me of 1943. Of Danceland. My legs trembled. All the pain and fright I worked so hard to forget. Was she staying in Saskatoon? I can't bear the idea of seeing her again.

23 November 1958

I couldn't bring myself to drive to town. Even though I needed Marina's company. I thought Tessa had swept from my life with no trace.

4 March 1959

I was summoned to the school. To the principal's office. Alone. Principal Dueck told me that Lark was banned from the school bus forever. Plus she was suspended from school for three weeks. She'd covered William's eyes as he drove the school bus. Her actions had almost caused a serious accident. But no injuries. He told me to ask her why. There was no appeal.

At home, Lark told me that she didn't care. Almost blithely.

I held my temper on a short leash. Donnervetter! I said it was not a game. She said again that she didn't care.

25 March 1959

Lark spent her suspension holding court in the kitchen. Without going to bed. Days and days awake. She talked nonstop, chatter I couldn't make sense of. The weather on the moon. What kind of peas liked butter. How many ways to send a message to someone on the far side of the globe. The real meaning of her math homework. At odd hours she started cooking. Making brownies, soda bread, meatloaf, coffee cake. Each time, she got a few minutes of cooking in. I would think, oh good, she's going to finish. But then something distracted her. She stowed the bowl in the fridge or on the stovetop. Where it inevitably hardened, or burned, or stuck, or spoiled. The house awash in dirty dishes and half-made food that I couldn't keep picked up.

I called Doctor Reid's office. Told the nurse that my beautiful daughter looked like a hag. She wasn't sleeping. Her face grey, eyes ringed with black circles. That wasn't all. Talked nonstop nonsense. She kept the radio cranked up. Some jarring melody that gave me a headache. Whenever I turned it down, Lark turned it right back up.

I tried not to think it, but when Lark chattered, I heard Simon. That nonstop babble. I struggled to keep my face from showing my dismay. My sorrow. Doctor Reid made time for a house call.

26 March 1959

Buddy Holly was blaring on the radio when I walked through the door. I couldn't see Paul or his new dog, that black-haired retriever Angus. No tractor in the yard. Doctor Reid was due within the hour. I found Lark sitting at the kitchen table. Knew trouble had landed.

Lark clutched something underneath the table. She raised her hands and threw what she held on the table. One of my early paintings of her. Slashed into ribbons. The spot on the wall where the portrait had hung smudged with raw lines of lipstick. My hands shook as I picked up the remnants. My portrait of Lark as a laughing seven-year-old. She never laughed anymore.

She talked in non-rhyming nonsense rhymes. *You are so apathetic. Systematic, really unsympathetic. Quit being so apologetic.* She didn't hear my responses. Stared at the markings on the wall as if they were clues. Finally she muttered that she wanted to live with Baba Marina.

I cried. The bitterest irony if my child leaves to live with Marina. Darling child, this is your home, I beseeched her.

She said she didn't care. Wouldn't live here. *This place has dogs. It's infested with frogs. Driven by cogs. Stricken with bogs. Festered with fogs.*

I looked around for the help that wasn't there. I didn't argue. Lark couldn't hear anything I said. Finally I left Lark at the table. Called Marina. The party line. But no avoiding it. The entire neighbourhood already knew.

My voice broke as I told her. I couldn't finish. But didn't have to.

Marina suggested I listen to Lark. That I take her to town to live for awhile. She could stay with them. The house had plenty of room. And Marina had tended difficult people before. She did say that even Gerard when he came back from the war was nowhere near as testy as my girl. Simon's blood, she thought. We knew nothing of him.

I remembered his spinning down from total wind-up. Marina thought he was ill too, in the same way Lark is. Marina was calm. Loving. Reassuring. Lark will do well enough with them. Poor darling, as Marina says, the wings of angels sound when one of their own falls.

I could hear Lark in her room, sniffling. No radio. I stuck my head in the door. Lark launched her stuffed pyjama dog. Hit the door.

I went to talk to Ma. She reminded me that I'd been a difficult child. Did I not remember taking my grandmother's shears to Ma's horse show coat to keep her at home? She counselled patience. My child is ill.

30 March 1959

Albert and I took Lark to the psychiatrist in Saskatoon after Doctor Reid had no help to offer. Paul begged off. Said he had things to do in the barn. Couldn't stand to see her suffer so. I didn't believe him. He'd stopped caring.

The psychiatrist gave me prescriptions. Anticonvulsants and sedatives for when she was wound up. When she was depressed, well... All he could tell me was to keep her safe. By then she'd quieted down. Huddled in his office chair like an exhausted toddler. I couldn't picture the earlier raving wild thing in the helpless child on the chair.

This illness. A list of fancy names. Manic depression, dual-form insanity, circular insanity. He insisted Lark was ill, not crazy. There were some who'd lock her up for life, or worse. Some doctors were experimenting with something called lithium. How on earth did they experiment? On patients as ill as Lark? She could be hospitalized, he said. Suggested shock treatment. Never! Would she get better? Outgrow it? He shrugged.

We took her to Marina's. On the drive home, I wept. My darling girl. I remembered being that age. Remembered hating Ma. Nothing like what that poor child endured.

When we got home, Paul headed for the barn.

Albert walked me to the house. His forehead crinkled into the heavy furrows he'd recently developed. He urged me to not whip myself so hard. Lark was ill. He told me her behaviour had nothing to do with her possibly finding out I never married her father.

How did he know that? Of course not, I said. I put on the coffee to brew. Measured the starter and flour for bread.

He told me to stop fussing. Told me what I already know – our family made him the keeper of secrets. He said Marina had told him my secret years ago. The truth about the flier – the real flier. Not William Jones.

My knees buckled. He motioned for me to sit down. Admitted that Uncle Pieter had helped him all those years back. He'd written up the fake marriage license when Albert explained how it stood with the pension.

Such relief. I'm not alone. After Albert left, I scrubbed the wall clean of lipstick.

Paul had no opinion. He'd given up hope of having a child. Withdrew. Buried himself in his chair. Listened to the radio after being out in the yard and field all day. She's your daughter, he said. Turned up the volume on the radio. Dragnet was playing.

Thirty

SECRETS WITHIN SECRETS, puzzles inside puzzles. Tragedy. I feel a rabbit punch of overwhelming sadness as I close the journal. Throughout all those decades, Anky kept her own counsel about so many things – her difficult life, the lifetime pension she collected under what she felt were false pretences and saved to leave to Con and me, her daughter's illness. How to reveal painful truths after years of secrecy? There is no right or wrong to guarding such secrets. Anky paid for her decision. The secret itself grew into a living thing, a snake eating its own tail. Mother's illness from such a young age is one more poisoned fang.

Two pieces of a torn black and white photograph and a yellowing bit of newspaper flutter from the last pages of the diary. I fit together the fragments and examine a two-tone rainbow spelling out one word in a band across the snapshot: DANCELAND. Beneath the sign, small against its arc and the blackening sky, a pair of young women, one short, one tall. Their arms are linked and faces tipped back, lips outlined in dark lipstick, skirts clinging to their legs, cigarettes held in front of them like a dare, the shorter woman's hair just like mine but bobbed. Anky. And the detestable Tessa. I find a bit of tape to hold the pieces together, then I mount the picture in a corner on the bedroom's bulletin board.

Everything I thought I knew about Mother – and my grandmother! – has melted away with the story Anky recorded in her diary. Years ago, my shrink told me that Mother was unfinished business, but I never understood what he meant. He said, too, that I should let go of any hope that Mother would have been better off if she'd stayed home instead of leaving. No one knew that for certain. If Mother hadn't run away, what would her life have been? It's ludicrous that I ever thought that I needed to forgive her. And Anky. What I didn't know about my grandmother... I know nothing, nothing. How incomplete our memories are, how inaccurate. Even if we pool them, there's still no guarantee of wholeness, or of healing. I read somewhere that grief is the price we pay for love. In full measure then, this grieving is in return for a full share of love.

I let the unanswered questions go, return to the diary, and read the final clipping. My grandfather Paul's death notice. I remember him as a private, silent man who spent most of his time alone with a book, indistinguishable music on the radio his companion. He rarely spoke to Con or me.

Saskatoon Star-Phoenix, 19 October 1985. Obituaries
Wipf, Paul – At home, near Goodfare, Saskatchewan, of natural causes.
Born 1916, in Goodfare. Survived by his wife, Mrs. Charlotte Jones Wipf,
adopted daughter, Lark Wipf and adopted grand-daughters, Connie
and Luka. The Lord is thy shepherd; thou shall not want. Rest in peace.
Visitation at Goodfare Funeral Parlour. Funeral and interment to be held
at Goodfare Country Hutterite Chapel, 25 October 1985.

THERE ARE NO more entries.

Jordan occupies my afternoon and evening, describing his school life in minute detail that I am oblivious to but grateful for. Later, I look at the diary beside my bed. Is it better to know? Maybe Con was right. Maybe it isn't. When I dial her number, she answers immediately.

"Listen, Con. About Mother. She got sick, I mean, really weird, and Anky sent her to Saskatoon to live with this woman Marina to avoid her having shock therapy. Shock therapy, Connie! Mother was bipolar."

The phone goes utterly silent, Con's boot heels stilled. "That explains it. I've been on lithium for five years now. Haven't you noticed that I've put on some weight? And Neal told me a million times that I turn into the worst of all possible bears when I go off it."

"You should have told me."

"Don't feel sorry for me. My biggest regret is that I've decided to not have kids. Your Jordy's it for the family reproductive line." I can hear Connie's heels again. Her voice slows and softens, the closest she ever comes to apologizing. "I thought you had enough on your plate without my saying."

"Did Anky know?"

"She nearly broke when I told her."

My dreams are filled with grainy images of unfamiliar masculine faces.

ONE AFTERNOON, as November comes to an end, Scout and Jordan chase each other in the snowy back yard and I stack a cord of split birch firewood in a stall in the barn. Earl's pickup rolls onto the yard. He puts on his work gloves without a word and helps me haul and stack, his nose and cheeks nipped scarlet by the wind.

"What brought you to this neck of the woods?" I ask as we finish.

"You. You all right? I got worried. You didn't sound like yourself last time we talked. Luka, we go back a long ways. I hate that we have this crappy distance between us. Friends help each other. Tell each other the truth. Inspire each other. Seeing how hard you've been working has lit a fire in my writing, Luka."

"That's good then." My mutter is barely audible.

"Luka, it's always been you."

"What are you talking about?"

"It occurred to me that I should be a little bit clearer. Franker. About you. Me. Us."

"There is no us, Earl. You're married."

"Yes. And I'll never do anything to hurt Suzanne or Claude. My happiness is not going to be paid for by them. Ever. I tried to tell you months ago –"

"Tell me what?"

"Suzanne and I are heading toward a separation."

"She told me."

"Thought so. I tried to tell you at the market but you brushed me off," Earl says quietly. "It'll be amicable enough. Been a long while coming. She married me because she needed a business partner she could trust to keep the farm, and a dad for Claude, and I married her because... well, because there was no one around I was interested in settling down with. She met someone. Before you even arrived she started sleeping in the spare bedroom. Long and short of it, I want her to be happy, to have a shot at real happiness. So I'm waiting to see what happens with her and this guy. When I need to think about something a long ways from here, I hit the desk and write. And I just finished my first draft of this manuscript about old Dunbar." He turns back to his truck. "That's all I came to tell you."

"Wait, Earl. That's great news. Congratulations! What happens next?" What's the best response to a declaration that includes fidelity to his wife? And it hits me: joy. "On all counts, Earl, I am happy." I reach out and touch his wind-burnt cheek. "I've been tearing myself apart. So now what?"

"We wait. I'll be at my desk doing revisions. Keeping myself buried. Send me notes, okay? Tell me how you are." He kisses my cheek. "Bye for now."

Thirty-one

ON CHRISTMAS EVE, the clouds unleash a blizzard. Connie stays home. Instead, we are Hannah and Mick's guests for Christmas dinner. They give us a new leather collar with "SCOUT" and my phone number engraved on its dangling blue tag.

Hannah keeps her face turned away from Jordan and her voice low as she asks, "Have you made up your mind about Scout? I wasn't sure about the tag..."

"I can't keep him on that run line no matter what I try. You know that. He ends up here every day. So I had a thought, yes. But it breaks my heart. I'll let you know if it goes anywhere."

When we get home, I send a question out into the cyberworld, then retreat to the shelter of Christmas movies with Jordan: *A Christmas Carol, It's a Wonderful Life, The Muppet Christmas Carol.*

ON BOXING DAY morning, I drink coffee in bed and check my email, looking for a response to last night's query. A note catches my eye, and I key in Suzanne's phone number.

"I got your email, Luka. And yes, I'm interested in exploring the possibility of adopting Scout. He's a gorgeous dog, and you're right, he needs a job. Are you sure you want to give him up?"

"I hate the thought. But I think it would be for the best."

"Claudine suggested a goat a while ago. We have a couple to spare."

"I don't know, Suzanne. It feels like one more thing."

"Maybe you should give it some more thought, Luka. A little time. Have you talked to Jordan about it?"

"I haven't."

"Why don't you leave off that part until we can show him things here? He's your kid, and you'll know better than me, but that's how I'd do it."

"I can't give Scout a fake job, Suzanne. I have to get this done."

"All right. What say you all come over day after tomorrow? I'll ask Earl to be around to give you the royal tour."

"WE'RE GOING OVER to see Earl and Suzanne's farm," I say to Jordan a couple of days later without elaborating. Scout is already in the truck, and I have misgivings as I watch him greet Jordan. Am I over-reacting?

"Sure, Mama. I'm hungry. Did you –"

"In the bag on the floor by your feet."

Jordan hasn't finished his snack by the time we pull into Suzanne's and Earl's yard. He studies the large Maremmas in the field with the sheep and goats, the dogs' white coats making them hard to spot against the snow. The pair of them sit on a slight rise, heads raised, watching their charges. "Look, Mama, guard dogs!"

"You know that's what Scout is too, right? A different breed, a guard dog. Do you think he'd be any good at guarding sheep and goats?"

Jordan looks suddenly guarded himself, in a way I haven't seen on his face in months. "What do you mean?"

"In Spain and France, dogs like Scout live in the high mountain pastures with flocks of sheep, without any humans. Isn't that cool?" Anxiety is creasing his face by the time Suzanne and Earl greet us at the door.

"Hey buddy, I'm glad you brought Scout to visit us," says Earl.

"He came to visit your sheep. Mama says you have sheep dogs. I saw them."

"I've missed your company," Suzanne says to me. "But the market's slow this time of year anyhow. I might have to take a month off – my cheese supply is dwindling. We only milk part of the year. Come visit more often."

We spend half an hour touring the farm, the barns, the lambing sheds, the dairy, the cheese aging closet. We don't enter the pens and fields where the goats and sheep congregate, overseen by their impassive guardians. Scout is reluctant to enter the buildings, and Earl ties him up outside. Every time I check on him, he's sitting up straight, head raised in a charming puppy imitation of the huge dogs on the slope three hundred meters away.

Finally, standing on the porch beside Scout and Lennox, there's no avoiding the issue.

"Jordan," I start, but Suzanne shoots me a look – I've got this, it says, plain as day. So I lie back in the weeds and let her run with it.

"Pretty amazing dogs, aren't they, Jordan? Like your Scout."

He nods warily.

"Our dogs live outside, with their animals. Except for Lennox here." The big black pup is sniffing at my heels, so I crouch and greet him, as does Jordan. "The others have double coats, like Scout, so they don't get cold. In fact, in the summer, they need to stay in the shade so they don't get too hot. They don't shed all their fur, so it's like leaving on your long underwear." She smiles, and finally, Jordan cracks a grin. "Do you think your Scout would like to live with some animals too?" She waits. Jordan waits. "Okay, let me explain. I think your dog is lonely for other animals. And your mom is feeling overwhelmed with trying to take care of him."

"But she has me! And Scout has me!"

"Yes, sweetie, he does. But this kind of dog needs animals he can take care of and guard. Like those sheep and goats. I wonder if Scout needs a job. Like you have school, right? Some dogs are work dogs, and they need a job or they go a little crazy and head off to find a job, some animals to guard themselves. Scout's like that. You know he's been wandering."

"So you want Scout to live with your sheep and goats? Outside?"

"Yes, but only if you are willing, Jordan. And you can come see him whenever you want."

I can read the struggle on his face. Finally he cracks and reaches for me. "Mama? Should we give Scout to Suzanne's sheep?"

"I think so, sprout. We can try it for a bit and see if it works for him. If not..."

He buries his face in my hip, then turns to Scout and kneels beside him. No one speaks as my son rocks and cries, his face hidden in Scout's ruff.

Sitting in the truck a few minutes later, holding Jordan's hand, I ask if he wants to come visit Scout. "No," he says quietly. "He's not my dog anymore. I don't want to see him."

I know exactly how Jordan feels, to the power of ten. In my rear view mirror, I watch Earl walk away, leading Scout toward the other dogs.

Thirty-two

I BARELY SLEEP all night, and wake to a familiar puppy voice whining outside. Jordan runs to swing the door wide, and Scout tumbles in, rolling over his own feet as he gallops over to me. Jordan, his face alight, squats and hugs the wriggling furball as I ruffle his cold ears, let him lick my face, then reluctantly call Suzanne. Have I made a mistake? Her face when she arrives is a mix of discomfort, regret, and sadness, and I'm sure that mine is bittersweet. I can't bring myself to look at Jordan as she leads Scout into her truck. Scout's persistence surprises and confuses me – we all had him pigeonholed as a guard dog. Is he a people-loving dog after all?

Scout runs the five miles from Suzanne's to our home every day for the next three days. With each reappearance, Jordan begs and begs for him to stay, then withdraws into silence when we put Scout back into the truck. On the fourth day, New Year's Eve, I succumb. It appears that being a surrogate mother to a pup is as permanent as raising a child. "All right, Jordan. I made a mistake. He's obviously decided that we're his people." I call Suzanne, and I hear the same relief in her voice as I see on my son's face. Then Claudine comes on the line.

"Mom says we've got to bring you a goat. Scout loves a little Nubian, Alessia. She's so darling, and no trouble at all. For a goat, I mean. She can live in your old barn over the winter. We'll bring her over later today. That should keep Scout happy, Luka. Okay?"

I can't do anything but agree. That afternoon, when Alessia leaps nimbly out of the back of the pickup truck and rubs her head on my knee, I immediately understand why our puppy fell in love with her. But then a second goat, just as small and entrancing, with the same floppy ears, follows Alessia out of the truck. Alessia is black and tan, the other rusty brown and cream. Jordan whoops with excitement as he gallops over. The goats are unfazed by his enthusiasm.

"That's Clea," says Suzanne, hugging me. "They're sisters. I'm so relieved, Luka. Honestly, it broke my heart when you brought Scout to us, and then again when he ran home. Here, you want this." She puts a large rolled-up fabric tube with flexible metal hoops in Jordan's hands. "It's a goat toy, a tunnel. They like to play."

Claudine appears from the back of the truck, her arms full of buckets and tiny halters and leadlines. "You're going to have fun. They're both escape artists."

"Just like Scout, but smaller," Jordan pipes up.

"Exactly." Claudine laughs and hands him a bucket.

Suzanne interjects, "Let them out into that paddock back there. It has a good high fence, and there's still the old watering tank from your granny's day. Maybe add a coyote roller around the top of your fence. I'll show you how to make it. Little rascals climbed out of our paddock last summer. They can come and go in and out of the barn if you build a little dog-and-goat door to block the wind and weather. And here – we brought a few bales of alfalfa for you to get started."

Claudine isn't done with her advice. I can hear her talking to Jordan about tether balls and wading pools as I write a cheque for the goats, gear, and hay, and hand it to Suzanne. They help us settle the goats in the barn, in four large box stalls facing each other across a wide central corridor where a stack of straw bales still stands at one end, and we leave all the stall doors open. We haul in several old tires and wooden pallets, organize a goat-jungle gym, and Scout takes up a position on top of the straw bales. The goats nose around, investigating everything, bounce up the bales and snuggle briefly with Scout, then bound down to check out the rest of the stalls.

"See?" Claudine says, sounding satisfied. "They're going to love it here. And he's all set to guard them. I bet he never runs away again."

We're all smiling as we swarm into the house for tea and cinnamon buns. It feels like a party I don't want to end. Claudine talks nonstop, telling me how to feed and water the go-girls, as Jordan names them, and she suggests lots of playtime and physical contact. When she offers to check in each week until we feel settled, I accept gratefully.

In bed that evening, I marvel at how I thought giving away Scout was a reasonable idea. And at how the goats fit so seamlessly into our life. Then I wonder: what about my apartment in Vancouver? The sublet is up at the end of March. This new addition feels irreversible.

Scout stays home. He spends his time with his goats in the barn or paddock. After school, Jordan and I play with him, then put him on his leash and work on his heel-sit-stay. When we release him, he licks our faces and ears, then returns to Clea and Alessia, content in his animal kingdom.

BY LATE JANUARY, the farm is snowbound, framed in white. I stop counting how many times I hear "record snowfall" on the news. The north wind blows in a drift that blocks the house from the rest of the yard, a drift almost as high as the building, wind-blown and hard enough enough for us to clamber up and slide down in a tangle of legs and snow suits. Jordan misses a few days of school and spends the time romping on his snow-shoes with Hannah's boys. They all love playing with the goats and Scout. I send round after round of pictures to Earl and Suzanne. In separate texts, I give each of them varying degrees of information about how we're adapting to life with goats, interspersed in the messages to Earl with more private updates.

The evenings settle into a routine, me at the counter reading Connie's political column online, and on weekends, her "local living" column, as far removed from politics as she can persuade her editor to let her roam – this week's a hilarious rant about all that can go wrong when snowplows are stolen. Then it's me at the stove, boy playing in the parlour and up and down the staircase before we both pull on coats, boots, mitts, and make the trip out to the barn for our evening visit to Scout and his charges. After our meal, Jordan clears the table and hits the bathtub, and I finish my wine. All that's missing is Earl.

Tonight I pick up the diaries and flip through them. As I close the last page, it occurs to me: Tessa. The ancient woman at Anky's visitation in the fur and fascinator. The woman with the personal-care attendant hovering beside her wheelchair. The woman that no one knew. Who else could it have been? But why would she still be in Saskatoon? And how would she have known that the Charlotte Wipf of Anky's obituary was her Lottie? We'll never know the answers, but it must have been her.

Ah, Mother. Whatever her childhood had been, she had no wish to set it on paper. Mother was never one for sharing. Those brief letters from Vancouver offer clear proof of that. Come to it, none of my family really knows how to share. It was Earl who taught me how to accept a hug. Mother as an adult was unable to share – her manic shopping and gardening, bouts of depression and retreats to her bed, were all indicators of her illness, and pain so deep that nothing would help except oblivion. How far she ran to escape. Who did she meet? What happened in Vancouver? Whatever Rockmore might learn about my mother, it might lead me to closure. To some form of peace. I hope he's learned something. Maybe. Con's been right so far about knowing or not knowing.

Instead of falling asleep, I scuttle downstairs, rummage in the schofbonk, and pull out the quilts. Two for Con, stacked on the kitchen table; one I drape over the back of the couch; the remaining pair I carry upstairs, gently tucking one over Jordan, the last one over my bed. Its soft cotton comforts me as I rub a length of it between my fingers and wait for sleep.

Thirty-three

ONE MORNING IN EARLY February I wake feeling as grey as the landscape, with an achy head and body. Sorrow or an incipient illness? Aching for a missing man? I don't know. Don't care. Yoga doesn't interest me. My attention, held during my intermittent reading of the diaries, has finally released, a whistle that leaves me deflated, my arms loose in their sockets, my body drained. All day, snow falls heavily, blows in from the fields, creates rippling dunes. Anxious for a breath of fresh air, I step outside. The flat light weighs me down. Bitter cold bores into my cheeks, settles around my shoulders like a cape, penetrates the exposed skin of my hands. The silence turns into an echoing cavern, disorienting me.

"Mama! Where are you?" Jordan's voice from the open doorway sounds dull. When I retreat into the shelter of the house, my heart falls away, borne into a void without a struggle, my body bereft of essence and meaning. Cold seeps in. I call Hannah, tell her I'm getting sick, ask her to come for Jordan, and please feed the goats and Scout. Then I take to bed. Fever comes, stays, makes itself welcome. I descend into nightmare, raving, the diaries' collective burden of suffering a stone bound to my body.

Hannah would tell me later that snow fell for a week. That Jordan and her crew missed school when the roads became impassable. That pneumonia took hold quickly. I don't notice, caught in fever. In my dreams, I struggle to escape boulders compressing my skin. A rock ledge takes hold in my chest, outcroppings of ancient fieldstone that pins me. I gasp and flail in the bedcovers, chest pounding as I dream. Horses tugging at stake-out lines, enlarged nostrils blown violently red and engorged. Freighters weighted with concrete blocks and granite slabs, crashing free of moorings and tipping downwards into the boundless ocean. My breathing shrinks and struggles.

One afternoon I wake, chilled, bathed in sweat, pyjamas drenched. Light pours in through the open curtains. Connie slumps on a chair beside me. She opens her eyes and takes my hand.

"Welcome back, sweetie."

I mop my face with a forearm, my head encumbered by gravel and sand that shift with each movement. "What time is it?" I vaguely recall being lifted from bed to car to doctor's office, the doctor's hands cool on my forehead.

Connie moves her hand up from checking my pulse to my sleeve. "What day is it, more like. Today's Wednesday, the day before Valentine's Day. You've been sick with pneumonia for a week. Hannah called me. I've been here all week. You're not contagious any more. Jordy's been beside himself, not being able to see you. Here, you're drenched again. Hold on, I'll get fresh pyjamas."

When I wake next, Jordan sleeps in the chair. Con appears in the doorway. She smiles and speaks, but she's as distant as a spectator on a faraway pier. She disappears, reappearing later with a tray.

"Eat this." Several spoonfuls of soup reach my mouth without spilling, then Jordan wakes and launches himself, upending what remains. Connie mops up the mess and re-makes the bed, re-organizes us so Jordan lies beside me, his face buried in my neck.

More slipping between the waking and dream worlds. One morning I wake almost clear-headed, stumble downstairs, lie down on the couch and tug the quilt over me. My sigh doesn't relieve the pressure in my chest. Jordan climbs in beside me. Con doggedly offers tea, soup, toast. My voice when I thank her emerges in a whisper.

Hours later, I manage a muted word of thanks when Con brings more tea and toast. It's a relief to realize that my body no longer aches and my head is clear. I slowly sit up, looking around for Jordan.

"He's gone to school," she says, and helps me downstairs, then pops a DVD into the player. I fall asleep to the clash of wizards colliding in *Harry Potter*. An hour later, I wake and stare out the window at grey sky. All day, I drowse and wake. My brain is caught in the grooves of 1917 and 1944 and 1959, spinning my ancestors' lives round and round until the images blur. Scenes from the diaries play over and over like a surreal reel of clips: Anky struggling to escape on the verge of the lake, Danceland's rainbow sign a lurid backdrop; a man tumbling down a wellshaft, an unheard scream ricocheting off the hard-packed earthen walls above his head; Mother covering the bus driver's eyes with her hands in the white glare of midwinter. When Con reappears with yet another cup of tea, I turn my face away.

That evening, I stagger over to the roll-top desk and pull out the diaries, haul them back to the couch and flip through them, reading and re-reading the darkest scenes. Then I rummage for the DVD Con gave to Anky and slide it into the player. Anky's face appears on the screen behind the credits. I muffle the sound, flip though a dozen interviews with other people, hit the volume control when Anky's face reappears. Anky speaks, recounting the start of her Victory Garden in 1946. A smile opens her face and the wrinkles she earned. My heart somersaults.

"Something joyful came out of those years, Luka." Connie appears beside me and tucks the quilt around my shoulders. "It wasn't all gloom and despair. That's worth remembering." A last yank at the quilt. "Earl's called a dozen times. Hannah told him you've been sick. Today I said you're back from the depths." She looks at me sideways. "Something you want to tell me? About Earl and you?"

I roll away to sleep. As the curtain drops me into oblivion, I see Anky on the same couch, her hair a net of silver, then Mother in one of her rare quiet states.

By the weekend, I have enough strength to shower alone. Back on the couch, I return to the diaries. I dully realize that Connie is watching me closely, and her tone has sharpened as she brings bowls and mugs. It doesn't matter. I don't stop to wonder how long she's been living in my house, caring for me. I just go back to the television, delighting Jordan with uninterrupted hours of *Harry Potter*. As the junior wizard labours repeatedly to save his friends from the Dark Lord, I slide gratefully into the darkness of the script and conceal myself among the ruins.

A cough behind me. My sister, scowling with impatience. She holds out another DVD – *Sense and Sensibility*, my favourite. "Watch something cheerful."

"IT'S BEEN TEN DAYS," Con says. "Jordan's at school and I need to go to town for some salad greens and a couple of steaks. Speaking just for myself, I can't face another pot of soup. Stay put."

When her car is out of sight, I struggle into my winter gear and wobble outside, truck keys in hand. The bright sunlight refracting off ice crystals and snow nearly blinds me. The truck coughs twice, hard, before the engine catches. I let it run, dig out sunglasses and make my way to the barn. When I go in, the goats bounce up, nibble at my jacket, bounce away. Scout regards me from his perch atop the bales. All is well in their world. Seeing them should make me smile but it doesn't. I retreat to the truck, ease into low gear, hands shaking. The kilometres unwind like chilled caramel. With each fencepost, Mother is with me, and Anky, and Klara, too, driving from the farm into town, and returning, always returning.

In Saskatoon, rolling south, traversing the Broadway Bridge. Halfway across, the truck slides on a patch of ice. I try to steer out of the skid but the truck doesn't respond and its unfamiliar controls fluster me. I sit paralyzed, hands raised in surrender as oncoming cars slow and swerve, missing me by a nose. My entire body shakes as I guide the truck off the bridge and thread through the snow-lined streets to the district of Nutana, avoiding the street where Connie lives.

I turn onto Temperance Street, broad and heavily treed, elms meeting overhead to form a canopy of naked boughs iced with white, looking for the distinctive fence Anky described in the diary entry about her wedding at Marina's house. I pass a weathered red house with a glassed-in sunroom at the front, an ornate metal scrollwork fence surrounding the yard, dried rose brambles and ivy vines tangled among snow-covered fence rails and uprights. Is that it? I circle the block a couple of times, the truck growling in low gear while I debate. The house looks newer than I expected. Is this it? Someone must love it. It makes sense – Marina would have only sold her home to another family who would treasure it.

The truck rolls to a halt. I shut off the key and drop my head to the steering wheel, breathing heavily, my heart knocking. A minute or two pass before I can climb out and approach the fence. I lay my hand on the tall gate and jiggle it. For a second, I consider walking into the yard and knocking on the door, but a dog rackets behind the shuttered windows. The snow crunches as I retreat.

Pounding head. Aching body. That doesn't matter. This does, this house, Marina's home, where Anky made so many decisions, where Mother lived, too. I can see them clearly: Anky as a young woman sitting in the yard; Mother as a teenager perched on the broad steps; Marina, who mothered them both, standing in the doorway, a bastion of safety and love.

It takes several tries to fit the key into the ignition. Finally it fires. I creep through the city and along the highway, onto the snow-packed grid road. I nearly overshoot the driveway.

When Connie returns with groceries, I am collapsed on the couch, the TV silent. I don't tell her. Instead, I fret. What if? If I am bipolar, like Mother and Connie? And Jordan? What if he is, too? Scenarios of the uncertain future spin like records – the school bus Jordan travels on each day careening into the ditch; my health declining into a bog of inaction; Jordan ill. Earl. Earl. I want to text him but my hands are too heavy.

Con can't rouse me.

"What if?" I mutter when she sits down opposite me, a plate in her hands.

"You want a bite of steak? A bit of baked potato? Salad, maybe? No? You aren't your mother or your grandmother, Luka. What happened to them... that's the past. You aren't –" She pauses. "It was pneumonia. Nothing worse. I wish you'd never found those damn diaries. I'm glad I never read them. Watching you go through this was more than enough. You need to live in the present. Let go. Get up, sweetie. I can't stay much longer. I've been working online, my boss needs me to show my face at the newsroom."

"HOW ABOUT SOME fresh air?" Con says the next day. "A walk? Visit the goats?" Then she insists. Coat. Boots. Cozies a toque on my head, fits fuzzy mitts on my hands, tops my snugged-up scarf with a pat. We step outside. But I won't leave the porch.

"You're making yourself sick," she says. "I can't just stand by and watch you destroy yourself. I'm going to hook you up with a counsellor."

"Seeing a therapist doesn't help. I've tried it before."

"Try again." She stalks into the kitchen, her muffled voice speaking to someone unseen, then the door slams. I straggle into the parlour and toss my coat aside. Some time later, she stands in front of me, dressed for the outdoors, holding out my coat. She tugs me to my feet and leads me to her car with Jordan at my side. I sit motionless in the back beside him while Con goes back to the house. On her return she hands me the diaries. "Here, let's bring the evidence along." During the drive into Saskatoon, she says quietly, "I have a friend who's a psychologist in private practice. She's made time to see you after hours. Luka, you have to come back to your life. I need to go home."

Thirty-four

DOCTOR ABEL LEADS us into her office, a large and open room with windows overlooking the river. Her fine white hair is cut short, her hands and face wrinkled. She stands no higher than my shoulder, and holds herself like a dancer, with an aura of taut fitness tempered by composure. Her small hands are light on my arm as she guides me past the dainty uncluttered birch desk to two stuffed armchairs positioned in front of the window.

She turns to Con. "We encourage an interactive family and support a team approach, tonight I need to speak with Luka on her own. Would you mind?" Con quickly retreats with Jordan to the empty waiting room.

Doctor Abel seats herself, pen and notebook in hand. "Now, Luka. Why are you here?" I freeze, unwilling to admit that Con acted unilaterally in bringing me. "Have you seen a psychologist before?"

"I saw Doctor Wesley in Vancouver."

"Why was that?"

"My mother was... I didn't know then what was wrong with her. Depressed, I thought. Now I know she was bipolar. Like Connie. I was afraid –"

"What are you afraid of, Luka?"

"That I am, too. That my son might be."

"We can figure that out. Do you have a history of depression?"

"I – I can't tell. What's depression and what's normal anxiety?"

Doctor Abel chuckles. "That's a very good question. How are you feeling about being here with me?"

"Anxious," I admit with a small laugh. I look out the window to the ice-bound river. Surely there is movement somewhere under the ice.

"It can be a scary thing, seeing a psychologist. Connie told me on the phone that you've been reading your family history. How interesting. Of what you've read, what's had the biggest impact?"

The doctor's skin from her hairline to the collar of her white blouse lies in shallow wrinkles, like ice that has frozen, melted, and frozen again. "All the things I didn't know."

"What do you mean?"

"The secrets. I keep seeing the worst of them. Danceland and my grand-mother being raped. Mother covering the bus driver's eyes. Yoppela at the well. Over and over, like a loop of broken film. I don't know what to make of it all. Or how to turn it off."

"Those are big secrets. We'll talk more about them. Meanwhile, what do you think would be the safest way for you to work through this so you *can* turn them off?"

"Surely that's for you to say. Isn't it?"

"There's never only one way, Luka."

"I don't even know the options!"

"Fair enough. What helps you feel better? How do you like to spend your time?"

"Um. Hanging out with my friends and talking." I stop abruptly. "No, that's not true. I only have a few friends. Gardening. Yoga. My son."

"Lovely. What age is he?"

"Six. Connie gave us a dog. Scout." Why did I volunteer this information?

Doctor Abel looks up alertly, the textured skin of her cheeks indenting as she puckers her lips. "Gave you a dog, hmm? Sounds like something Connie would do. Dogs are empathetic souls."

"We couldn't – keep him. At first. But we got him two goats."

"Oh, I see. Tell me about your friends. They'll want to see you feeling better, I'm sure."

"There's Hannah. Connie took care of me and Jordan while I was sick."

"Do you talk to either?"

"A bit. Con won't want to hear any more about my stuff."

"Well, give it some thought. If it feels safe, talk with her."

"She won't want to."

"How's your appetite?"

"I had pneumonia for a week."

"So you haven't been eating."

"Food doesn't interest me."

"Understandable. But you look too thin for a woman of your height and frame. Are there things you've enjoyed eating in the past?"

"My grandmother's kuchen."

"Tell me about when your grandmother would make kuchen."

Anky at the kitchen table, her hands deep in the mixing bowl, talking over her shoulder to us, or standing beside the sink, the stove crackling, the pungent drift of cinnamon cutting the air. I start to talk, and the room fills with images.

Forty minutes later, Doctor Abel sets down her pen. "I think we can work together, Luka. Would you like to?" At my nod, she says, "I'd like to see you once a week. I can fit you in on Thursday evenings, at seven. Yes?"

"Yes. No drugs!"

"Agreed. For homework, I'd like you to think of some good times with your grandmother, times when you and she were happy. Every day, sit down for a little while and think about the good times. I'll see you next week."

ON THE DRIVE HOME, Con takes a direct tack. "What about the greenhouse? Valentine's Day has come and gone. Should I turn on the heat? It'll take awhile to heat the soil. All those seeds you ordered – tomatoes and peppers and eggplant, they need planting soon. They need you. So does Jordan. He's wandering around looking like a ghost. I'm leaving tomorrow morning."

Anky. Admonishing Mother in much the same way. A dull voice like a rough wood-saw growls in my head – things will surely worsen if I speak.

At home, I collapse on the couch, pick up my bracelet from the table beside me, spin the amber pieces. Imagine I am walking hand in hand with Mother down East Hastings Street. Minutes later, Jordan tiptoes in and slips under the quilt beside me. I must have been mad, or under the influence of too many glasses of wine, ordering so many seeds. Thinking I could start a market garden.

Later that evening, I wake from a nightmare of Yoppela forcing my son down a wood-cribbed well. The house is silent. I creep upstairs, find Con asleep in the guestroom bed, Jordan dreaming peacefully in his.

Connie leaves the next morning. She hugs me before she heads out the door. "I'm just a phone call away and Hannah is right across the road. She's taking Jordan until you can cope. There's soup on the stove and salad greens and leftover steak in the fridge."

I am saddened to see her go. There's a new tenderness between us. I move like Anky in her last weeks, slowly, deliberately. The yoga mat unrolls like an old friend, and I get through several poses before exhaustion stops me.

"HOW DID YOUR homework go?" Doctor Abel asks a week later while Jordan is safely ensconced with Hannah and her boys. When I shrug, she hands me a notepad and a pen. "Write down three instances of times you had fun doing something with someone you love."

"I don't feel like remembering happy times."

"I know you don't, Luka, but I insist. Here, we fake it 'til we make it. Depression is an insidious beast." Doctor Abel grins, suddenly looking years younger. "Oh yes, the beast. We say its name here. It helps. I believe in demystifying the healing process. Another therapist might say that means we're working toward effecting a shift in your emotional mindset." A giggle. "Now, that list." She looks off into the distance, humming quietly as I write. "Now let's hear what you wrote."

"Flying kites with Jordan on the beach." Doctor Abel nods. "Talking about gardening with Hannah." I want to add Earl but don't know how to bring him up.

"Good. Any more? No? I want you to add to that list this week."

"Homework? Really?"

"You bet. Now, did you feel like talking to a friend this past week? No, hmm? What do you think makes it hard to talk?"

"We're private people."

"Privacy is learned behaviour, Luka. How do you feel when you share something you like to eat with a friend?"

Anky's kuchen. I scribble a brief note.

"You aren't sleeping well."

I tell Doctor Abel about my nightmare of the well.

"Why might you have dreamt of a well?"

"Someone might be in the well."

"Well, Luka, if you're going for effect, it worked. Who?"

I give her a brief synopsis of my family's history.

"There are decades of pain in those diaries," Doctor Abel says when I stop talking. "We can talk more about them and your mother in the next session. I want you to do your homework this week." She peers at me. "Try to get some exercise, maybe not near abandoned wells. And eat. Fuel for the machine. To my mind, this sounds like complicated grief. Also known as persistent complex bereavement disorder. Not that labels help. All right, do your best. I'll see you back here next week."

On the drive home, the late-evening sun beams in through the truck's windshield. When I stop at a corner, relief spreads through me like morphine.

The sensation doesn't last. On Saturday morning, I'm back on the couch, in my nest, walking Vancouver's Downtown Eastside alleys alone in my head. Finally, I pick up my phone and find a dozen texts from Earl asking how I'm doing. Confusion and dim hope elbow each other for breathing room. I send a two-word answer: better, thanks. I don't know what else to say.

A while later, I hear the front door open but I don't get up. The scent of coffee and cinnamon drifts through the air. Hannah and Con enter the room, a plate and mug in Connie's hands. She plops down and hugs me. Hannah perches on the arm of the couch. "We heated up some cinnamon buns and made some coffee," Hannah says. "You have a little munch-up and we'll go on out and look at your greenhouse. We'll start those seeds together. You need a little exercise to get the oxygen flowing. Come, my girl."

"I don't want to."

"I know, but you need to feel like you again. Here." She puts a plate in my hand. The bun is heavy with icing. "Can you at least tell me what's on your mind? Is it Jordan?" I shake my head. "Well, that's a relief. Let's get some air."

I stay on the couch, watching Jordan eat the bun.

The next day, Hannah shows up alone. This time she brings warm apple kuchen. As I take a tiny bite, tears well up. Anky's recipe. Turning to Hannah, I say, "Keeping secrets hasn't done my family any good so far. You might as well know." The diaries and their secrets spill out, and a slow swell of relief washes through my body. Why didn't this happen while I spoke with Doctor Abel? It doesn't matter – I am simply grateful.

"It's no surprise you're mourning," Hannah says.

"Mourning?"

"Of course. Sounds like you have every right to mourn." She holds out the kuchen. "Keep your strength up. Mourning's hard on the body. You look a bit haggard, my girl."

Another bite. Apple and cinnamon explode on a current of buttery caramel. I sit up and eat the entire slice, the flavours intense after my diet of soup and toast. After the kuchen disappears, Hannah makes fresh coffee. The first sip sends its wake-up alert through my system. I sigh in capitulation.

Inside the greenhouse, I wander along, dabbling fingers in the soil that fills the elevated tables.

"Where are those seed packets?" Hannah asks as she digs gardening gloves out of the basket by the door and hands a pair to me. We slowly move around the greenhouse, our gloved hands in the soil. "Now why don't you tell me more about these diaries while I get things organized? Tell you what, I'll come over every day and we'll go out on those snowshoes I saw in the mudroom. Pretty gorgeous out there. All silver and sparkle, like a fairy tale."

THE SEEDLINGS SPROUT. Hannah comes by faithfully each day, marking off days on my fridge calendar, calling out dates to me. "March third, Luka." "March fifth." She brings meals and a whoosh of fresh hope with each arrival, carting Jordan in her wake, back and forth between her house and mine. But the seedlings wither and die. Too early. I tried too hard, planted before the ground was ready. In private moments, I add events to my slowly growing list of happy times. The smell of soil as I garden with Hannah. How soil feels between my fingers. The final moment before falling asleep as I lie in bed. Patting puppies and watching goats. Jordan shouting as he careens across the yard on his snowshoes. I want to add something about Earl, but I can't.

We re-seed the eggplant, peppers, tomatoes. "We'll make up recipe cards for your market clients so they'll know how to make ratatouille and moussaka." Hannah gestures at the soil where the seeds lie sleeping. "I'll be back. You'll see – they'll grow, and you'll feel sunny again."

Each Thursday evening I head to town for a session with Doctor Abel. In the greenhouse and in Hannah's kitchen, I talk. With each conversation, a small flash of relief ignites like a flame. But the feeling always fades and the rainclouds roll in.

Thirty-five

EARLY ONE SATURDAY MORNING in the second week of April, I am outside in boots and raincoat, digging trenches, directing water flow across the driveway and yard toward the edge of the field, trying to salvage a parking spot among the puddles. Since my bout with pneumonia, I have dreamed that Earl has slept beside me every night. I tell myself he's close to leaving Suzanne, but I really don't know. I am afraid to ask for fear of hearing the word "no." How frightfully easy it is to hurt someone you love, how thin the membrane between misunderstanding and good intentions! What if I need Earl and he changes his mind, doesn't need me? If I hurt him past bearing? The fragility of love has never occurred to me before, has never seemed so fraught. It jousts with my ongoing anxieties about my mental health, and my son's. Then I realize – this is the first thought I have had for my son, for his well-being, in ages. Have I been buried in a well of my own making, a well of self-centered despair?

When Hannah and Jordan show up after school, I hug each of them. When I try to thank Hannah, she nods. "You're back. Good. Go watch the dog and goats play. That'll do your heart good."

Sitting on the straw bales stacked in the barn, watching Jordan run after Scout and a soccer ball, the goats running circles around both of them, I catalogue more happy times to add to my list. Watching my boy play ball surely qualifies. Watching the goats climb and frolic. Scout looking settled and happy in his guardianship. Then I look up at the sky through the open barn door. Grey doesn't help. Weekly conversations with the doc do, though, as does the return of prairie spring sunlight.

I have expanded my conversations about the diaries to include Connie. Since my illness, she exhibits her sunny side when we talk. I muse with her about the diaries – I know all the characters as well as a reader would know the characters in a beloved novel. Somehow, my close blood relationship to the diaries' characters has added an element I describe to Doctor Abel as 'curdling': that sense of outrage and horror that close kin are capable of keeping corrosive secrets. I ignore the hard fact that I have done the same thing in withholding Jordan's parentage from him, and his fatherhood from Marlon.

I head out to the meadow with Jordan, where I fall to my knees and show him how to pat the grasses to find the lady's slippers. The plants look healthy, leaves developing, but no buds have taken shape. I sit back on my heels and stare blindly at the ground in front of me. When will they bloom again? The stillness is an opiate. The sky shines like glass, beams of sunlight leading straight to the spot where Scout sits on guard duty.

Something akin to adrenalin fills me. I don't believe in fate, or much in a god. But there has to be some spirit that moves across the water, through the night sky – the natural world is too perfect, too gorgeous. This is our home. Our family's. Mine. We're staying. The mothers in the diaries stay with me as I sit in the meadow with my son.

Thirty-six

DESPITE MY CALM, I barely sleep, and wake at two A.M. that night, chest thumping, coyotes carolling, and spend the next two hours trying to forget what I read in the diaries. At four, tea. The cup cools untasted on my bedside table. Some time later, I wake sweating, heart at a mad gallop from a nightmare about echoes in a well as a body plummets. At eight, Jordan and I roar down the driveway to meet the bus.

Jordan's goodbye hug has an element of desperation in it. "Are you really better, Mama?"

"I'll be right here when the bus brings you home, sprout."

In the greenhouse, the eggplant seedlings are ready for transplanting. Immersed in the job, my hands deep in soil, the headache that has hounded me since last night's nightmare slowly recedes.

That evening after bath time, Jordan slumps cross-legged on his bed as I dry his hair, his eyelids drifting south. "Are you afraid of anything, Mama?"

"Yes." I can't come up with a single funny rejoinder. "Now lie down. We're safe and in our home." Six-year-olds don't need to know that what their mothers fear most concerns them.

I stretch out on the couch and close my eyes. Immediately, an image of Mother in the garden appears. Instead of struggling against the image, I embrace it, imagining myself with Mother, both of us adults, both of us wearing amber necklaces and bracelets. I visualize myself standing eye to eye with Mother, hugging her, and I move my lips as I say the words: I love you. I fall asleep within seconds.

Next morning while studying the photographs on the bulletin board, I pull the pins from the photos and carry the pictures downstairs, find the album in the parlour and empty it, sort dozens of images, and arrange them chronologically on the long planks of the kitchen table, from the first Jordan and Klara with the puppy on her lap, through the generations until I arrive at Mother in boots and jeans with us as young girls, and finally, my Jordan with Scout. From half a pace back, I appraise the line-up. My family. I pick up the phone.

"Con?"

"Yeah?"

"Thanks. We're staying. I love you, Connie."

A moment's silence. "I love you too. I'm glad – about everything."

I look away abruptly, exhilarated and terrified, then reach out and touch a photo of Con. I love my sister. I've always known it, but neither of us has ever said so. The tyranny of silence and reserve bequeathed by our heritage and the fallout of what happened at Danceland closed our mouths as effectively as duct tape over a vent. Actually saying the words has lit a small candle in my heart, its faint glow illuminating my path to Mother.

Thirty-seven

THE PHONE RINGS on a mild late-April morning. At the sound of a sharp unfamiliar English accent, I have no idea of what to expect.

"I'm Andrew Rockmore with Vancouver Police Department. Luka Dekker, right?" My throat closes. "I got an email from you some time ago," Rockmore says. "We have reviewed the notes you submitted and may have a candidate for a pig farm victim ID. We have some Jane Does – some unidentified belongings and body parts from the farm site. I need to review your mother's details, if you can bear with me."

Bitter bile climbs through my body, sorrow and outrage for my beautiful mother as Rockmore painstakingly reconstructs her last week at home, her clothing, hairstyle, height, weight, habits. A smoker, I say, remembering the red cigarette pack always close by her hand, then other habits: vodka neat, mah jong, learned during her early years in Vancouver.

"Remind me: any drug use? Illnesses?"

It takes a minute to answer, to formulate the words. Truth. No secrets. "The doctor at Insite told me that she was on lithium and olanzapine, but went off sometimes. She was bipolar. He last saw her in 1995."

"Tattoos? Piercings? Distinguishing marks?"

"None we know of. No." When he asks about jewellery, a nerve twitches in my throat. "An amber necklace. Just like my bracelet." I describe it.

"Right. This is the reason for my call." I go silent as the possibility hovers unsaid. "Luka? You with me? We have a necklace. Amber, I am told."

My heart skids into my belly with dismay, and I realize how much I hoped I wouldn't hear anything back from my last throw of the dice in Vancouver. I touch my bracelet with shaking fingertips.

"I just emailed you a photograph, lass. Have a look."

A moment passes before the email arrives. When I click on the image, it opens into a circle of sunshine, the gleam of amber offset by a tiny helix of seashell set in the largest piece. It's the same necklace I handled as a child on Anky's lap, the same necklace she asked me to untangle. Mother's. A rattle of adrenaline shakes through my lungs, eerily similar to the rattle of the amber on my wrist. "It matches my bracelet. That's my mother's. My grandmother gave it to her." I start to shake.

"All right, lass. Steady on."

My fingers clutch the amber, smooth as skin, warm to the touch, the past captured in its depths.

"Do you have any of your Mom's personal things packed away? Toiletries? Old lipsticks? What about her hairbrush? We're looking for a source of your mother's DNA, Luka. Think you can find her old hairbrush? Let me know as soon as and I'll get in touch with the Saskatoon police service. They can collect it and send it to us. We need conclusive evidence."

"I don't understand."

"It's called a chain of evidence. This isn't evidence in a court case, but we need to ensure it's handled securely." Rockmore repeats himself several times, I know with bone-deep certainty that the amber necklace was around Mother's neck when she vanished. Even if she was desperate, she wouldn't have hocked or sold it.

Upstairs, after hanging up the phone, I rummage through the last box of Mother's things that Anky packed away. I wrap the hunt in a prayer, and find Mother's hairbrush buried at the very bottom, a few strands of long chestnut hair still wound around the bristles. I stare at the brush for several minutes, my hands sweating on the wooden handle. This is not just DNA, but the last tangible evidence of Mother's existence. It sounds too cold to countenance, too harsh. Amber. I still have the bracelet. Amber beads are warm, resin. Amber preserves evidence of life in a golden bubble. My bracelet's beads click like a rosary, realization setting in. What horror they represent. Mother's final hours are too shocking to contemplate, and my fingers rub my bracelet, seeking whatever comfort and memory the resin still holds. If I close my eyes, I can see Mother's face, lit with gold, caught within the amber like the helix shell on her necklace. Artifacts caught in amber survive for millennia, the perfect time capsule. After I email Rockmore, I lay the brush gently on the bookshelf in my bedroom. Tears, oh tears flow.

WHEN MY TEARS STOP, I don't want to call Connie. Not yet. Not out of fear that she might crow about being right – knowing *is* worse – but because I don't have the words to say what needs saying. This particular news can wait. How can this horrifying violence be the outcome of Danceland? Of the secrets and half-truths that filled the diaries?

Then I remember my phone call with Roger Arnett, whose sister perished in Vancouver. A memorial, he suggested. What kind of a memorial can I create?

Eventually my heart slows, a pattern that echoes in my bloodstream, its certainty underlaid by peace. The garden.

Thirty-eight

I'M NOT CERTAIN what causes happiness – surely not just the bells-ringing and lights-flashing of good sex, or the inbred urge to love my baby. What causes it? May's green twigs emerge, nubbins of pussy willows beating out winter, rose blossoms, tightly furled and unfolding like flags, sunflowers growing with a tight amber spiral at their heart, Jordan growing from baby into toddler, toddler into preschooler, preschooler into the busy boy he is now. Magic. It's magic, this happiness idea. There's no understanding it, and maybe it's foolish to even try, best to simply accept the small, sometimes invisible details, just as I'm practicing saying "I love you" to Con and Jordan. Maybe happiness just takes practice. I feel my face lift from grief into the unfamiliar shape of happiness. Happiness seems attainable. Concentrate on that. Then I catch myself humming. Wasn't it Albert who hummed? My need to forgive Mother has transformed, along with my need to be absolved, into acceptance.

The house is silent, Jordan still at school. I walk into the kitchen and examine the rows of photographs still lying on the table: Klara and Jordan, Anky and Marina, Anky and Tessa, Mother and Dad, Connie and me, Jordan on snowshoes with Scout, Connie with her arms wrapped around Anky. My family, my own place in it clearly defined.

Outside on the deck, staring up at the sun, looking for lotus blossoms to open in its shadow, like koi dreaming of koi dreaming of me dreaming of a dream. Mother's face is with me. She is more present now than ever before, a ghost that doesn't taunt or accuse, simply follows my breath. Beyond the yard, I can imagine the field, the barley Mick has sown, sprouting into an ocean of new green. In the darkness, I imagine the lady's slippers, visualize the buds appearing in their folds.

At what point do acres of land become something else? I imagine my nascent orchard of fruit-bearing trees and shrubs, the rows labelled with plaques: cherry trees, for rebirth, and rebuilding; plum trees, for youth and fertility; apple trees, for peace; grapes, for abundance and artistry; pear trees, for longevity; and raspberries, for kindness. My Victory Garden. The idea of this market garden began as a work project, but it's grown into more – a link to my grandmother and mother, an offering of gratitude to the goddess of plenty, and footsteps in Anky's path, feeding people. I can see hosting farm tours and a bi-monthly meal in a new greenhouse, among my soon-to-be-built raised beds, in the orchard after I plant it, tables and chairs set among the saplings and new plants. That would please Anky. I'll name it for Mother, Lark's Lunch. We'll put the money it raises towards providing food – and clothing! Mother would want her women to be warm and well turned out! – for women living on the street in Saskatoon and Vancouver.

My soundings take out a mortgage on imaginings, bank the outcome as if they were rands or doubloons. Value ascribed to land equals what, exactly? A drop in the bucket. An echo. A sigh. A dog's wet nose. A dream of a missing woman come home to sleep in peace.

I make a cup of tea and walk out to the greenhouse. As I open the door, the spicy green scent of tomato plants leaps into my nostrils, and I stoop over the pots, assessing the Green Zebras, Brandywines, and Black Krims: they've shot up. So too the salad greens, radishes, green onions, sunflower sprouts. Good – they'll be market stars soon.

The bus. Time to meet Jordan.

Jordan leaps off the bus and lands lightly beside me. "Mama! Watch me! Look what Claudine taught me!" He hauls out his soccer ball. Walking in place in slow motion, his knees high, the ball bounces from one knee to the other – five times before it drops to the ground.

"Someone's been practicing!" I swoop him up and kiss him. "I m so proud of you, sprout. And in case I haven't told you, I love you."

Jordan looks only momentarily puzzled. "I know, Mama."

"What do you think about staying? We can ask Cherie and Keesie to come visit whenever they can. What do you think? Do you want to stay?"

"I always thought we *were* staying, Mama. Anky asked us to."

SITTING IN THE BARN an hour later while Jordan plays with the goats and Scout, my fingers tap out a text to Earl, hope drifting into the ether with my typing, a short, simple message: "I'm thinking of you, hope you are writing. Jordan and I are staying. Come when you can." Then I add a row of X's.

His rejoinder is rapid: "Revised first draft approaching the finish-line for submission to publisher. Nearly finished all else. Hang tight." Relief washes through me, followed by a sense of unexpected, unaccustomed sense of surety.

Thinking of Earl reminds me of Jordan, how he asked, on meeting Earl, "Is he my daddy?" Jordan deserves to know his birthright, his blood, and so does Marlon. It's time to tell them both. Love swells through me, a kaleidoscope of images of Jordan playing with Scout, his round eyes as he queried Anky about her childhood, his solemnity in the church yard, his glee with the goats, with a soccer ball. Mother lives on in her grandson.

Then I call Con. Our conversation is slow, punctuated by tears.

When we finally sign off, I call Cherie and fill her in on what I've learned and what I've decided. After more tears, I describe my new garden and my plans for the CSA. "First, though, I've arranged to have a booth at the farmer's market. It won't be indefinite, just to build up clientele."

"Make it so, Number One. Sounds good, but a lot of hard work."

"You and I thrive on hard work, Cherie. Come visit. Maybe you'll like it. There's room in the house, if you and Keesie want to leave Vancouver."

"Yeah, right. Leave Vancouver to live in Saskatchewan. Not too likely. Why don't you move back here and do this thing where it's warm?"

"Land's cheaper on the prairies. I might add a tropical angle, orchids, maybe, in a year or two, if I can figure out a cheaper fuel source for more greenhouses. Maybe wind turbines. Lots of big wind on the flatland. Anky would love it. Mother, too." My eyes brim with tears.

"Orchids in Saskatoon sounds promising, you crazy woman. We'll visit. I am and always shall be your friend. You go on and cry. I gotcha."

THE FIRST RUSH of farmer's market customers has swelled and subsided, and my list of potential CSA clients already has names scribbled on it. I sip my coffee, marveling. It still seems unreal that I sit here, selling vegetables under the Victory Garden banner my sister the quilter made, a rainbow of colours like Danceland's sign, repatriating it and my memory of Anky and my mother – last month I consigned her hairbrush to Saskatoon police, who sent it off to Rockmore's team of DNA genies.

First thing this morning, before the market opened, when I went over to greet Suzanne at her stall, she hugged me. "I hear we're going to be market neighbours," Suzanne said. "Congrats, Luka! How very cool."

"How's Claude? And Earl?"

"All good. Claude could be a great vet. She's so good with lambing and kidding. Earl's fine, too." She grins sideways. "Listen, pop back after market closes. There's someone I want you to meet."

AT ONE-THIRTY, footsteps approach my stall.

"Time to go soon, miss. Market's closing in half an hour." The manager, Melissa Weeks, pauses beside my stall. "Do I know you?" She looks like she's in her mid-seventies, with muscular arms, a lived-in face, and wiry hair like worn heather set into an eroding hillside.

"No. But maybe you knew my grandmother? Charlotte Wipf?"

"Charlotte! Of course. You have the same hair. A little taller, though, aren't you? How was your first market?"

"I'm exhausted," I admit. "But thrilled. This is all I have left." I hold up the last packet of greens and one bunch of radishes.

"I'll take the greens for tonight's salad. What's your name?"

"Luka Dekker."

"Right. Charlotte would be proud of you, Luka." She pays for the greens, and I start packing up. I can see the men clad in plain black clothing and cowboy hats or caps, women in long skirts and vests with polka dot headscarves – the Hutterites, my distant cousins – do the same at their tables several meters down from my stall. I catch myself staring at them, my new "us." The diaries and Hannah's recent offer to teach me Hutterisch have strengthened my sense of connection to my kin. What my life would be like if Yoppela and his contemporaries had formed colonies on their arrival in Saskatchewan instead of homesteading on privately owned farms? I could just as easily be one of those Colony girls with the old-fashioned rolled-under hairstyle and headscarf. If I were a Colony girl, if my great-grandmother and her family had lived in the communal shelter of a Hutterite Colony, none of this would have happened. No well, no studhorse woman, no Danceland, no bus accident, no death in Vancouver. I'd be some other woman.

One of the Hutterite men approaches as I pick up the packet of French breakfast radishes, red and white, sharp and sweet, like memory.

"Nice-lookin' radishes," he says, his English overlaid with an accent. A year ago, I would have thought, *German*. Now I know: Hutterisch.

I smile at him and hold out the radishes.

"Maybe you know my family," I say. "I'm Luka Wipf Dekker. Charlotte Mueller Wipf's granddaughter. My great-grandmother was Klara Walter Mueller, my mother was Lark Wipf Dekker. We are Prairieleit. Have some radishes. A first-day-of-market gift." Maybe we're fifth cousins, or grand-niece and great-uncle four times removed. I hope his Colony's men are respectful and kind, the women safe and happy, the children beloved.

A smile eases across his bearded face as he takes the radishes. "Family, are we then? Wilkommen, cousin."

Then I scoot over to Suzanne's stall, dragging my empty cooler behind me. "Sold out!"

"Perfect. Exactly what you want for your first day," Suzanne says. She gestures to a stocky bearded man standing just behind her. "Luka, this is my friend, Andrew Klassen." Her eyes and face tell me he's a special friend.

"I feel your joy, Suzanne," I say. And I do, tinged with the bittersweet thought of Earl leaving his partner and friend to join me. I have to ask – "How is Claude?"

"With the change?" Suzanne tilts her head toward her friend. "She likes Andrew. And she likes you and your crew. It's good that you're close by." She leans closer and whispers, "Earl told me. I'm so happy. For all of us, I mean."

As I leave the market, I pause to text Earl. His response – "Nearly finished" – lightens my step.

JORDAN AND HANNAH are waiting on the chairs beside her garden. Hannah pours lemonade and we toast my empty cooler and full garden, then I hug Hannah, make my excuses, pack up my boy, and head for home. He and I sit together on the lowest step of the front porch, watching Scout and his goats rambling within the confines of their new pasture and their mini-gym. Home. I suddenly remember the sight of Claudine's kite soaring against the sky.

"Let's learn how to make kites, sprout."

Jordan beams. "Like Claude's? Maybe Earl can teach us. Why don't you ask him, Mama?"

"Great idea, sprout."

LATER, AFTER JORDAN is asleep, I tap in Earl's number. My message is brief: "Jordan and I are going shopping for silk for kites. I thought we'd make four – ours, and a new one for Claudine. Will you show us how?"

After that, Marlon's cell phone number comes easily to mind. I key in the digits, then sit motionless, confounded by the enormity of telling a man he has a son, that he became a father almost seven years ago. What should I say? All the love I feel for Jordan swells through me, a kaleidoscope of images of him playing with Scout, his round eyes as he queried Anky about her childhood, his solemnity in the church yard, his glee with a soccer ball, his love for Scout.

"Marlon? It's Luka."

Marlon's voice is stilted. "I never expected to hear from you again."

"No. I'm sorry. Can you talk? There's something I need to tell you." I can hear the sounds of papers being shuffled, voices receding, doors closing.

"Now is fine, Luka. I'm still at the office, and everyone is heading to the bar. How are you?"

"Well enough, thanks. Listen..."

"Right to it, then, yes? You haven't changed. All right."

"You have a son. His name is Jordan. He'll be seven in July."

"You're kidding, right?"

"No." I pause, imagining again how shocked I'd feel to receive such a message out of the blue. "I am so sorry I didn't tell you. We live on my family's farm in Saskatchewan. You're welcome to see him. He's wonderful – he has your wit and humour."

"Wait a sec. Turning seven. So when you chased me away –"

"Yes. I'd just found out and I couldn't figure out how to tell you. Because – well, you know why."

"Luka, for chrissake, you should have said! We'd have figured it out."

"How? You still married?"

"No. I'm divorced. Shawna and the kids moved back east. It's been a few years. I had it coming. Send me a picture. Jordan, you said?"

I send him a picture of Jordan chasing Scout, then wait. Finally, when Marlon remains silent, I speak. "He doesn't know, and it's past time I told him. Can we talk in a few days? Do you want to see him? We can make arrangements."

"Yes," Marlon whispers. "I do. Thanks for telling me."

FOR BREAKFAST, I make waffles, Jordan's favourite. As we mop up the last of the maple syrup, I say, "Jordan, do you remember asking me last summer if Earl is your dad?" He nods solemnly. "Well, I've been thinking, and I realize that I should have told you about your dad years ago." I pause, then hold out a photograph – the only one I have of Marlon – that I pulled out from the back of the top drawer in my bedroom.

"This is your dad. His name is Marlon Andersen. You have two families."

Jordan studies the photograph for a minute. "I'm an Andersen as well as a Dekker. Why didn't you tell me?"

"I thought I knew best. I'm sorry, sprout. I made a mistake."

Jordan's hazel eyes are guileless and open to everything. "What's he like? Do I have brothers and sisters?"

"He's funny, like you. Smart, like you. Pretty wonderful. And yes, you do. I'll leave it to him to tell you all about them."

"I want to see him."

"I know, sprout. I've been talking with him. He wants to see you too. He didn't know about you, sweetie, so please don't blame him. So let's put your dad's photo with the rest of our family photos when we go inside."

Detective Rockmore's email two weeks later is brief and pointed:

> Advise DNA sample from your mother's hairbrush is a perfect match with forearm bone fragment sourced from convicted serial killer's farm site as discussed. The department therefore IDs Jane Doe Number Seven as Lark Wipf Dekker. Both brush and necklace will be returned to you when our files are complete. My personal condolences for your bereavement, Luka. I know the loss is eternal, but I hope this data offers conclusive relief from uncertainty.
>
> Best regards, Andrew Rockmore, VPD.

I call my sister. We both weep. Then we start making plans for a memorial service.

EARLY ON A COOL MORNING a few days later, I've finished watering the greenhouse and raised beds. Jordan is still asleep. Scout and the goats are nestled in a tangle of paws and hooves in the pasture adjoining their paddock.

I set down the hose and head east, toward the meadow. When I reach the lady's slippers, I can see how happy they are, yellow faces beaming toward the sunlight like long-lost cousins greeting one another. I kneel and run a gentle finger over the blossoms, marveling at the simple perfection of existence, spiraling out from infinitesimal beginnings and opening into infinity to encompass the universe. The Milky Way. Sunflowers. Spider webs. Fingerprints. Human lives. Flowers. Home.

My phone jangles with an incoming text. "Finished here," it says, then, "Do you still want me?"

As I tap "Yes," up ahead I see a figure, tall against the sky. As I get closer, I can make out the kite strings, near-invisible tethers, running from Earl's hands to the cluster of red silk phoenixes afloat in the clouds.

ACKNOWLEDGEMENTS

I live and write in Treaty 6 territory, home of the Cree, Dakota, Lakota, Nakota, Saulteaux, and Dene people, and the traditional homeland of the Métis Nation. I live on land my family has had the care of for 75 years. I gratefully acknowledge my relational bonds to the People and to the land, creatures, sky, and water.

It can take years to write a novel. Especially if – as I was – the novelist is a beginner in novelizing. The resulting village of helping hands and hearts all deserve their own ponies, or at least the best wine and pizza party ever, with chocolate cake and gratitude.

My first thanks and my last are to Dave Margoshes, a writer's writer, my first reader, frequent editor, husband, and partner, who has seen me through the ups and downs of writing this novel. You helped me learn that writers play the long game. Love always.

Many thanks to Debra Bell, John Kennedy, Tania Wolk, designer, and press asistant Mia Bell at Radiant Press for your faith, hard work, attention to details, and for producing a gorgeous book.

My editor, the amazing Susan Musgrave, deserves champagne and all manner of chocolate for patience, wit, and humour in the midst of perseverance, troubleshooting, big-picture thinking, and small-detail focus. I feel honoured and humbled to have your insights and support. Thank you again, origami dove.

The first draft of this novel was my creative thesis as I earned my MFA in Writing at the University of Saskatchewan in Saskatoon. Thanks are due to Professor Jeanette Lynes, friend, poet, novelist, and fearless Director of the program, and to the committee who read my thesis. Thanks to my cohort in that program for feedback and friendship. Thanks especially to Sandra Birdsell, who so patiently mentored me as I took the first steps of learning how to write a novel.

My appreciation to the University of Saskatchewan for the Innovation and Opportunity Scholarship. It provided financial assistance while I researched and wrote the first draft of this novel.

Many thanks to the sharp-eyed and thoughtful members of our writing group, Visible Ink, friends and fine writers, all.

Thank you to Miriam Toews for ten days of rewarding interchange at
Sage Hill Writing.

Thanks to Guy Vanderhaeghe for teaching me that motive is queen of the
novelist's hill, and to Doug Glover for insisting on the same thing. It's no reflection
on either that it took me so long – and so much mess! – to learn the lesson.

Thank you to the Saskatchewan Writers Guild and its team of genies for the
many ways the guild supports writers and the literary arts in the province,
especially the annual Writing Retreats at St. Peter's Abbey, and the John V. Hicks
Long Manuscript Award.

I am grateful to SK Arts for grant funding that allowed me to work fulltime on
this project.

Thank you to Helen Humphreys for modelling the bravery of cutting unnecessary
text, and for your close eye and compassionate, hard-nosed style.

Thank you to Lorna Crozier for permission to use a quotation from her late
husband Patrick Lane's memoir, *There is a Season,* as an epigraph.

I am so grateful to David Thauberger for the use of his stunning iconic prairie art,
"Danceland," for this book's cover.

Thank you to the librarians and writers across the country who kept us sane and
reading for the past two years of isolation and lockdown.

To my darling friends who know who they are, my love and gratitude for wine,
coffee, good food, friendship, encouragement, and patient ears.
Let's eat together again.

Thanks and love to my family. For everything.

dee Hobsbawn-Smith's award-winning poetry, essays, and short fiction has appeared in publications in Canada, the USA, Scotland and elsewhere. She earned her MFA in Writing and her MA in English Lit at the University of Saskatchewan. Her debut poetry collection, *Wildness Rushing In*, published in 2014, was a finalist for Book of the Year and Best Poetry Collection at the Saskatchewan Book Awards. *What Can't Be Undone: Stories* was published in 2015. She's a local foods advocate, active in Slow Food for more than twenty years, and has written a stack of books about food, including the award-winning *Foodshed: An Edible Alberta Alphabet*. She served as the 35th Writer in Residence at Saskatoon Public Library in 2015. *Bread & Water: Essays*, published in 2021, won the Saskatchewan Book Awards nonfiction prize. A new poetry collection, *Among the Untamed*, is forthcoming next spring. dee lives on the remnants of her family's farm west of Saskatoon.